W9-AFA-743

Praise for
Life, Sex, and the Pursuit of Happiness

"Oh, my goodness. . . . A novel in which the psychiatrist does NOT sleep with one of his patients?? You've got to be kidding! But in this sexy, surprising story you DO get hypnosis, Masters and Johnson, a nymphomaniac, a guy who just can't stop masturbating, and a lot of bagels. Quite a trip!"

—James D. Weinrich, PhD
Author of *Sexual Landscapes—Why We Are
What We Are, Why We Love Whom We Love*

"Since the publication of his book *The Bisexual Option* in the early 1990s, Dr. Fritz Klein has been the dean of bisexuality studies. With *Life, Sex, and the Pursuit of Happiness,* he displays unexpected talent as a novelist. Following the intersection careers of businessman David Randy Gold and psychiatrist/actor Dr. Paul Manes, Klein's novel does not simply explore the complexities of sexual desire. It gives a more general overview of turbulent politics and rampant promiscuity from the hectic 1960s through the stable 1980s. Moving from Switzerland to New York to San Diego, the story examines life and love between parents and children and between heterosexual and bisexual couples with equal sensitivity. By the end of this exhilarating read, one feels enlightened not only about the psyche but also about the human soul."

—David Van Leer
Author of *The Queening of America:
Gay Culture in Straight Society*

NOTES FOR PROFESSIONAL LIBRARIANS
AND LIBRARY USERS

This is an original book title published by Harrington Park Press®,
an imprint of The Haworth Press, Inc. Unless otherwise noted in
specific chapters with attribution, materials in this book have not
been previously published elsewhere in any format or language.

CONSERVATION AND PRESERVATION NOTES

All books published by The Haworth Press, Inc., and its imprints
are printed on certified pH neutral, acid-free book grade paper.
This paper meets the minimum requirements of American National Standard for Information Sciences-Permanence of Paper for
Printed Material, ANSI Z39.48-1984.

Life, Sex,
and the Pursuit
of Happiness

To LGBT Center

F K

HARRINGTON PARK PRESS®
Bisexuality
Fritz Klein, MD
Senior Editor

Bisexual and Gay Husbands: Their Stories, Their Words edited
by Fritz Klein and Tom Schwartz

Bi America: Myths, Truths, and Struggles of an Invisible Community
by William E. Burleson

Eros: A Bi/Cultural Journey by Serena Anderlini-D'Onofrio

Life, Sex, and the Pursuit of Happiness by Fritz Klein

Life, Sex, and the Pursuit of Happiness

Fritz Klein

Harrington Park Press®
An Imprint of The Haworth Press, Inc.
New York • London • Oxford

For more information on this book or to order, visit
http://www.haworthpress.com/store/product.asp?sku=5601

or call 1-800-HAWORTH (800-429-6784) in the United States and Canada
or (607) 722-5857 outside the United States and Canada

or contact orders@HaworthPress.com

Published by

Harrington Park Press®, an imprint of The Haworth Press, Inc., 10 Alice Street, Binghamton, NY 13904-1580.

© 2005 by The Haworth Press, Inc. All rights reserved. No part of this work may be reproduced or utilized in any form or by any means, electronic or mechanical, including photocopying, microfilm, and recording, or by any information storage and retrieval system, without permission in writing from the publisher. Printed in the United States of America.

PUBLISHER'S NOTE
This is a work of fiction. Names, characters, places, and incidents either are the products of the author's imagination or are used fictitiously, and any resemblance to actual persons, living or dead, business establishments, events, or locales is entirely coincidental.

Cover design by Jennifer M. Gaska.
Design concept by Jeff Miller.

Library of Congress Cataloging-in-Publication Data

Klein, Fred, 1932–
    Life, sex, and the pursuit of happiness / Fritz Klein.
        p. cm.
    ISBN-13: 978-1-56023-577-4 (soft : alk. paper)
    ISBN-10: 1-56023-577-2 (soft : alk. paper)
    1. Psychotherapist and patient—Fiction. 2. Bisexuals—Fiction. 3. Widowers—Fiction.
I. Title.
    PS3611.L445L54 2005
    813'.6—dc22
                                                                    2005009231

CHAPTERS

PART I:
PAUL AND RANDY

1. Paul—June 1984

"Nowwwww," Paul said, dragging out the vowel and slowly lowering the volume until it trailed off into the silence of the room.

Paul Manes sat back in the Morris chair, relaxing his tall and lanky body even more. It was the only time during a session that he permitted his mind to meander, to idle in neutral.

Though he had been in an altered state these past fifteen minutes, his attention had been completely centered on Laura, the woman sitting opposite him. She was a good trance subject and had gone under as soon as he had changed his voice to a slower word rhythm, a monotone cadence, and a lower pitch. His colleagues admired Paul's inductions. He succeeded in getting almost all his patients into trance. Fellow hypnotists often sent him their "trance resistant" clients.

Paul now permitted his mind to wander into whatever byway it chose though he carefully kept his eyes on his patient. Just as someone waiting at a red light is brought back from idle thoughts at the exact moment the light turns green, he made certain that he would immediately notice her slightest change of expression or movement.

He reviewed the metaphor he had just given Laura, the thirty-six-year-old patient who still found sex aversive though she'd had years of therapy. Her latest therapist, a Jungian analyst who could not make any progress with her, finally sent her to Paul.

After the rapid, deep induction, Paul had continued, "That's right. Enjoy this time, enjoy this peace. Let me tell you of someone I know quite well who reminds me of you. A beautiful girl, a girl with dark hair and light skin just like you. She is my daughter, Anna. She is eighteen years old and has the same bright smile that you have. When Anna was half that age, she owned a lovely doll named Little Evi that she played with all the time. I watched her many times when she was totally engrossed with Little Evi.

"I remember once when her doll fell off the table and landed on the floor with a loud thud. She immediately took Little Evi in her arms and gently comforted her, consoling her pain with warm murmured words and with her mother's gentleness. I know that she would today, at age eighteen, look at you when you were nine years old and tell you how much she grieves over the pain you suffered at the hands of that awful, horrible, molesting neighbor. She would tell you how you did the best you were capable of at that young age, just half her age, as she is now just half of your present age.

"She would forgive you and understand that you were not able to resist. She would take you, the nine-year-old hurt girl in her arms, hold you tight and whisper how she loves the brave, quiet, silently suffering girl. She would stroke out the guilt, smooth away your jagged and tormented fear.

"Yes, Anna would love and forgive the nine-year-old Laura with the wisdom of an eighteen-year-old. And you, who are doubly mature, can understand Anna's love and forgiveness. You can accept her love and forgiveness.

"As you imagine, see her. As you visualize her love, you can move forward in time to the present you; going deeper into yourself, understanding your love, knowing your capacity to forgive, enjoying this time to feel peaceful. Feel calm. Enjoy these next two minutes . . . all the time in the world . . . before you return fully refreshed and wide awake. Enjoy it. Nowwwww. . ."

Paul intuitively felt good about this intervention. He knew that the next step would be to have Laura herself forgive and love her nine-year-old self. By reinforcing this a few times with Laura in trance, he was sure she would begin to respond sexually to her husband in a much more positive manner.

As Laura sat absolutely still, her eyes closed, her breathing slow and regular, Paul kept one part of his mind focused on her while he permitted another part to journey into his personal life.

Right from the start, Anna had always given him great satisfaction and joy. As a child, she showed her deep love with frequent hugs and kisses. These feelings of love had continued to grow each year. With passing years, she added the dimension of genuine affection. Just last Sunday, they spent a glorious sunny afternoon at Seaport Village: wandering in and out of shops, snacking at Upstart Crow, then finally driving home for dinner.

Mary was glad to see their smiles and feel their closeness as they walked into the house. She completed this circle of happiness by hugging and kissing Paul.

"Did the two of you have a good time?" she asked Anna.

"Yes we did. Daddy bought me this," showing her stepmother a blue mug which was embossed with a pale beige whale. "From now on this will be for my morning hot chocolate."

Paul unwrapped another mug, this one with the word "Mary" printed on it. "And this is for your morning tea, darling."

She responded to the gift with another warm hug and a quiet, "Thank you" whispered in his ear.

This Norman Rockwell scene was interrupted when Johan, a younger version of Paul, came hurtling down the stairs from his room.

"Are we going to eat soon?" he asked his stepmother. "I'm missing out on a party at Mission Beach that is already in full swing."

"Johan, you'll sit down at the table with all of us when the food is ready and you'll remain there until we are all finished. I'm sure your friends can manage without you for a while." Paul immediately realized that he had spoken to his son more sharply than he meant to.

"It'll be ready right away, Johan," Mary said in a tone that attempted to placate her energetic twenty-year-old stepson, though she unconsciously took a deep breath and sighed.

Paul knew that his son did not feel warmly toward him. They treated each other with the good manners of a civilized family, the good manners that Johan's grandparents had instilled in him. This toleration on both sides had existed for many years. If Johan were not going away to Wisconsin for his third year of college next year, the underlying tension of father and son would have boiled over into open hostility.

Paul's attention suddenly switched back to his patient when her head nodded a couple of times. A slight smile touched her mouth, then faded as she returned to the stillness of her deep trance. Paul continued to watch her closely. When he was satisfied that she wasn't yet ready to come out of the trance, he allowed his mind to wander again.

With his thought process unfocused, Paul's peripheral vision took in not only the atrium's palm tree but also three photographs on the wall. The scene depicted in the middle photo brought to the surface his speech in act 1 of O'Neill's, *The Iceman Cometh:* ". . . But I didn't mean booze. I meant save you from pipe dreams. I know now, from my experience, they're the things that really poison and ruin a guy's life and keep him from finding any peace . . ."

Yes, Paul thought, that's what troubles people. For some it's the pipe dreams of the future, while for others it's their past dreams, their memories which they carry as a burden—the old, heavy weight of unforgettable fears. Laura still carries with her the fearsome anxieties of a nine-year-old.

At this point, Laura began the slight movements that would lead her out of her trance. Paul's attention immediately was focused on her. As she became fully conscious, Paul carefully followed her every move and gesture so that when she opened her eyes, she saw her doctor sitting comfortably in his chair, smiling at her.

"Do you remember anything while you were in trance?"

"No, not a thing," she answered. "But in some way I feel so much better, so much happier, but have no idea why."

"Knowing why is not the important thing here," Paul explained. "Your unconscious knows and will make good use of your new thoughts and feelings." As he got up, he reinforced the idea suggested during the hypnotic trance: "You are most capable of loving and accepting your nine-year-old-self."

He wished her a good week and saw her to the door. After she left, he made some notes on her chart before rereading the referring doctor's report on his next patient.

David R. Gold was the name on the urologist's report which concluded that his problem was not organic. Paul was curious about David's unwanted baggage. The cause had not been found in the body, so David was referred to Paul, the psychiatrist.

Priapism had been ruled out: his penis did not remain erect all the time. Mr. Gold's constant erections were neither due to faulty venous blood flow, nor were they the result of a malfunction in the autonomic nervous system. Paul was intrigued. No patient of his had ever complained of too many erections. "I wish I had that problem," he thought to himself. Paul was an expert with impotence. "I wonder what drives this man, what makes him so sexually excited." After finishing the report, ready to meet his new patient, he thought: "Strange how one man's neurosis is another's strongest desire."

2.   Randy—June 1984

I finally found a metered spot a half block from his office. The building, a renovated, two-story, white Victorian mansion converted to office suites, was a stately example of twentieth century practicality combined with nineteenth century grandeur. Fumbling with the change, I dropped a quarter onto the sidewalk. *Can't anything go right and if nothing is wrong why am I here?* It was a ninety-degree early June day; I felt drops of sweat dribbling down my lower back as the Santa Ana desert heat blew into San Diego. The glaring sun pasted the front of my short-sleeved, tan shirt to my chest and my shorts clung to me like a wetsuit. I was uncomfortable and early—no need to go inside as yet. After feeding the meter, I leaned against the cold, black, iron fence in the shaded cool of the street's purple and still-blooming jacaranda tree.

The traffic was minimal. Though quiet and peaceful, the street, lined with flowering shrubs and neat lawns in front of the well-cared-for homes, did not ease my inner churning, an anxiety centered in my chest. The door of a black VW Beetle opened across the street and a young, blonde, full-bosomed woman stepped out. As she slowly sauntered toward the corner, her lilting hip movement was made even sexier by her delightfully tight jeans accentuating her round ass. The cock, *damn it,* began its upward expansion in my jock strap. It was full-length hard by the time she turned the corner, and I was achingly horny.

Now I had no choice but to go in. I carried *The Tribune* in front of me to hide my boner and opened the front door. I hurried past the only two people in the waiting room before reaching the door marked MEN. I was relieved to find it empty. Locking the outside door before entering the stall, I got to my cock at last. I began jerking off, fantasizing about the blonde's delicious ass. I saw myself fucking her. I pumped faster and faster, my hand stroking in rhythm to my imaged thrusts. She moaned and came. So did I. Though still somewhat hard, I felt more relaxed now. I wiped up the jism that had shot all over the toilet seat and floor, then washed my hands. At last I was able to go into the waiting room to talk sensibly to the receptionist.

Though things were falling apart and my head was in a swirling turmoil, I did manage to fill out the form correctly. I even had my Blue Cross number with me. The buxomly and heartily *zaftig* woman behind the open window of the small, tidy reception office took my completed paperwork.

"Your appointment is for two o'clock. Dr. Manes will be with you in five minutes," she said warmly, then continued her work on a large appointment calendar.

The beige walls with standard birds of paradise prints did not calm me. Nothing seemed to these days. My eyes were drawn to the sunlit atrium, with its lavender and white impatiens surrounding the trunk of a stately palm tree. I could see the top fronds through the room's skylight. I shifted my attention to the impatiens and waited for one of the four closed doors to open. *What will Dr. Manes look like? And more important, can he help me?* I thought.

My mind wandered as it had done these past months. The atrium's vivid greenery triggered a thought of tomorrow's deadline. I needed to come up with a hook for the zoo's new brochure. Last year the client had been delighted with the monkey theme. *What about flamingos with tropical pale pink as the main theme color? No, it's been done too many times,* I decided.

We found out this year that two other firms are also submitting designs to the zoo. I couldn't afford to lose this account, with Baltimore Bagel taking their account to another agency and Taco Bell cutting their billings in half. It is such a dog-eat-dog field. Though I was one of the best, I couldn't manage to get beyond the half-million-a-year billing plateau.

What's going to satisfy them as well as make good graphics? Bears are in but too overworked. Birds? Maybe a colorful parrot. No, too many people dislike them. Elephants? Tigers? No. Zebras? Lions?

No. Leopards? Llamas? *That's it*. Llamas, with their soft fleecy wool and foreign mystique. Ah, I had it:—*The Llama Extravaganza!* As soon as I got back to the studio I would start John, my assistant, on it.

"Mr. Gold?" I suddenly heard a male voice say. I don't know how long I had sat there worrying about work. I was lost in the swirls and circles of business thoughts. I snapped back with an automatic nod as he continued, "I'm Paul Manes." I almost tripped over myself getting up from the soft sofa to shake Dr. Manes's extended hand. He smiled warmly, then motioned with his left hand, inviting me into his office. I trailed behind his loping strides noticing a small bald spot in the center of his graying blond hair.

He stopped just inside the office and waved me to one of the two light oak Morris chairs. After closing the door, he sat comfortably in the other. Somehow he had my filled-out form that was now clipped to a manila folder. Once again, I saw the atrium, the tree trunk, and the impatiens, this time through the two large windows practically covering one narrow wall. A floor-to-ceiling bookcase covered the other wall and several titles with the word "Sex" caught my attention.

I nervously looked at the third wall which displayed three black-and-white photographs. They were obviously scenes from plays, but which plays and who the actors were I couldn't guess. Slowly I turned back to Dr. Manes. He looked about fifty, with an ash blond mustache. He was dressed conservatively with a cerulean striped tie and an expensive-looking gray sports jacket. His rimless glasses highlighted rather than hid his smiling, smoky blue eyes. With his long, angular arms and legs, he looked taller sitting than he did standing. Even his shiny black loafers were large—probably size thirteen. I was drawn to his quiet smile.

"Do you like David or Dave?" he asked softly.

"Actually, everyone I know calls me Randy," I answered. "The middle initial R. stands for Randolph."

"What brings you to my office, Randy?" he asked in a neutral conversational tone.

"Didn't . . . didn't Dr. Perry get ahold of you?" I stammered nervously.

"Yes, Dr. Perry was in touch with me. He did fill me in on his urological findings which, as you know, were normal." Dr. Manes paused. "However, the difficulties and problems you carry are best known to you."

"I don't know where to begin," I complained. "It's driving me crazy. It's complicated and I can't untangle it."

"What is the biggest problem?"

"It's not big. It's huge." He waited for me to go on. "Well, as Dr. Perry probably told you . . ." I finally plunged in: "Doctor, I can't stop fucking. I always have a hard-on; it never goes down."

He leaned forward. "Always?" A slight pause, then "Never goes down?"

"It seems like I always . . . I can never get enough. No matter how much sex I have, it isn't enough. I always want more, need more. Like I told the urologist, even after coming I still stay hard. Sometimes it hurts so much that I have to jerk off to make it go down."

"So it does go down sometimes," Dr. Manes asked gently as he leaned back slightly.

"Yes, but never for long. The least thing makes me hard. All that's necessary is someone to touch me, look at me in a certain way. Maybe see a nice ass, anything. Vaboom, there's my hard-on again." I began to sweat as I recalled the scene from just a few minutes ago. I told him how I got hard after I saw the woman with the big boobs and lovely ass. "Only after I jerked off in the men's room did my cock go down."

"What did you fantasize about when you jerked off in the men's room?" Dr. Manes asked.

"A big bed. I saw me fucking her and fucking her until I felt her begin to moan and writhe," I answered. What I didn't tell him though was that I had also fantasized sticking two fingers up her ass.

"How often do you pick up women and fuck them?" he then asked.

"As often as I can," I laughed sheepishly. "But I get turned down too many times."

"When was the last time you tried and succeeded?"

"Let's see," I tried to remember the last woman I met and fucked. "Oh, yes, a week ago. It was with Joyce, a real estate broker. She was showing me some new office space; I lost the lease on my present quarters. . . . Anyway, she took me to a building with an empty second-floor space on Seventh Street in the Gaslamp District. The key didn't fit properly and she had trouble getting it into the lock. Standing behind her, I noticed the elastic panty lines on her thighs under her nice, curvaceous, round ass. My cock started its usual shenanigans. At first, I tried to ignore it. However, when she finally opened the door and we were alone in the empty office I was fully hard and knew, outside of fucking her, nothing would make it go down.

"It was easy with her because I saw her eyes kept glancing down to my bulging crotch. After the third or fourth time, I just took her hand and laid it on my hard-on. In no time at all, we were all over each other on the floor, our clothes jumbled about us and fucking like crazy. But I can't count on that happening as often as I want it to."

"When was the last time you tried to pick up a woman and didn't succeed?" he wanted to know.

I remembered the incident all too well. "Betty and I were at a vernissage last week and . . ."

"Betty?" he interrupted.

"Oh, I'm sorry, my wife." I paused, "and . . ." then stopped altogether. "I've lost my train of thought."

"Vernissage," he prompted smoothly.

"Oh yes. Last week Orr's Gallery had an opening for an exhibition of English watercolors—mostly landscapes and horses, late nineteenth century. Not bad, considering it's San Diego. Betty was talking to the gallery owner while I was somewhat bored and perturbed, as I'm not that comfortable in crowds. A short, dark-haired woman was in front of what I considered the best piece in the show, a sea view by Sir William Russell Flint. She was lost in the painting and didn't see me approach. She had on a wonderful floral type of fragrance as well as a red-rose-printed silk blouse. That's all it took. I began throwing a rod.

"I opened the conversation with, 'Fleur Elegance?' She was startled out of her reverie and looked up at me. 'Your perfume, is it Fleur Elegance?'

"She was surprised that I knew it and we continued talking for several minutes during which time I was fully conscious of my straining cock hard against my jock strap. Though in all honesty, I really was not all that interested in her. Short and thin is not my favorite type of body but the cock didn't pay any attention to that. It wanted to get out of my pants and into hers. As I was commenting about her blouse of roses and comparing it to her scent of flowers, Betty came by. She took one look at the woman and another at my full crotch. She raised her eyes to glare at me and turned around, practically running out of the gallery.

"After excusing myself to the once-again-startled woman, I hurriedly followed Betty to the car. Betty didn't stop crying 'til we got home. After a while she calmed down but in no way did she want to have sex with me. We already had a loving sexual encounter just before dinner that evening, around six. Shit, my cock stayed stiff during the ride home and continued hard even as I tried to smooth things out between the two of us. I finally had to jack off. It was hurting and just wouldn't go away." I stopped talking.

"How often do you usually have sex with your wife?" Dr. Manes asked when I did not continue.

"It's getting less and less," I said quite unhappily. "I do love her a lot and she loves me, but love has nothing to do with it."

"How much is less and less?"

"When we first got married four years ago, we had sex once a day, sometimes twice. Now I'm lucky if it's twice a week even though I'm always ready to trot." I felt awful. It used to be so good with Betty, but lately with all the problems and disagreements, I just didn't know. "She used to be all over me. She loved my cock, called it 'her big man.' Couldn't keep her hands or mouth off of it. I'd come home from the studio and she'd have my hard dick out of my jockey shorts in a jiffy and would begin stroking it ever so slowly back and forth while I kissed and held her tightly with one hand while with the other I gently massaged her cunt. But not anymore. These days she stays away from 'her big man.' I continually have to seduce Betty. That's not good—having to seduce your own wife, especially since these days I strike out more often than not. It hurts, as I dearly love her. It's truly painful. She's the only woman who brought out a gentleness in me and a deep affection apart from the sex." My feelings of tenderness toward her welled up and I remained silent.

"Is your wife monogamous?" he asked after a short pause.

"No. We had an open marriage right from the start. She had a couple of short affairs, nothing important. Our understanding was that as long as I didn't take anything away from her, I could fool around on the outside. In fact, she knows about Joanie. I've been seeing Joanie regularly for over a year. She works at Frazee's Art Store and we usually manage a quick one in the back room when the store is closed for lunch."

"So you regularly have sex with both Joanie and Betty, and yet it's still not enough. Hmm." He looked out the window for a few moments. "How often do you jerk off?"

"It varies, but on the average three, four times a day."

"Did you jerk off three or four times a day when you first got married?" he wanted to know.

"Uh, well I . . ." I felt off balance for the first time since we began. "No, I don't think so. Yes, I'm sure I didn't. I remember that Betty and I joked about masturbation and how seldom either one of us did it."

He shifted gears. "How long has this problem of your hard-on been going on?"

I shook my head. "I don't know. It has come on gradually and is getting worse. At least a year, probably longer."

"Did anything happen to trigger it?"

"I . . . I don't think so." I suddenly felt nervous. I swallowed a couple of times and noticed that my palms were moist.

"Let us return to your relationship with Betty." He had obviously noticed my anxiety and I was glad to switch subjects again. He continued, "Besides the problem with sex, how are you and Betty getting along?"

"Not as good as before." I still was skating on thin ice. "That is also going downhill."

"Do you fight a lot?"

"No." I continued to feel shaky. Oh damn, I sensed my dick had begun to expand. I couldn't imagine what Dr. Manes would make out of that. "No, we bicker from time to time over small things. It's more like guerrilla warfare."

"When exactly did your big fight occur?" he darted in.

"Two years ago," my voice quavered. "We had gotten somewhat closer but . . ."

I couldn't go on. I fell apart. The tears started, then the shaking. I began to sob softly. I took one of the tissues on the small table next to my chair and wiped my wet face. I felt ashamed and looked down at the carpet. The small sobs that broke through every couple of seconds finally began tapering off. It was a couple of minutes before they stopped at last. My hard-on had gone down—thank God for small favors. I closed my eyes and breathed slowly and deeply a few times.

It was only then that he pulled me back to the present moment with, "What happened?"

"I came home late one night," finally able to control my voice, "and we argued over it. Nothing important, just a blow-up that happened from time to time. But during the fight, I got angry at her—really upset at some comment Betty had speared me with. Without thinking I yelled, 'Even if you don't trust me, the one thing you don't have to worry about is my running off with another woman.'" I did not go any further.

"And?"

"And, nothing. The fight ended; we kissed and made up. I thought that that was the end of it. But it wasn't. She continued to think about my remark. She did not understand it. It bothered her like a pebble caught in her shoe. And two weeks later all hell broke loose." It was difficult to keep the quaver out of my voice. The tears welled up and the shaking began again.

Dr. Manes waited a couple of moments while I calmed down once again. He asked softly, "So, Randy, the first fight was just a preliminary to the main bout?"

"Yes." I clearly remembered that horrible evening. "It had started harmlessly enough. We were discussing the possibility of going out to the theater and I didn't know which night I had free in the upcoming week. I was watching the Padres. I asked Betty to get my calendar out of the attaché case I had left on the hall table. She came back holding the red calendar as well as a black notebook I used for sketching. She didn't say a word, just threw both of them at me and ran out of the room." Again, I began to cry and couldn't talk.

"What had you drawn?" he asked gently.

"Phil. Someone I was seeing." I finally managed to get out. He waited patiently. "The trouble was that some of them were sketches of him naked. Why I hadn't left the sketchbook at the studio I'll never know. But for Betty it clicked. The penny had dropped."

"You had never told her about Phil," Dr. Manes nodded with calm understanding.

"Well, there was no need to," I answered defensively. "That side of me had never been important before. In fact, I used it only for quickies when a woman wasn't available . . . for a release of tension. Phil, however was different from other men. He was the first man to see my resemblance to Michelangelo's statue of David. Most of the women have noticed, but Phil was the first man.

"That meant something to me. I don't know why, but it did. *He* meant something to me. So of course I felt guilty. It was one of the few things I hid from Betty. So when she reacted so hurt and angry, I flew off the handle myself. I said things I'm still sorry for; but once it's out of your mouth you cannot swallow it back."

"Do you still see Phil?" he asked.

"No," I shook my head slowly and began to get teary. "It just didn't survive Betty's anger. I stopped seeing him shortly thereafter. I still regret that. He and I had really connected." I paused, ruefully shaking my head, upset at my loss. After a few moments, I continued, "Now that I think of it, since that night I haven't really been balling men all that much."

"How often do you have sex with men these days?"

"Not often," I responded sadly. "I used to enjoy going to gay bars, having a couple of drinks, and then get into the cruising aspect of those places. I had no trouble finding men who were attracted to me and wanted to satisfy me sexually."

Dr. Manes wanted to know when I'd last had sex with a man. "About three weeks ago," I finally said after having sat there for a minute trying to remember just exactly when the last time had been.

"Yes, I remember. Betty had a late class that evening and I was fidgety. Since I couldn't concentrate on the work I had to do, I decided to go to One Fifth, a dark but pleasant bar in Hillcrest. In fact, it's just one block from here. A handsome, fair-haired man came up to me within the first five minutes I was there. He began with small talk but propositioned me shortly thereafter. I agreed and quickly finished my second beer. Ten minutes later we were at his place having sex. I was back home within an hour of leaving—relaxed and much calmer. Not only did I enjoy the physical release of sex but had also felt the delight of someone who physically wanted me."

Dr. Manes segued to my family with, "As a child, did you experience being wanted?"

I told him of my warm feelings toward Father as well as my younger sister. I had mixed emotions, however, toward my extremely domineering but loving mother, who was without doubt the matriarch of our family. We then delved into my schooling, adolescence, and work histories. He was particularly interested in what drugs I used and how much alcohol I consumed.

Returning to the sexual problem, he asked, "What if any arrangement do Betty and you have with respect to telling the other of outside sexual adventures?"

"Since she found out about my bisexuality," I answered, "she doesn't want to know anything. Not about men, not about women. We do talk about safe subjects—the work at my agency, her computer courses, but not about sex."

"Does Joanie at the art store know of your bisexuality?"

"No—once bitten, twice shy," I shook my head. "There's no need to throw a stone into calm waters. We have a good relationship and I don't want to jeopardize it with something she might not understand."

"When you first met her, how did you know that Joanie was interested in you?" he asked.

I did not understand his digression but did remember what turned me on with her. "When she showed me some paper I had asked for, she managed to touch my arm in the process. I like women; I really do. They're so, so . . . I don't know how to say it, but they're so wonderful. I guess it showed. She must have reacted and I felt something in her attitude that made it obvious to me that she was attracted to me."

"You are an attractive man, Randy, and yes, you do resemble that famous statue."

That surprised me.

"Also, you are exquisitely aware when another person is attracted to you, sees you as sexually desirable. With that ability, you find it easy to establish sexual liaisons. That skill allows you to create situations in which the other person will make the first move or permit you to make an assured advance without worrying about rejection."

"But I do get rejected," I protested.

"Of course," he responded, "nothing in life is one-hundred percent certain. But your sensitivity does greatly increase your chances of success. You get better at what you do, then you eat the fruits of your accomplishment. However, there is an even more elegant method I learned some time back."

For the first time in the session he began to talk about himself. I was all ears as he told me about the classes he had taught on and off for many years. Like me, I thought, having given lessons in graphic arts and design a number of times in the past five years. He also loved to teach and his classes were well attended. He related how the students worked hard, spent time preparing their assignments, and continually sought him out for advice and encouragement.

"There was one seminar at the Gifford Clinic, attached to the medical school, that I remember well," he reminisced. "Twelve third-year psychiatric residents were taking a course in sex therapy . . . theory and techniques. Four or five residents began to stand out as the ones who were both interested in the subject and already competent therapists. They asked many insightful questions and crowded my study period schedule. I concentrated on these doctors to maximize their learning experience and excite their imaginations. Sure enough, they improved noticeably over that six-month period. Their final papers were outstanding."

Then he related how one resident presented a truly brilliant case study. Dr. Manes overlooked him during the seminar, as he had sat in the back of the room and asked very few questions. He had simply not noticed this particular student, this doctor. Only after Dr. Manes read the excellent paper did he invite him to his office. From that point on, they developed a closer teacher/student relationship. The resident turned out to be an excellent therapist and, more important, a wonderful human being.

"I almost missed it," he said sadly. "Why? I waited for the students to show me they were competent and interested in what I had to say. Those that let me know were the ones I paid attention to. The others who were quiet, shy, or nonaggressive, I hardly noticed. I did not make an effort to discover the diamonds sitting in the indistinct background.

"As an artist you are aware that the obvious is not always the most beautiful—the showy, not always the best. I became a better teacher when I began digging deeper to find the dedicated student. What I risk is some time lost; what I gain is immeasurable. This is true not only for teaching but for many aspects in life."

I agreed, nodding my head.

"Let us return to your problem," he said. "It is important for us to establish a baseline and know exactly just how often you have sex, with whom, and when. Please keep a diary, jotting down the day, the time, and the sexual situation itself."

"How about jacking off?" I asked. "If I leave that out we'll miss a lot of orgasms."

"Of course, include jacking off," he grinned. "In my view of the world, masturbation is definitely included in the category of sex."

He asked me to repeat the assignment, which I did. After reassuring me that my problem could be solved in a short period of time, he raised my spirits by saying that my defenses against anxiety were pointed in the direction of enhancing life forces. We agreed that the next session would be the following Wednesday afternoon, again at two o'clock. Dr. Manes got up and escorted me to the waiting room where he warmly shook my hand.

I looked at my watch. Five to three. Boy, did that hour disappear. I must sort out what had gone on. I did feel better but didn't understand why. Maybe just getting it off my chest was what did it. One

Fifth would be a good place to mull it over before I headed back to the office. I fed the meter another quarter and strolled to the bar.

The darkness of the place overpowered the low lighting and the vague visibility inside was worsened by my eyes' slow adaptation from the outside brightness. I ordered a lite beer and wandered to the back to sit on a stool around the black baby grand piano. The bar was mostly empty. Only four other guys in the whole place. It was a good time and place to concentrate on the session.

Strange how similar we were. So Paul Manes also taught classes. He seemed nonchalant when I brought up my fooling around with men. I wonder if he ever did? One never knows. On the other hand, he also understood my problem with Betty and other women. I don't think my constant hard-on was going to be solved as easily as he implied. *Damn cock!* I thought, *You think you're so smart but you're dumb, a dumb, throbbing prehensile prick. You're nothing but a grasping, aching, horniness.*

I went to the front bar for another beer. A tall man walked in while I was waiting for the bartender to bring me the bottle. Just my type: athletically strong, stocky and powerful, late twenties, blond, and a good face. After getting a beer, he wandered toward the back and self-assuredly stood with his back touching the mirrored wall, one foot raised onto the barstool rung. We began the dance of eyes that led to both of us smiling.

My hard-on was already strong and straining. I waited for him to make the first move. He didn't. To my surprise, I did. Later I realized that I didn't think about possible rejection. I let my desire lead me to him with, "Hi, my name is Randy," hand extended.

"Mine's Jim," he grasped my hand firmly, still looking directly into my eyes.

"Has anyone told you that you look like a taller and blonder version of Steve Garvey?" I opened the verbal play.

"No," he said, "but I did play professional baseball several years ago. In fact the Chicago Cubs called me up for spring training in 1981."

A real ballplayer! I got more excited. I found out that he never did make it to the majors and now is out of sports altogether, working instead at the San Diego Natural History Museum as the bird curator. I told him about my public relations and advertising company as well as my bent toward art. When I remarked on the gold band on his left hand, he confirmed that he was married.

"I find you real hot," I couldn't stop myself from saying. "I'd like to play around with you, have some fun and games."

"You're a handsome dude yourself, Randy, real classic looks," he smiled. "I'd like that myself, but it'll have to be on my terms."

"Terms? I don't understand."

"Yup," he eyed my full crotch. "I give the orders. It's done my way. I dictate what we do in bed. Nothing kinky, but what I want goes."

Well, there's a first time for everything, I thought. The shoe's on the other foot this time. I service him. Why not? My cock agreed, that's for sure.

"Sure," I said quietly.

"My wife is away visiting her folks in Denver so we can use my place in Cardiff."

"It'll have to be after work, as I have to get back to my office."

"That will work for me. Is six o'clock okay?" he asked.

I smiled and said, "Works for me."

"You'll like it," he promised. He gave me his address and with a salute left the bar. I went to the men's room. No way would I be able to return to the office with this driving cock. For the second time that day, I jerked off—this time to Jim's image.

As I headed toward the car, I decided on impulse to call Clara who was both wild in bed and always ready to party with her husband. I found a pay phone on Robinson Avenue.

She answered on the second ring.

"Clara, this is Randy."

"Oh, Randy," she said. "Haven't heard from you in a real long time. Since that roudy party in March, wasn't it?"

"Yes, it was wild and loads of fun. I'm calling because I'm going to be in your neck of the woods, in Cardiff," I felt my cock once again starting to expand. "How about me dropping over tonight around nine? Are you free?"

"Of course, we'd love to have you over," she said quickly. "You know that both of us like threesomes. It's the next best thing to swinging with another couple. Especially you, Randy, you horny bastard."

"Well, it's not every day I make it with such a gorgeous woman as you," I answered. "See you tonight. Keep it warm in the meantime." With a smile I hung up.

I continued to the car. Almost contented. Now if Betty is in the mood later that night, I think I just might be satisfied—not satiated, but satisfied.

PART II:
PAUL

May weather arrived early in New York that year. April hovered over the city, its colorful Aphrodite's wings billowing gentle breezes, its nascent light enveloping the haughty skyscrapers. New Yorkers didn't actually laugh, though now and then a smile broke through their guarded set faces and usual protective stance. The evening air, though cooler, still contained the daytime's open and clear shimmering warmth. The streets seemed cleaner, the metropolitan fervor calmer.

Spring had claimed its season. Riverside Drive, with its rolling park of trees and bushes, had begun its annual rebirthing bloom. The wispy, anemically thin trees on the side streets already brandished their tiny, leafy buds. In two small, oblong boxes on the fourth-floor window ledges outside Carl's apartment at 313 West Eighty-eighth Street, the crocuses showed off their first flowering with colorful blossoms.

Eighty-eighth Street between West End Avenue and Riverside Drive never had to be reclaimed from a rundown state. It was situated on the right side of Ninety-sixth Street, a sad and squalid, all-too-visible poverty line. The right mixture of apartment houses, brownstones, and well-cared-for ground-floor professional offices contributed to a loyal local neighborhood. Block parties were not necessary to mold the populace into a cohesive fellowship, nor were private security firms hired to police this street. Two apartment houses, tall and massive, stood watch at each end of the street. These sentinels of stone guarded a strip of safety in a city of bolted doors and gated windows.

Carl Saroff must have felt secure. His windows were not barred—not even the bedroom windows behind the orange-coated fire escape: the burglar's usual entry point. Carl lived in 4C, an apartment consisting of six large rooms: out-of-date wooden kitchen cabinets; old fashioned toilets with hanging chains; and door-hugging telephone wires, still noticeable though they were painted the same off-white as the walls.

The kitchen nook was the usual eating place, but dinner that evening was to occur in the rarely used dining room, as its large, round oak table sat six people quite comfortably. Jeanette was not yet at home. She was still shooting wedding pictures. The job had taken more time than she had optimistically estimated and much too long for the money earned. Carl had cooked the beans the previous evening, and he was in the kitchen finishing the cassoulet and licking his lips noisily as he helped himself to a large ladleful of beans, pork, and lamb. They had agreed that cassoulet was the right dish to celebrate the Trinity of Easter, Passover, and the one-year anniversary of Paul and Evi's first meeting.

The downstairs buzzer sounded. Carl went to the foyer and buzzed back, permitting the celebrants to open the locked inner-lobby door. Carl had moved to this place in 1960 and in the ensuing three years Paul Manes had become inured to the elevator's mulish fits of starts and stops the many times he had waited for its tardy arrival.

"It's a wonderful week," Paul said joyfully, squeezing Evi's waist, "even if this elevator decides to remain stuck on the fifth floor forever."

Standing in the cool marble lobby with its burgundy pair of crackled leather easy chairs in the corner was an appropriate place for Paul to brace and gird himself. Meetings with Carl required inner strength.

"Just two more days," Evi responded and on tiptoes kissed him on the cheek. "Tonight we celebrate, tomorrow's the dress rehearsal, and Thursday's the big day, *Schaetzli*."

"Evi, who would have thought I'd ever get this far," Paul shook his head to emphasize the unreality of it all. "And Carl made it happen." He owed Carl so much: his stay in New York, his budding career, and, in a way, even Evi.

"But don't ever forget that you're the one with the driving talent and intelligent sensitivity," Evi said seriously; then she added playfully, "and what's most important, your good looks, my golden treasure."

Before Carl, Paul had discounted his good points and concentrated on his failings. Years of therapy had only emphasized his insufficiencies. Even these last six vaunted and changing years with Carl calling the shots, bull's-eyes more often than not, did not allow Paul to extinguish that hidden insecurity in the core of his being. The externally successful achievements still dragged along his inner jagged failings.

The elevator finally arrived and his inner musings stopped. Paul opened the door and then the inner gate, holding both for Evi to enter first. During the ride up he embraced her tightly and held her in a long and loving kiss until the fourth floor.

"Happy anniversary," he whispered into her remarkably soft and full black hair. Even in the dim hallway, Evi's dark eyes sparkled bright happiness. Paul, whose prominent ears were partially hidden by his long, straight hair, brought to view his best feature, a teddy bear smile that widened his clear blue eyes and flattened his slightly dimpled chin. However, as they stood in front of the brown metal door waiting for Carl to answer the two short rings of the doorbell, Paul kept nervously brushing back his well-groomed hair.

"Come in, come on in! You're prompt as usual and nothing's ready. Jeanette is not home yet." Carl ushered them in with a wet kiss on Evi's mouth, a dry one on Paul's, and bear hugs for both.

Though he was of average height, Carl was an imposing man, not only with his solid weight and strength but through his strong facial features: heavy graying eyebrows; a large rounded nose which if red would have signified alcohol abuse, and fleshy lips surrounding teeth that would have been straightened if Carl had come from a home where the children were given over to the orthodontist; instead he grew up on the Lower East Side, the son of a Polish mother who supported five young ones by taking in sewing to make ends meet.

"What's the wonderful smell?" Paul asked, sprawling into a beanbag chair, feeling at home in this room. In the past few years he had spent almost as much time talking, studying, and arguing with Carl here as in his own place just across Central Park on East Eighty-fourth Street.

"A dish fit for the lovely couple," Carl said, though he did not reveal what it was. "It's a special recipe that fits the holiday spirit as well as tasting just right for anniversaries. Let me get you a scotch and soda, Paul. You'll have the usual spritzer, Evi?"

"Yes," she said as she got up from the daybed. "I'll help you. I know where things are." On the way to the kitchen she took the bottle of Black & White from the sideboard.

"She's a find," Carl said. "You're lucky, Paul, that I introduced the two of you. If it weren't for Jeanette, I would have kept her for myself."

"Stop that Carl!" Paul said softly but with a spring-coiled tension. "A couple of times in bed do not signify having her." Then louder, "It takes two people to decide if they have each other and in this case *we* have each other."

"And that, of course, is what we're celebrating tonight," Carl answered with a forced smile. "I'll send Evi back with the scotch. I must see if the meal is ready," he said with forced gaiety before he returned to the kitchen.

Paul tasted bitterness. He pushed back some loose strands from his forehead, usually smooth and pink, now wrinkled in annoyance. Carl always found ways to be one up on him. Even though it was he, Paul, who lived with Evi, Carl's sufferance to it was intolerable. No, he decided he definitely would not go to Maine with him. Anyway, it would have meant changing Evi's plans and he didn't want to do that. Besides, summer was a long way off—no need to decide anything right away.

Now was the time to celebrate. This past year had been a great one, the best ever, and Evi was such a big part of it. *Evi,* he thought, *my first true love; loving Evi and being loved by her. Lovely, god how lovely. I do hope she likes the heart. I still don't know if I'll give it to her here or wait 'til we're alone at home. It'll depend on how things go, though this has not been a good beginning.*

The kitchen door swung open. Evi had a drink in each hand. "Hi, I'm back," she said, handing him his glass. "I've never been to a Passover Seder before. Is Carl religious?"

"No, but he loves ritual," Paul said, taking a long swallow and draining almost half of the tall amber-filled glass. "To celebrate two holidays and one anniversary at the same time is his sense of humor. Three variations on a theme. It also releases him from the tension of directing rehearsals day in and night out."

"And it's good for you also. You do . . ." she stopped as she heard the front door opening. Jeanette, with short red hair topping a lightly freckled nose and a finely boned, oval face, bounced in. She beamed when she saw both of them. She dropped the camera, tripod, and large case on the coffee table and ran to hug Evi.

"Evi, it's so good to see you. You look radiant." After hugging her Jeanette held Evi at arm's distance to get a better look. "It must be Paul. I know it's *not* your job at the box office." She then bent down to peck Paul on the cheek. "And you also look great, fantastic. I know it's Evi's doing, though Carl tells me you're a real ball of fire in the rehearsals. How does it feel to be a star?"

"Jeanette, I'm not a star. In fact, we haven't even opened yet," he said, laughing, obviously pleased nonetheless. "How did the shooting go?"

"The bride was beautiful," she answered, "but the parents were impossible. Insisted on corny shots. I told them I won't be responsible. But I did get a number of the newlyweds getting dressed that were great." She gathered up her equipment. "I'll change into something more comfortable. I have to help Carl. Though if I know him, there'll be very little left to do by now," as she rushed into the bedroom.

"Are all American redheads so vivacious?" Evi asked, putting her almost untouched drink on the end table. She sat down on the daybed and tucked her legs under her. "I knew another redhead from the States who worked with me in Zurich who was just as animated."

"It's probably not the red hair but rather the American aspect that makes the difference." Paul took another swallow. "Swiss women are much more sedate. And not only the women—the men as well. You just grow up to a slower tempo."

Two drinks and a half hour later found the four of them formally seated in the dining room with plates full of food, their wine glasses filled with Manischewitz red wine. An intricately painted Easter egg graced each of their place settings. Evi wore a large purple orchid, while Carl's gift to Paul, a good luck horseshoe, was propped up next to his plate.

"What does the wine-filled silver goblet signify?" asked Evi. She looked at Carl for the answer.

"That's right, it's your first year with us," he nodded for emphasis. "At a Seder, the extra goblet is for the prophet, Elijah. He comes in with the proper prayer, takes a sip, and blesses the gathering."

"And the extra setting?" she continued.

"That's for Judy," Jeanette interposed. "Nothing to do with holidays, just Carl's daughter."

"She won't make it," Carl spoke to Jeanette. "She called before. She has a hot new date."

"For a sixteen-year-old, she sure has a lot of boyfriends," Paul said.

"You know my opinion," Carl said with a mouth half full of gefilte fish. "If love and sex are good for adults, they're also right for kids. In fact, she's been fucking since age twelve and I've lost track of all the boys she's been with. Never seems to get enough."

"Too bad she's not here tonight to celebrate with us," said Jeanette. "She's full of fun, and I think she needs more home life, what with her mother never having time for her—drinking and all."

"Jeanette, enough of that," and Carl switched subjects with a turn toward Paul. "Well, how do you think you'll do tomorrow? How's the long monologue?"

Paul was annoyed by Carl's crass regard for his daughter and it took a moment before he finally answered, "You know as well as I do. You've worked on it with me and I'm confident it'll wow the audience. However, in the third act, when Larry tells me I've brought him the peace of death and I answer, 'That's a lie,' I would like to say it softly, almost a whisper. Show inner fury."

"No, you'll yell it and damned loud at that," Carl answered in a loud voice, displaying his own temper. "I'm directing this, not you."

"Okay, okay, it was just an idea," Paul quickly backed down.

As the dinner continued, Carl and Paul dissected the play, the roles, the lines, each relieving his own tension by easing the other's. In a concurrent conversation, Jeanette and Evi relived their time together in Zurich, then continued with light, bubbly talk: the subjects not of import, their contact and close feelings being the real topics of the interaction.

Afterward, back in the living room, they sat comfortably stuffed. Even Evi, whose narrow waist reflected her food intake, had eaten too much. They had topped off the feast by completely finishing the last of the chocolate-covered angel food cake, another holiday symbol, though all had laughingly agreed that was stretching it a bit. They still continued to nibble at Passover macaroons and chocolate Easter eggs to go with their large mugs of coffee. Even the conversation had been satisfyingly full. All they wanted was to digest the evening's offerings leisurely.

To change the tempo, Paul was ready to take out the gold locket and share with Carl and Jeanette his affection and affirmation for Evi. At that moment however, Carl switched the subject and time frame with, "It's a shame that we don't exactly know how long the show will run. If we have a hit and the seats are still filled after two months, we'll take the extra month's option on the old Greenwich Theatre."

"Yes, that means we either go up to Maine in June or, with a hit, in July," Jeanette took up thread.

"It'll be a great summer," Carl mused. "Evi and Jeanette doing their thing while you and I, Paul, will work hard preparing for the fall season. New plays to decide on, with at least three new roles for you."

Evi looked up from her mug and quietly said, "Carl, I've been meaning to let you know that Paul and I have been invited this summer to my parents' home in Mürren."

"What?" Carl was stunned. He turned cherry red, his mouth dropped, then remained open.

"For one month only," she tried to placate him.

"You know that's impossible." The red now turned to angry splotches.

Paul recognized the surfacing vicious temper and immediately raised his emotional fence by damping all his feelings.

Evi was even quieter with, "We've already accepted."

"Well, you'll unaccept it," Carl raised his voice in reply.

"I can't. They expect us," she murmured.

"And I can come back earlier," Paul finally spoke up. His voice was steady, the barrier in place, though the widening tension on the inside began to wriggle through the solid-steel slats.

"What? You've also accepted?" Carl fumed, his fury now turned fully on Paul. "It's one thing to lose time if the play's a hit; it's another to while away the time doing nothing when there's so much work to be done. How are you going to be a success if you waste time with foolishness?"

"Spending time with Evi is not foolishness," Paul countered.

"Come on, Carl, cool down," Jeanette interceded. "I'm sure we can work something out."

"Keep out of this, Jeanette!" Carl got up yelling. "Things were all set, Evi. You fucked them up. Now you change it back."

"I did no such thing," she said weakly, her voice quivering. "Things were not firm, and I haven't been back home for almost two years. I miss my family. They miss me."

"There you go again, Evi," Carl shot out. "It's one year, not two. You're always messing things up. Even when I was fucking you, you almost managed to fuck things up between Jeanette and me. You're the typical devious bitch."

Evi began to cry, her face disappearing into her hands. She looked ever so fragile. Carl continued with venom, "Once you seduced me you didn't want to let go, admit it."

"Carl, don't go . . ." Paul began.

Carl did not let Paul continue. "And you shut up, you snake. Here I give you the opportunity of a lifetime to get your career into orbit, one that was nonexistent before I picked you up from nowhere, a nonentity. And what do you do? You shoot me in the back. You still need a lot of work, young man. And if you think you can make it by yourself, you're welcome to try. What about your learning to become an assistant director? I have big plans for you Paul. And all you want to do is relax in the mountains!" The volume of his voice was now a bellow, an amplifying system gone awry.

"I told Paul he could stay in Maine," Evi came out of her sobs.

Without a pause, Carl switched back to Evi, "Oh yes, sure you told him to stay here, while at the same time engulfing him in you. Oh sure, 'you can stay,' you said with smooth words, all the while holding his ass and pulling him by his unthinking cock to follow you where you want him to go."

With new-found courage, she answered, "You're talking about *your* penis, not his and it's you who uses it to . . ."

"You're not the one to talk," Carl laughed loudly, "not with the way you just laid there not moving a muscle, dead both to me and dead inside yourself. One would have thought you were a JAP. I didn't know what to do with dead meat so I handed you over to Paul, who is becoming just like you."

Evi heard these spewed intimate details warped into a web of untruths. Her sobs began again and now turned into loud moans, her teardrops turned into streams. Carl became quiet. No one said anything; everyone was listening to Evi's pain.

Jeanette was mutely curled up in a tiny space on the sofa while Paul was shocked into inaction, into a mute stare. He had heard Carl shout and rant before, but this was incomprehensible; this was crazy. What should he do? Nothing and let Carl get it out of his system; or should he take Evi home right away? And what about summer? His thoughts whirled, his emotions lost in checkmate.

But at that moment Evi decided to act. She suddenly stood up. Still weeping, she ran to the door, quickly unlocked it, and with a bang shut it behind her. No one spoke; no one moved.

"Let her go," Carl said, now quite calm and in control. "It'll do her good to have a good cry."

"No, I must go," Paul said and stood up to follow.

"Wait, we must decide about the summer. I cannot just let you disappear. You need me and we must set up the fall schedule."

"I can't think now." Paul stood still, not moving. "Why don't we compromise; I'll go with her for two weeks, ten days, and fly up to Maine directly from Switzerland."

"You don't understand. I don't compromise! It won't work otherwise. We'll lose too much time."

"That's it," Paul cried, "it always has to be your way. I'm not so sure that that is what I want. My father also made it always go his way. I don't need this at all."

"Look Paul," Carl said with assurance, "you always seem to tie your past to the present. I'm not your father. I love you and cherish your fulfilling yourself. I want you to succeed and you do know that. But this summer you're going to be in Maine and that's that," he paused with effect. Then, firmly, "No ifs, ands, or buts."

"I'll think about it." Paul felt himself giving in. He really had no choice and Evi would understand. She always did. "I'll let you know tomorrow."

"There's nothing to let me know. We'll do a bang-up job together and this fall will see your career skyrocket."

Paul, dispiritedly, went over to Jeanette, kissed her on the cheek while grasping her hand tightly, and left without saying anything to Carl. He got into the hallway just as the elevator door closed. Damn, he missed her. He jumped down the stairs two at a time. He reached the ground floor out of breath, but in time to take Evi in his arms and comfort her with, "It'll be alright; it'll be alright."

They slowly walked across the park, tightly holding on to each other, both needing the closeness, each other's warmth.

Wednesday saw New York tamped down with layers of thick gray clouds. April gloom descended, bringing steady rain. During a period of wet drizzle, Paul began his four-mile walk to the theater in Greenwich Village. He needed time to think, time to get ready for the dress rehearsal of *The Iceman Cometh*.

Paul walked slowly, dressed warmly in the lavender sweater Evi had knitted for his twenty-ninth birthday the previous February. He kept dry in a long tan raincoat, under a large black umbrella. The weather matched his mood; the long slow steps; his somber pace. Normally, he would notice the activity in the city's streets during these city walks, taken as much for stimulation of the pulsating life as to keep physically fit. Today, though, his attention was focused inward.

Crises arise at the strangest times, he thought as he turned the corner. *I'll walk down Park Avenue; less traffic, less stimulation, and better air for my breathing exercises. Out of nowhere, critical moments appear. Here I thought everything was set, all was well. The climb was tough and I finally saw the crest of success looming. And now this! How the hell am I going to give it my all feeling this way? Can I truly lose myself into Hickey's role, compartmentalize my problems, and concentrate on the play?*

His mind wandered over his personal terrain, skipping hither and yon. Scenes with his father kept intruding. "You're dense; and with your big flapping ears, you're a real Dumbo," he vividly recalled how his father in a moment of anger had pinned the name Dumbo on him at the age of eight, a nickname that was immediately adopted by his older sister, Sally.

Another evening, another scene, when during dinner his father, a successful lawyer, yelled, "You're grounded for the next three weeks, young man," an unjust confinement that should have been administered to Sally, for it was her infraction. As a lawyer, his father ran argumentative circles around Paul. Even as he got older, he never won their verbal battles. In addition, there seemed to be no way to please him. This was especially true from the time he had won a single term to the California state assembly. Sally yes, him no. Sally the bright one; Sally the good child who followed Daddy's every lead, so today she is his right hand in the law firm and a well-known attorney in her own right.

"You're going to law school come hell or high water," his father intoned. The first maturing step Paul took was one of refusal. Though accepted to Yale Law School, Paul had said no. For the first time, he did not follow Father's commands. As a result he was given his marching orders. If it weren't for Paul's mother, the break would have been totally clean and absolutely final. Father, who usually ignored her, eventually yielded to her in this case and allowed a reconciliation. Mother's warmth kept him whole when he thought he'd crack; her love right from the start saved him. And now he had Evi. No way is he going to give her up.

He switched the umbrella to his left hand and waited for the light to turn green. Fifty-ninth Street. That's twenty-five blocks, one third of the way. *Damn Carl,* his thoughts circled back. *I hope he's not really going to make it an either/or decision. It doesn't have to be. Better think about what I'm going to tell Carl about Maine. Why does he give these deadlines, cre-*

ate these false crises? In one way, he's just like Dad: a need to have it his way, a Fascist's need to control.

At Forty-seventh Street, just before reaching the Pan Am Building, he stopped. He raised his hand with a majestic flourish and from the depth of his diaphragm intoned "STOP" to a passing cab. It did, though a passenger was already settled in the back seat. He smiled at the success of the acting exercise Carl had given him. Total commitment was the necessary condition for its realization.

His mind wandered back to the time he had rejected his father's command. Instead of going to Yale, he traveled to Europe—got away from the family, lengthened his horizon, and broadened his outlook. The first year helped, especially Rome, *la bella Citta*. It was a happy place of piazzas and marble, trattorias and pasta. The city also introduced him to Anne, his first love. When summer ended so did the romance. She returned to a small college town and he left the Eternal City. This was followed by a three-year interval of treading water in San Diego.

Vividly, he recalled that memorable day: Paul was sitting in sunny Balboa Park complaining to Herbie, who, with easel and brush, was creating a new canvas. "Eight meaningless jobs, some mediocre acting classes, and a small amateur part is all I've got to show for these last years," Paul grumbled to his close friend. "No goal, no purpose."

Herbie looked up from his painting. That was when he told him about Carl. It was Carl who had changed Herbie's life, had given him direction. As a friend of the family, Carl, acting as teacher, friend, and mentor, took him under his professional wing. In just two years, he had Herbie mesh his painting with architecture: his life's art and work into an artistically satisfying weave, a pattern of unquestioned success.

"And he isn't even in my profession," Herbie said, putting away his paints. "He's a director right here in the park's Old Globe Theatre and a natural for you."

So they trod through the park to see if he was in the theater. They entered the door next to the box office and heard mewling noises in front of the glass door marked "Director." Herbie knocked with two short raps. The noises ceased. Nothing happened for twenty seconds. Suddenly, Carl opened the door. He was sweating and, if one looked carefully, the ghost of a bulge in his pants could still be seen. Jeanette was on the sofa, face red and hair disarrayed.

"Herbie, you pick the oddest times," Carl opened the door wider. "Jeanette just climaxed. We've been at it for a while. I've already come twice, so you're not disturbing."

Paul was not reassured and felt awkward. Herbie, on the other hand, laughed, "Knowing you, I almost expected it. I'm glad you two got your rocks off. Listen, if you're not finished, we'll come back later."

"No need to," Jeanette answered, having come down from her plateau. "Herbie, you're a delight for sore eyes. And who's this tall, good-looking man?"

With that introduction to Carl and Jeanette, Paul's life changed: the start of six "quick years." It was intense living and quantum life changes, all held together by the rainbow arc of Carl's vision.

At Forty-second Street, he turned east and headed for the Automat on the corner of Third Avenue. Though a couple of blocks out of his way, he wanted to escape the driving rain. Besides, he was early. He exchanged a half dollar into nickels at the elegant marble change booth located just in front of the cubbyholed bread and roll section. Paul got a corn muffin from a display whose window could only be opened with four of his nickels and then coffee from the brass dolphin spigot that flowed only after paying three more. Carefully balancing his food, drink, and umbrella, he sat down at an empty table for four, unoccupied now that the lunch-hour crush was over.

He poured the sloshed coffee from the saucer back into the cup and reminisced over the many times he and Carl had been here. It was Carl's favorite restaurant, cheap and unpretentious. Having experienced fine cooking in his youth, Paul usually preferred fancier fare. Paul had gotten to like the Automat, though, and through habitual use it had become invested with an "old shoe" comfort.

These past years, his new experiences had changed him. Carl had cast his influence over Paul through their frequent and lengthy talks and the example of his own behavior. Less fear, more feelings, and the ability to take chances were some of the changes Carl had sown and whose fruit Paul had borne. His feelings of diminished worth had abated, and Carl was the agent of this change. Though not a therapist, Carl achieved much more than the two psychiatrists Paul had seen for so many years. The progress astounded and delighted him.

He now felt closer to people. Carl and Jeanette had become his substitute family, trusted and relied upon. Now, even his love life had opened up. He had a lot to be thankful for. Carl did demand payment, though, its coin in the form of complete obedience. Since the start of rehearsals, the cost had become more exacting and expensive. Just last week, Carl had demanded they meet at the Automat at eleven in the morning, which necessitated canceling a dental appointment. Nothing special about the meeting, just a get-together, but he had submitted. Carl commanded and he jumped. *Where will it end?* he pondered.

Yet, in the past six years, the two-man team of Carl in the wings prescribing the moves and Paul on stage following directions had resulted in a continual string of smash hits. The first had been a Q-Tips commercial. Carl had hauled in a favor owed him by a Los Angeles agent. For thirteen weeks, Paul had saturated American television as a friendly pharmacist. Hard work with Carl, a new voice coach, and several small roles—first in San Diego then in Los Angeles—led to his role as Algernon in *The Importance of Being Ernest*.

He had to stretch himself for that one. And now his first Off Broadway role! How far he'd come. Yes, how close to the top he had climbed.

He finished his coffee and began the last half of his wet walk to the dress rehearsal. He spent a couple of minutes on his daily exercise of breathing quickly through his nose, getting as much air as possible into the diaphragm depths of his chest.

To stay sharp, he practiced his lines and cues for one of the acts every day. Today it was act 1 of *The Iceman Cometh*. He began:

ROCKY: Here's the old son of a bitch!

HICKEY: Hello, Gang! [Singing] It's always fair weather, when good fellows get together!

It went letter perfect until he came to:

. . . I finally had the guts to face myself and throw overboard the damned lying pipe dream that'd been making me miserable . . .

Here, Hickey disappeared and Paul took his place. What was his pipe dream? What did he have to face? Being a successful actor was no pipe dream; it's rooted in reality. Paul's thoughts continued to rush in and out: Carl's anger, Evi's love, the summer in Maine, Mürren. Hickey's dilemma made Paul wonder, what would he have to do to make peace with himself? He knew that he was at the breaking point with Carl. He could not give in much more and still be free. What was his pipe dream?

"Ah yes, I have it," he thought. "Carl will make me a star. I need him to make it happen. Didn't I leave the legal quest because, deep down, I knew that I'd succeed only if father made it happen, would lead me into victory. Now for six years I have had these same feelings. Only through Carl can I succeed. My fantasy is that others pave the streets of my victories. But! Oh yes! It's a sure way to lose no matter how high I fly in the theatrical sky. My god, the cost is already too high. I'm not an actor. I'm the slave to a sadist director whose every whim I must obey."

He had to reach Union Square before he finally decided what his summer plans would be. With that decision, he signed an inner peace treaty.

Serenity did not last long. As soon as he entered the theater, Carl collared him.

"Get ready; it'll be a great show," he said maniacally. "Don't forget to have them make up your jowls to age you. Did you make Evi comfortable with the idea that you'll be in Maine with us?"

"No, I didn't." Paul nervously brushed his hair back. "I've decided to compromise and go with her for only one week. In that way everyone involved will be happy."

Carl stared. Then glowered. And then with slow malice, "You're stupid if you think you're going to change the rules at this late date. I don't have time now to convince you. But you better change your mind, or else you will . . ."

He stopped when he saw Paul shake his head from side to side. Paul, with another nervous stroke through his hair, insisted, "It's a fair compromise."

"We'll see." Carl turned away, dismissing Paul.

Paul trudged slowly to his dressing room. On the way, he passed through the set's dreary saloon—sawdust on the floor and melancholy peeling walls. Even the light coming from single wall brackets matched his dense and foreboding mood. He must pull himself together. Become an upbeat salesman. If Hickey, with his murderous problems, was able to do it, he could. He would. With a last run through his hair, he straightened himself and began turning into the bald, life-of-the-party Hickey.

The papered house of friends and relatives, who filled over half the seats, loved the first act. Evi, seated in the rear, smiled broadly when Paul appeared on stage late in the act. Carl had interrupted the action only two times for minor changes.

Act 2 flew by with only one glitch—a glass fell off Larry's table and broke. They ad-libbed and were right back on track. Enthusiastic applause followed the end of the act.

The tsunami began to build in act 3.

Hickey had just lost his temper for the first time and yelled at Larry,

"That's a lie!" He then grins and continued with, "Well, well, you did manage to get . . ."

"Can't you manage to get it right?" Carl yelled, stopping the play dead. "Show us your intensity with a coiled-spring low voice," he continued to shout.

"But you insisted that I yell it." Paul looked at him, confused.

"That's a lie," Carl hollered. Then angrily but in normal volume, "Look Paul, the dress rehearsal is not the time or place to change the rules or direction of a scene. If you don't know how it should be played we'll let Jason show us. I'm sure *he's* prepared."

"Okay, okay." Paul shook his head indignantly and with embarrassment. "I'll say it softly. Just as you want it." He said the last with a trace of sarcasm.

Carl stopped Paul twice more. Nothing important, but it made Paul jumpy and on edge. Finally, the act ended. On his way to his dressing room, Carl stopped him and wanted to know if he had come to any decision regarding Maine.

"There's nothing to decide, Carl. I'll be gone for only one week. I'll even memorize a new role while I'm in Switzerland, so no time will be lost."

"I'm sorry you feel that way," Carl looked at him with disdain. "There'll be more than time lost. Get yourself ready for the fourth act. The last one was miserable." He turned away without giving Paul time to respond.

In the dressing room, Paul took off his wig and bow tie. For the next fifteen minutes as he sat alone, the cast intuitively stayed away. They knew Carl's temper all too well and did not wish to be near the center of this particular cyclone. He sat with eyes closed, thinking, "How far can he let Carl dump on him? Where was the limit?" Not until the final buzzer did he open his eyes to get ready for his big scene.

The explosion erupted near the beginning of his monologue.

. . . I can't figure it—unless it's just your damned pigheaded stubbornness! Hell, you oughtn't to act this way with me! . . .

"That's the last straw," Carl interrupted with fury. "Jason, please come on stage and show Paul how this should be acted."

"Carl, if I've done it incorrectly, let me know what you want. But don't do this to me," Paul cried. "Not in dress rehearsal. It's humiliating."

"Mr. Paul Manes, don't you understand English? Get off the stage," Carl clipped in cold wrath. Then in a normal tone, "Let your understudy, Mr. Robards, give you an idea how this is to be done."

"Mr. Saroff, if you go through with this I'm not getting back on stage today," Paul said decisively, shooting off this small stone of a threat, the only weapon he possessed. The battle line had been drawn here; the line in the sand was crossed.

"Don't threaten me, Paul," Carl narrowed his eyes. "I just want Jason to render the first minutes of the monologue."

"No!"

"What do you mean, no?" Carl was shocked. "No one says no to me. Now get off that stage and see how it's to be done."

"Well, he'll have to finish the act as well," Paul shouted.

"You leave, and you're finished," Carl warned him.

In answer, Paul pulled off his wig and slowly walked off the stage.

"Paul, come back here," Carl yelled, but Paul did not hear. In three minutes, he changed back into his street clothes, not taking time to remove his makeup. He pulled on his sweater and raincoat, grabbed his umbrella and ran out of the theater through the side door.

Evi was waiting for him outside with tears in her eyes. Distraught, he ran into her open arms.

Into the evening, the rain continued to pelt New York. They forced down some of their late dinner but left most of it uneaten; their appetites reflected the deflating events at the theater. Paul phoned Carl to apologize, but got only Jeanette on the other end.

"Carl wants you to know that Robards was brilliant and who gets to play Hickey in tomorrow's opening is up for grabs," Jeanette opened the conversation. "And, no, he won't speak to you unless you change your mind about Maine. Paul, why don't you see it his way? It's very important for him that the two of you work together the whole summer. You can give in just this one time. It's not that important and you must think of your career. Besides, Evi has already agreed."

"Thanks, but no thanks," Paul was firm. "I cannot cross this ridiculous and impossible line and still feel whole. Jeanette, I have a feeling it's going to be a long, long time till we speak again. I'm truly sorry to lose you. If ever . . ." he stopped, choking with emotion. After a couple of seconds, he continued with, "Evi sends her love. Good-bye Jeanette."

Until bedtime, Paul held his emotions together with defiance and determination, but once in bed, the black clouds of feelings thundered down his soul and out his eyes. He cried and sobbed. Evi held him with tenderness and love, allowing him to weep his tears of hurt and loss.

"So close, so close," he repeated over and over. "It was a pipe dream, after all. That's all it was—a pipe dream. Magic. Thinking that Carl, the Svengali, would pull my career out of his hat. But he's black magic and I signed a devil's contract with my own blood. I cannot sign it with yours as well. I can't. I can't."

"It'll be alright," she murmured, "it'll be alright."

She continued to hold him as he sobbed and cried. She rubbed his back, trying to stop his fitful shaking. Evi caressed him gently, softly. Reaching down, she stroked him in rhythm to his sobs. Slowly his crying diminished. When he finally stopped weeping, she did not need to caress him any longer. He was erect. She guided him into her warmth and love. He now followed her rhythm, gentle at first then faster and harder, the rhythm of life.

A Swiss summer is devoted to vacations and children's holidays, autumn to the serious work of earning money, and winter to the joys of skiing down the towering and invigorating snowy mountains. Spring, the time of rebirth and romantic strivings, is practically ignored. Resorts are empty of tourists and the mountain chalets lay snugly deserted by their wealthy owners.

In the late spring of 1963, Herr Professor Doktor Stocker gladly let his daughter, Evi, make use of their vacation house in Mürren. Even when Evi was young, the Stockers went up into the mountains only during the winter holidays for skiing and in the summer holidays to breathe the cool, fresh air of the *Berner Oberland*. So when Evi showed up in Zurich two months early with Paul in tow, the professor quickly arranged to give the lovers use of the empty house, a wooden chalet always kept in ready for guests.

With his head turned to the bright sun, his eyes protected by sunglasses and seeing neither town nor mountain, Paul lay comfortably on the redwood chaise lounge looking only at his wandering inner visions. To focus on his thoughts and gentle mood, he closed his eyes while taking in a deep breath of cool air. By doing so, he eliminated the bright white rays of the sun with their reflections of Murrensteig in the foreground and the high Trinity of Jungfrau, Mönch, and Eiger in the clear distance, the three mountain peaks that always brought radiance into his being.

He marveled at the height's healing power. No wonder tubercular sanitariums exist in the high Alps. For Paul they were truly magic mountains: with each additional foot of altitude, he had shed another mottled layer of hurt, anger, and worry. It was just over one month since that night he yearned to forget, that evening of the dress rehearsal fiasco. Nothing had seemed to help the deep wound from the loss of imminent stardom. He had opened the door, started through it, and just as he glimpsed the white golden light on the other side, Carl fiercely shut it, hurling Paul back down life's dark vortices.

Evi tried to expunge his hurts, soothe his fears, and massage his wounds, but he barred her calming efforts. He withdrew into himself and entered into depression's domain. Initiative was set aside. He took up a role of inactivity of both mind and action. To break this gray granite, Evi suggested sunny Switzerland, to which they had planned to go anyway in a couple of months' time. She hoped their leaving New York for new scenery would open a new vista for him to explore. He did not actually and actively agree. He just let himself be packed onto a plane and transported over the ocean.

And lo! Just five days later, here he was lying relaxed at the Stocker chalet with his oceanic depression practically gone. Life started taking care of itself. Healing had begun even as they took the taxi from the railroad station up to the house. The scenery around Mürren was majestic; the village itself a blue-white jewel. For the first time since that tragic O'Neill night, Paul lost his inner-mourning mood. He began to notice the external world, the bracing clean air of the mountains.

Upon returning to her home and homeland, Evi became the efficient Swiss homemaker. Every morning she went shopping at the local stores. She prepared nourishing hot soups, introduced Paul to fondue and raclette, the renowned melted-cheese dishes, and "riz orientale," the meat, rice, and fruit course that the Swiss had adopted as their own. They took long walks along quiet paths. Instinctively, she knew when to stay away from him. She busied herself with cleaning, sewing, or reading. As she spoke fluently and read avidly German, French, Italian, and English, she was always in the midst of several novels or books on European history.

Just as Evi came out on the patio with some coffee and home-baked butter cookies, she first heard, then saw the black BMW rounding the curve in the driveway.

"Schaetzli," she said softly, gently bringing Paul back to the present, "my parents are here."

Paul slowly opened his eyes. Evi looked wonderful, her dark eyes bright with love, her smile filled with joy. He knew that this happiness of hers was caused by the imminent presence of both her parents. Next to Paul, her parents were her best friends. She quickly put down the refreshments, and ran down the steps to greet her father, a tall, imposing man with a thin but prominent nose and a neatly trimmed Vandyke beard. After receiving a warm but formal kiss on the cheek, Evi hugged her mother, a small, nervous woman. Mrs. Stocker was haunted by squinting attacks, which in recent years had increased both in frequency and intensity. They masked her regular and pretty features, facial qualities that Evi had inherited. Professor Stocker took Evi's arm and led her up the stairs to the patio, leaving his wife to gather up the two small valises from the back of the car and hurry after them.

Paul got up to greet her parents. Professor Stocker reminded him of his own father, a man quick to judge and sure in his movements. His father's arena of action lay in the body of law, the professor's in the body of man. Whereas the elder Manes was tall and lanky, a body well toned by regular exercise, the doctor's tallness was filled out in front with a noticeable potbelly. However, the most important differences between them centered in the large sphere of their emotions. They each reacted to others in a manner indicative of their respective profession: The lawyer dealt with life's relationships in an adversarial stance; the doctor positioned himself vis-à-vis others in a healing posture. While both ruled their world with autocratic authority, one emulated a cold and distant feudal king, the other a firm but understanding monarch.

Paul got up to greet the man, who in his mind was already his father-in-law, with a respectful, "Good morning, Professor Stocker." They formally shook hands, with Paul following the other's lead by bowing ever so slightly.

He turned to greet Evi's mother, a woman he pitied but understood: She had to live in her husband's long shadow. The doctor's friends were also hers, his honors decorated her bosom, and his wishes became not only her orders but also her desires. Paul appreciated how difficult it must be for her to see what went on in the world's galaxy outside the binary system of her tiny planet revolving around his shining sun. She reminded him so much of his own mother, a woman who also did not attempt to glance outward. She had totally involved herself with loving her children and caring for her husband. When the children left home, she narrowed her focus to her fingers as they knitted and purled day after day.

Paul took Frau Stocker's small hands in his. "I'm glad you are able to spend the day in the mountains. It's so peaceful here. It's just what the doctor ordered." He turned with a smile to Evi's father.

The men stayed on the patio while the women went into the house to prepare the meal and set the table for lunch.

Professor Stocker sat down opposite Paul and took out his gold pocket watch. Nodding his head, he said, "Yes, we made very good time. We left after my morning rounds. Luckily there were no emergency operations." Dropping his fob watch deftly back in his vest pocket, he looked carefully at Paul, permitting the silence to mount.

Paul felt he was being judged. He took a swallow of his coffee with one hand as he smoothed back his hair with the other.

Putting down his cup, Paul looked at him directly and said, "You brought up Evi to become a wonderful human being. She's very good to me. I want to thank you. I don't know what I would have done these past months without her love."

Doktor Stocker nodded. "Yes, we all love her deeply. She's a good child with a big heart. I can see that you reciprocate that love. That is also good and it pleases me that she found someone. But . . ." he stopped. He did not continue but let the questioning quiet reign.

Paul moved forward in his chair. "Yes?"

"But . . ." again the doctor paused. Then with a slight nod, he finally put his concerns into words. "But what are your plans? How are you going to support her?"

Paul flushed. "I, I don't have any right now. As you know things did not work out. It's only this week that I've finally gotten back to normal. I had a big shock and it was only Evi's concern and caring that helped me overcome it. I've had no time as yet to think about the future." Then smiling, he continued, "I have just came back to the present."

"Do you want to get back to acting?" the professor asked.

"Possibly. I'm not sure."

"Do you have in mind any other possible directions?" he continued his interrogation.

Paul shrugged. "None comes to mind with any sort of real desire. The one profession I do not want in any shape or form is law."

Evi, who appeared on the patio to bring them into the house for lunch, interrupted their talk. Mrs. Stocker served the meal by herself, making Evi sit at the table. After the main course, Professor Stocker interrupted Evi's description of the two new shops she had discovered in Mürren by turning to Paul and continuing their earlier conversation. "So, as of now you do not know what you will be doing. How about a brand-new direction? Have you ever thought of being a doctor? I'm sure you can get into Zurich University without any difficulty. I do have some good connections," he said, smiling.

"Medicine," Evi perked up. "Yes, Paul, you would make a good doctor. You are intelligent, caring, and do have sensitive hands."

Even Mrs. Stocker in her strong Swiss-German accent chimed in with, "Ja Paul, it is a good profession, good for you and good for the others."

Paul was amused at this unified family offensive. He was certain that each of them worried about Evi's future and security. Though the advice was given with love and concern, it was not well thought out. He really was not the one they were considering; it was Evi they were thinking about.

"Evi," he said, putting his hands on hers, "you know that the sciences were not my strong suit. In college, I studied the humanities and majored in theater."

Dokter Stocker answered for his daughter, "But Paul, do you really dislike medicine? Do you have an aversion for it?"

"No, not really," he looked at his "father-in-law" across the table. "It just never entered my mind. It's a world apart, an unthought-of idea."

"But *Schaetzli,* you do love to study new things," Evi broke in, sympathetically but hesitantly. Paul knew she only wanted what was good for himself in the long run.

"True, I am curious about life, about people," Paul admitted. "However, I've not taken any of the sciences except for math. I don't even have a single course of biology under my belt."

"Well then," Doktor Stocker sat back, satisfied both with the meal and the conversation's direction, "you'll be in good company with the rest of the first-year students. Medical studies begin with physics, organic chemistry, and biology. In Switzerland, as you probably do not know, the study of medicine, including the basic sciences, takes seven years."

"Seven years," Paul was surprised. "That means I'll be thirty-six before I become a doctor and able to support myself."

"That's not a large problem," the doctor countered. "What have I worked so hard for if not to help Evi and the ones who love her? The government does not charge tuition in this country. It therefore is just a question of providing a roof over your head and food on the table. I earn enough to feed three families in comfort. There is no one else besides my wife and Evi that I wish to support."

Paul shook his head. "I cannot accept your money. As of now, Evi and I aren't married. What happens if we decide to break up? Not that I want to or envision it, but one never knows what will happen."

"Father can lend it to you and you can pay it back when you finish school," Evi volunteered.

"Even hardheaded Swiss banks are delighted to lend money to medical students," Professor Stocker nodded.

Frau Stocker got up from the table. "Why don't you *drei* go onto the patio? I'll bring out the fruit *und* linzer torte."

Once on the patio, the doctor intuitively backed off direct arguments and began talking about his patients, the fulfilling nature of being a surgeon, and then onto Zurich's charms and attractions as a city.

Paul knew that all three Stockers had planted the seed of the idea and now it was Paul who would have to decide whether to water and nourish it or let it remain dormant in the ground. He therefore was happy when the conversation veered to other subjects. For the rest of the afternoon, the four of them leisurely talked about politics, both international and departmental. They argued about America's intentions in Vietnam, agreed that Swiss neutrality was good for the whole world, and were amused and chagrined at how fierce the election battle for next year's rotation of the medical school dean had become. Professor Stocker was in the running but with only an outside chance of winning.

When Switzerland's version of high tea, *Z'vieri,* was served, Paul began to talk about his family, concentrating on his mother and sister. As he started to open up, he was able to verbalize his past struggles as a budding actor and the recent disaster with Carl. Medicine was not mentioned again that afternoon, but the thought hovered above the group, darting in and out of Paul's awareness.

At six o'clock the older couple bid Paul and Evi *adieu* and took off for Zurich. This had been the first time that Paul had spent time with the Stockers. Yes, he thought, Evi does have caring parents, and a father who is both successful and loving.

The thought of medicine as a profession was not the only new idea for Paul that particular Saturday in May. That night, when Evi and Paul got into bed, she brought this new concept to light.

Turning to him and holding him closely, Evi whispered in his ear, *"Schaetzli,* I have something to tell you."

"Yes?" Paul tensed slightly. While Evi hesitated and waited a few seconds to continue, he thought, "What now? I do hope it's good news."

With a deep breath, "I haven't had my period." She paused again. "I'm never late."

"But aren't you using your diaphragm?" asked Paul, stunned.

"Yes, Schaetzli, I've used it every single time except that one night. You were so angry with Carl, so upset and hurt. I did not think we would make love or you would be in the mood. But it was beautiful and right, and I felt the moment was more important than my getting up to get it. In fact, I didn't think of it until the next day."

"How sure are you?" Paul wanted to know. Then, becoming gentler, he loosened his strong and unconsciously tight hug.

"As sure as I can be without having the doctor confirm it," Evi said softly, and Paul knew she was smiling at him. "For the last three days, I had to throw up. You know, morning sickness."

Evi having morning sickness convinced Paul. His heart knew that she was pregnant. It dawned on him he was going to be a father. The thought radiated throughout his body and turned into feelings of awe and joy, wonder and delight. He let go of Evi, twisted to turn on the light on the night table, and turned back to look at her with a new vision and glowing light. "My god, she's beautiful," he thought. He held her once again and began repeating over and over, "My love, my love."

Evi held him tightly, her arms fast against him, her hands gently stroking his back. She was ready to lower her hand to his penis, stroke it and make it hard, when she felt his erection growing against her. She was surprised. In the year they had been together it had never gotten hard until she had touched and fondled it. Necessary caresses that sometimes took as long as fifteen minutes before he became erect.

"Yes," Paul said throatily. "I want you; I need you; I love you." He began rubbing against her, at first slowly, then faster and faster. Evi became excited and took hold of his penis and placed it on the mouth of her vagina. That was what he was waiting for. With one strong thrust, they became fully and deeply united, in body as well as in spirit. For once, Evi did not think about pleasing Paul or making sure he remained hard, and this time Paul did not worry about his erection. His thoughts were on Evi and on their tiny offspring. They began to cyclone in on a swirling circle of lust, gasping deeply and losing control. They reached higher and higher, tighter and tighter. With throaty yells and sweaty groans, they reached the loving peak and climaxed as one.

Adversity for some enhances growth, while for others the catalyst needed is good fortune. Paul, who tasted both, prospered doubly. With a maturity that finally described his almost thirty years, he aimed at a new set of life coordinates with laser quickness. The trajectories were set naturally and there was neither need nor time to hesitate.

The decision to marry Evi was made when he awoke the next morning. His body and spirit had spoken for him the previous evening. His love for Evi evolved into a deep commitment in the form of a lifelong union. In addition, their anticipated parenthood would require a legal license.

The decision to study medicine was more difficult. His becoming a father necessitated that he secure a strong base of success, a realm where he acted from both knowledge and strength. Medicine would be such a domain. No longer would he need to react to the wishes of others, nor would he always have to obey another's command.

That morning, Evi and he picnicked in the woods near a stream that gurgled and shimmered just outside Mürren. When Paul broached the subject of a possible medical career, Evi was unusually demonstrative in her reaction.

"How wonderful; how absolutely wonderful. First your proposal and now this!" She threw her arms around him with a force strong enough to throw him on his back. They lay there laughing, their faces touching in joy and glee.

When he righted himself, he went on in a more serious vein, "There are a couple of things we must think out before we announce this decision to your parents. I admire your father, but I don't want to create another *Carl* situation. The Professor is used to getting his way and dominates most situations."

"What do you have in mind, *Schaetzli?*" Evi, in the rarified atmosphere of love, marriage, and pregnancy, looked at Paul in a way that showed him she was agreeable to any condition he deemed necessary. He took her hand and closed his eyes while he thought through the various factors and possible permutations.

"What we must do is arrange conditions so that the two of us will remain independent of your parents."

By the time they returned to the chalet, they had agreed to a plan they both felt was sensible. They would indeed borrow money from her father, but it would have to be as a formal loan: an agreement legally recognized. Exact sums to be borrowed, length of time for repayment, and amount of interest to be paid were all to be negotiated and then given to a lawyer to notarize.

However, the most important part of the plan was not borrowing the money. It was that Paul was not to enter Zurich University. They both agreed they would not be living under the same roof with her parents. Therefore it made no difference where in Switzerland he would study. The cost would be the same. There were five universities, each boasting of a fine medical faculty. Zurich, Basel, and Bern were taught in German while Lausanne and Geneva were in French. Paul instinctively leaned toward German, so it was a choice of either Basel or Bern. It did not matter to Evi which of these two places they would live. Paul would consult with her father. He would know which of the two faculties were better, as well as which one was easier to get into.

When Paul and Evi returned three days later to Zurich, her parents were joyous at hearing about the baby and their decision for Paul to study medicine. The money and formal loan were no problem, but it did take two days to convince Professor Stocker that Paul truly did not wish to study in Zurich. When the doctor finally realized they were adamant in their resolve, he graciously bowed to the inevitable. He immediately helped Paul line up Bern University, the better of the two schools and the one with a strong surgery department headed by his longtime colleague, Professor Waller.

Both Paul and Evi had a full schedule that summer: first was the formal interview with the dean at Bern University, then the hours spent at the typewriter requesting transcripts in time for the fall semester, finding a suitable apartment near the university, buying furniture, and, not least of all, Paul diligently studying German—a task he devoted himself to with avid interest. He found that it was not unlike studying for a part in a play. Here the role was one of being a German-speaking medical student.

For Evi, the summer was filled with setting up home, the advancing pregnancy, and the preparation for their wedding, which was to be held on the first Saturday in September.

The simple ceremony took place in a small church and was officiated by the Stockers' minister. Afterward, they had the wedding meal at the Beau Rivage, the grand hotel along Lake Zurich. Only their families and a few close friends were invited, since it was quite evident she was five months pregnant. Only his mother, sister and brother-in-law, and Jim, his one remaining friend from his San Diego days, represented Paul.

Paul's father canceled at the last moment; an important case obligated him to miss the event. Instead of appearing in person, he called the morning of the wedding to wish his son all the best and sent a $5,000 check with his wife as a wedding gift. Paul, though hurt, was not surprised. *How true to form,* he thought. Time for his father was more important than money, and money in turn replaced time spent in affection and love.

The disappointment did not affect Paul outwardly. For many years he had to deeply inter his unanswered love toward his father, a man too cold and busy to pay attention to his son, let alone permit him to partake in life's joy of filial closeness. Paul's feelings toward his father were displaced onto other men, both the anger and hate on one side and love and respect on the other. He continually kept looking for his father, sometimes far afield, sometimes near to home.

Doktor Stocker, who neatly qualified as substitute parent and who now was his father-in-law, evinced a strong interest in Paul. So on a certain level, Paul was relieved that his own father was not there to compete with his recently acquired close and respectful feelings toward the professor. It was therefore no surprise that on that sunny wedding day, the two of them talked animatedly and interacted warmly, preparing the foundation for a closer relationship: a harmonious structure of respect and affection that was to be built higher and higher with each passing year.

Mrs. Manes and Frau Stocker also talked with an animated harmony, feeling an immediate link and comfort with each other. Both had to manage their families' homes and bring up the children by themselves while sitting at the side of and walking behind their successful husbands. With the children now grown and out of the house, their closed worlds kept getting even more constricted. Though the conversation revolved around the mundane, the contact was immediate and magnetically magical.

The two daughters also achieved close and warm contact. Evi admired Paul's confident and successful older sister, while Sally, though making a mark in the legal world, felt unfulfilled. She had been trying unsuccessfully to get pregnant for several years. Evi's glow was not only the one that every bride carries down the aisle; her carriage and step also shined with motherhood. Each woman complemented the other and rather than compete, they shared.

The day brought forth a successful wedding, a happy celebration.

The next day saw Paul's family departing from Zurich's Kloten Airport while the newlyweds left for their apartment on Brunnmatt-strasse in Bern. Both families returned to the usual; the new couple, on the other hand, sprouted the first leaves on their branch of life's tree.

⚬─⫻─⚬

"Darling, guess what?" Paul came bounding in joyfully. He lifted Evi in a hug and twirled her around.

When back on her feet, she pecked his cheek, and with a "What?" went back to changing Anna's diaper.

"I got the part. I got the part!" He skipped around the room, this time picking up his three-year-old, Johan.

"Daddy got the part. Daddy got the part!" his laughing, twirling son chimed in.

"Well, you always were a good actor," Evi said over her shoulder.

"But this time I'm speaking and acting in German," Paul continued to move rhythmically with his son in arm.

"See what rewards hard work brings? You kept studying the language all the time. You even speak *Schweitzerdeutsch* as well as I do, and I grew up in Switzerland."

Paul knew his strength was based in his uncanny ability to mimic any sound he heard. Languages were easy for him. It even helped him in his medical studies. While other students kept taking copious notes, Paul listened attentively and taped his lectures for review at home. He found he did not need to memorize the voluminous data pushed his way. Rather, he correlated facts and retained concepts in an almost three-dimensional sphere, a knack he had picked up while studying roles.

After they put the two children to bed, Paul told Evi how the director at the Keller Theatre, the Bernese version of an off-off-Broadway theatrical company that was located in an actual cellar, had called him back two times before giving him the role of mayor in *The Visit* by the Swiss playwright Friedrich Durrenmatt.

As was their habit, they both prepared dinner, with Paul cutting up the salad and setting the table while Evi heated the soup and readied the main course of veal, carrots, and spaetzli.

Evi informed Paul of the home news, with the most important being that Johan had built a wonderful structure with his LEGOs that he then named "Paul *Spital.*"

"I'm worried that Johan is mixing up the three languages he's bombarded with at different times of the day," she went on. "You speak to him in English, his playmates and I use Bernese, while he hears high-German on television."

Paul, instead of showing concern, laughingly said, "No doubt Johan is definitely a chip off the old block."

Breaking into the Bernese theater scene was not the only big news that Paul brought home that evening. He gingerly broached this new subject with Evi, "I made an appointment and saw Professor Waller today."

"Yes?" Evi must have instinctively known something important had happened for, as she waited for him to continue, she became absolutely still save for a slight dropping of her shoulders.

"I told the Professor I did not wish to specialize in surgery," Paul said, looking directly at Evi.

"Oh," she whispered. Evi's eyes began to glaze, but she managed to hold herself back from crying.

"I know you've set your heart on me joining your father's practice. I'm flattered and I do wish to please you. That is what kept me from making this decision until now. Even Professor Waller was disappointed. He told me how when they met these past years, your father would always boast about his wonderful and talented son-in-law. In addition, Waller himself wanted me as his resident when I graduate. He told me I have an innate talent and a maturity that he's not seen very often.

"However, I'm sure you noticed these past months how I enjoyed psychiatry. Well, what I haven't told you in detail are the exciting afternoons I've spent in the sex clinic under Professor Spoerri. The cases are fascinating and I've begun to learn all about behavior modification. There are only four universities with behavior therapists on their . . ."

He stopped. Evi's welling eyes had begun to overflow and tears ran down her cheeks. He got up and embraced her, realizing that she had stopped listening after learning that he would not join her father. Just like her mother, her father's wishes were incorporated into herself as her own desires. Her disappointment would be greater than Professor Stocker's. He knew this decision and the resulting dashed hope of the whole Stocker family would be the greatest test of their love. He was afraid that Evi, in some part of her being, would neigher be able to forgive Paul nor understand his need for entering an alien and incomprehensible specialty when he was assured a successful career in surgery. In addition, he would have been able to help her father, both in his practice and eventual retirement.

Paul knew himself well enough that as a surgeon he would be unhappy on two counts. First, he would have to perform operations on people who were unconscious. Patients eventually would be dehumanized into organs. Many were the times he had heard how the surgeons talked about yesterday's gall bladder or that morning's kidney without any mention of the patient. Second, he would be under the aegis of Professor Stocker. His past experiences with both his father and Carl taught him he would not be willing to pay the price that would eventually be demanded of him.

As they both feared, the decision did not sit well with the professor. He became furious and did not speak to or visit them for months. If it were not for the two grandchildren, the rupture would probably have been complete. As it was, it became clear that Paul was no longer welcome in the Stocker home, though Evi and the children were received with open hearts. Professor Stocker adopted a distantly polite mien toward Paul. While keeping his end of the financial bargain, he transferred his former affection toward Paul onto his grandchildren, Johan and Anna.

Paul writhed internally at the older man's treatment of him. He could not hide his feelings of yet another loss that aggravated his doubts about who he was and where he stood in the world. These stacked feelings were a repetition of older ones going back to early childhood, to the impossible demands made by his father and the ensuing years of distant coldness between them. In addition, those emotional and conflict-inducing tapes with Carl, so painfully played out in New York, were stored in the same psychic space.

Once again, many nights were spent crying in Evi's arms, arms that consoled his blackish moods and childhood fears. She loved Paul, her wonderful husband, with an unreserved loyalty. However, as he had feared, there was one area where she was unwilling to fully give him total commitment, the arena of Paul's misalignment with her father's wishes. It was her lack of complete acceptance that did not permit Paul to parry this latest emotional spear thrown by yet another dictatorial father.

It was ironic that the more Paul studied and learned about sexual dysfunctions, the worse his own sex life became. It had never been great, but with Evi their tendrilled arms of closeness overcame his cloudy sexual mechanics. Very early in their relationship they developed their own method for bypassing Paul's predilection for flaccidity. Evi would invariably begin his erection by stroking his penis and continue to manipulate it until it was hard enough for him to penetrate her. Once in a while she would fellate him, but they found the erection so induced would more often than not lose its potency by the time he wished to enter her.

Evi's second birth, her tiredness in taking care of the two children, and Paul's psychological setback with her father all contributed to their having sex less frequently, sometimes as little as once every two or three weeks. Paul, however, needed sex more often than that. He began to masturbate, an activity he had stopped when he met Evi. These acts he did not share with Evi, either physically or verbally.

Outside of the sexual sphere, though, Paul found their love was not only as deep and fulfilling as before but was continually growing. Their disagreements were few and usually occurred more because of tiredness than any real differences between them. Paul became a caring father, especially to Johan now that his son was old enough to respond with love and affection verbally as well as in behavior. He was a child very much like Paul used to be, precocious and with an uncanny ability to mimic his parents in words and tone, and he gathered to himself the fullness of their munificent love.

As a medical student, Paul had right from the start been outstanding. His maturity, a matter of being older than the other students by ten years, as well as his seriousness of purpose as husband and father, contributed to his becoming the brightest star in the medical sky of his class. His professors also liked him for his ability to mold the information they taught into meaningful responses rather than parrot back answers that flocks of students hoped would bring them the teachers' equivalent of a cracker.

Psychiatry in general and behavior therapy in particular became Paul's obsession. He read a lot and then studied still more. He visited Dr. Mayer in London and Dr. Van Eysen in Utrecht to study under them the various aspects of behavior modification as it applied to sexuality. Professor Spoerri accepted his dissertation's subject: "Behavior Modification, an Optimal Treatment for Impotence." By the time Paul had finished treating the ten patients in his research, he knew more about behavior modification's role in sex therapy than anyone in Bern's department of psychiatry and probably more than anyone in all of Switzerland.

Their family life flowed and flowered. The children grew, Evi blossomed as mother and wife, and Paul was nearing completion of the seven hard but rewarding years of his medical studies. Lately he had begun to feel like a "real" doctor, as he was now treating patients in the various clinics on a regular basis.

A few days before the start of the last six-month push of the oral finals—the exams that would give him his degree—he was paged out of the eye clinic. Professor Waller, chairman of the department of surgery, wanted to see him right away. Paul, having already passed through that rotation, could not imagine what the professor wanted.

"Thank you for coming so promptly," Professor Waller showed him into his office. "Please take a seat."

Paul slowly sat down. Something did not feel right. He waited for the professor to continue.

Switching into English, Dr. Waller began with, "Let me come right to the point. Doctor Berger of the *Frauenspital* consulted me this morning regarding your wife. She had visited him last week."

"Yes," Paul interrupted. "She has been irregular the last couple of months and seemed to get more tired than usual. What did Dr. Berger find?" He read the Professor's nonverbal movements as indicating anxiety. Paul absorbed this and multiplied it with his own level of icy fear.

"Professor Berger took the usual tests and gave her a complete workup. You know how thorough he is."

"Professor Waller," Paul interrupted again, this time showing his anxiety with a tremor in his voice. "Please get to the point. What did he find and in what way are you involved?"

"Well," he bought a little time with that one word, but then with a deep breath, he finally cut into the center with, "Your wife has cancer. To be more specific, she has a sarcoma in the retroperineal cavity."

"Are you sure?"

"I am sorry to say that in reviewing the X-rays and all the tests given, I am sure. They leave no doubt. We do not know if it has metastasized to the spleen or the pancreas as yet. However, the good thing is that it probably has not spread above the diaphragm, so it is only a stage two or three sarcoma."

Paul did not remember a single word after this exchange. The rest of the conversation enveloped him with a numbness that permitted no memory of words or sentences. He only knew they had agreed Professor Waller himself would operate and the faster the better.

On the way out of the clinic, Paul found an empty office. He locked the door, sat down in one of the empty chairs, and just stared at nothing.

With hurtling speed, a spinning internal carousel projected slides of his life with Evi. One scene, however, kept coming back again and again: A warm day in Mürren. The two of them alone near a shimmering brook. The sunny chalet nestled on one side while the majestically magical mountain peaks of Jungfrau, Mönch, and Eiger loomed on the other.

He began to sob. "In God's name, why Evi?" he cried. "My darling Evi, my poor Evi," he sobbed. His being shook with crushing moans. His soul grieved.

It was a day of good-byes, a day of losses. Such days occur in the life of every human being, days in which the sun's light is hidden from you even if it shines on those right next to you, days that cry out with a wail of woe, days that never allow the clock to go past midnight. There was so much to take leave of that Paul did not think he would ever rise from the shadow of his soul's depression: a shadow of darkest black, a soul that stared at departing ghosts, a depression woven out of blackest burlap.

"One suitcase, that's all that remains; one city, to leave and not return to." Those were the perseverating thoughts that Paul carried with him as he walked to the tram stop that dreary rainy Tuesday in June. When Paul boarded the tram, he did not know how long he had been waiting, as his mind had already left Bern. A ten-minute ride brought him to the train station. The construction to modernize it had started at the beginning of the year, and Paul wondered if the citizens of the city would mourn their old station, the one they were used to, the structure that had served them so well for over fifty years.

Paul indeed was carrying only one suitcase, which he put down to buy a one-way second-class ticket to Zurich. He looked up the timetable and saw that the express train from Geneva would be arriving in eight minutes on track four. Sure enough, the train arrived exactly eight minutes later, stayed in the station for three, and left at 2:24 on the dot for Zurich.

Wishing to be alone with his thoughts, Paul was thankful that he was the solitary occupant of the compartment. In the past months, he had not been able to separate his tears from his emotions. He would begin to cry, silently but steadily, whenever some emotion would touch his supersaturated sponge of grief. Sometimes the cause would be his thoughts, sometimes an external reminder such as a hairstyle or a child laughing as it held tightly to its mother's hand. These he could understand, but when out of nowhere, with no overt thought or conscious emotion, his tears would suddenly begin to flow down his cheeks, he just had to patiently wait for them to stop by themselves. His will had no effect, his desire useless.

The train began to gather speed as it pulled out of the station. For the last time Paul looked at the gentle Aare River, the arcades of the old city, and the lofty Munster Tower. As the city gave way to the suburbs, he finally and fully realized that he might never see these sights again. His studies were finished and this ride to Zurich was the end of an era, a time that had been both wonderful and devastating, fulfilling but full of loss. These seven Swiss years embodied not only the seven fat and milk-yielding cows but the nightmare of the seven starving and emaciated ones as well.

This time the tears did not flow silently. He began to sob. Once again his loss became unbearable and he could not contain his hurt, could not stay his grieving heart. He began to cry aloud, wracks of pain unsoothed by the water of his eyes. Saying good-bye to Bern had reopened his wounds, losses not as yet healed by time nor scarred over by forgetfulness. He continued to cry and cry. It was only when the conductor came through the car to punch his ticket that Paul's tears suddenly ceased. It had begun without his will and ended without being completed.

He now sat quietly looking out the window, not seeing the passing fields and not aware of buildings, cars, or distant mountains. Rather, his eyes were fixed on his first memories of the three mountains towering over Mürren, the icy peaks wearing their aprons of fog, the cold freezing heights of shadow and light. His eyes were focused inward, his feelings circling round and round, his memories alive with Evi.

Professor Waller had pronounced the dreaded news: sarcoma. Evi had intuited the verdict but did not lose hope. Two days after the discovery, they operated on Evi. They tried to relieve future pain by partially removing some of the encroaching tumor—it being already far too advanced to remove completely. During the operation, complications ensured from the moment of incision: Enormous loss of blood followed by a precipitous drop of blood pressure were the first catastrophes. A sudden heart stoppage required heroic efforts. To no avail! Evi died on the operating table.

Professor Waller had taken Paul aside in the waiting room and with heavy heart told him the awful news. Her sarcoma had already spread beyond the diaphragm and she would not have had long in any case. He explained to Paul that it was for the best; she would have suffered horribly the few months left to her. Months of pain, persistent and unyielding, pain not amenable to drugs.

Paul recalled vividly the Professor's face, remembered the weary lines around his eyes, heard the harsh sadness of death in his voice. Paul had become still. He stopped his breath. His eyes concentrated on the doctor, his ears on his own heartbeat. He just stood there not saying anything, not moving. In tandem with his muscles, his mind willed itself into numbness. He wished his own life to match Evi's death. He became a stone, a statue that began to lose its heat. His death wish ascended and life's force diminished.

With an instinct buttressed by empathy, Professor Waller snapped Paul out of his cataleptic fugue with two hard slaps on the face. The power of life manifested itself. He closed his eyes and his body collapsed of its own weight. The Professor, with outstretched arms, caught Paul before he fell and eased him into a leather chair. Paul did not break down, at least not then. The shock of Evi's death severed his emotions of grief from his rational mind. He encapsulated his feelings and began to take care of death's details with an efficiency of a doctor and the assurance of an undertaker.

He had the professor break the news to Doktor Stocker, his colleague and friend of over thirty years. For some irrational reason, Paul felt that his in-laws would in some way blame him for their daughter's sickness and demise. He also arranged for the body to be shipped to Zurich, for he knew that her place was now to be in the family plot beside her grandparents and, in the future, her parents.

The most difficult task was the one that concerned his son, Johan. Anna had already been sent to her grandparents two days previous when they had decided on the urgent operation. Evi had been able to take care of Johan the first night while a neighbor took over the second day. Now that Paul had completed the necessary phone calls, he knew what must be done. He took his son out of school and brought him back home, an apartment now missing the younger sister. An empty place that would never again experience a mother's care or the love and laughter of his Evi. Paul was silent and somber as he accompanied the boy up the steps and opened the door.

Though only six, Johan was mature in ways that often surprised Paul. Paul had not prepared the boy in any way for Evi's serious illness, let alone her death. The catastrophe had cycloned in from nowhere.

Johan suddenly went in to the kitchen, opened up the refrigerator, and brought back a bottle of beer. He asked, "Daddy, would you like a cold beer?" Paul drank alcohol only when extremely tense or if there were serious problems that needed a looseness of spirit.

"Why, yes, my big boy," Paul took the bottle from his son. He put it on the table and raised Johan onto his lap. He did not know how to begin. How do you tell a small boy that his mother is no more? How do I tell my son that Evi is gone and that she exists only in our minds, in our hearts?

He began by holding Johan tightly, then lifted his head and looked at him directly. "I just came back from the hospital and Mommy . . . Evi is very sick." Though able to keep his grief at bay, his voice still quivered when he said "Evi." He used the doctor's time-honored strategy of announcing bad news a little at a time.

But Johan heard Paul's unspoken news and unnamed loss. He promptly began to whimper. Paul once again took him to his breast and held on tightly, comforting both Johan and himself with, "There, there, it'll be alright, it'll be alright."

Suddenly Johan took Paul's head in his small hands, leaned over, and whispered in his ear, "Mommy's dead, Daddy," and now Paul couldn't hold back his tears. He also began to whimper, trying to hold back the flood. He shook, held on to his son, and shook some more. They both now heaved with gulping sounds and shaking sobs, each of them fighting for a semblance of control and neither able to. They began to stroke and caress each other's face, neck, and back. Since they could not control their emotions, they stopped their moving hands.

They began to cry deeply into the narrow space between them, clutching each other, Paul tightly and Johan spasmodically.

It was many minutes before Paul was able to stop and realize that he was not alone in his loss and that he needed to comfort Johan. Once again he was able to separate his feelings and begin to deal with the matter at hand: a son who just lost his mother. He began to speak slowly and rhythmically. Saying over and over again that it was for the best, that Mommy was at peace, that Mommy did not have to suffer anymore. He began to change the sentences. He began to talk of the present, saying that Johan has to be a big boy, a brave boy, that he would now have to care for Anna, be an example to his younger sister. With the love flowing from him, he was able to get Johan to stop his deep cry of loss. Slowly Johan began to whimper more than cry; at last he too was able to stop altogether.

Intuitively, Paul had Johan set the table while he prepared some sandwiches. It was the first time the two of them had shared in the preparation of a meal. For Paul it was the first step in a life without Evi; for Johan it was the first sharing with his father, now his only parent.

That night after Johan fell asleep, Paul talked to Evi's parents. They also were in shock and the conversation was mainly devoted to the burial service to be held in two days. They decided that Paul was to pack Johan's essential wardrobe and when they came to Zurich for the funeral, Johan would stay on with Anna and the Stockers. Paul had to study for his finals and was in no position to take care of his two small children. Paul did not like the idea, but at that moment could not suggest a better solution.

He then called San Diego and broke the awful news to Sally. She was able to say only "Oh God, oh God," over and over. Paul asked her to be the one to break the news to his mother and father. If they could make it, he would like to have his family at the funeral. He felt so alone. Sally finally managed to come down to speech level and told him that she definitely would be there and that she'd also try to get their parents to fly over.

So it was. Two days later, Paul and Johan arrived in Zurich with two large suitcases containing Johan's clothes, books, and toys. Paul, dressed in his dark gray suit, did not have any luggage of his own, as he planned to return the same evening after the burial. Upon arriving with Johan at Professor Stocker's luxurious home, with its magnificent view of the city from the top of Zurichberg, Paul was met at the door by Frau Stocker and Anna. His daughter ran into his arms and joyfully told him, "American Oma and Opa are here, Daddy."

Giving her a big hug and kiss, he put her down and told Johan, "Take care of your sister."

Turning to Frau Stocker, he asked, "Where are my parents?"

She led him into the living room, a room full of people—none of whom he knew except the Professor himself, his parents, and his sister. He nodded to Professor Stocker and greeted Sally with a warm hug and a kiss on the cheek. He then tenderly held his mother, who was already welling up with tears, and murmured, "Mother, Mother."

She in turn held on to him, saying, "Oh my darling, my darling. She was such a wonderful woman, Paul."

It was then time to let go of his mother and face his father. He had not seen him for over eight years. Outside of being grayer and his face somewhat more lined, his father still emanated the aura of strength and sureness of former years. Paul extended his hand and said, "It's good to see you, Father."

The elder Mr. Manes responded with a firm handshake. "You look fit, my son. I'm truly sorry that after all these years we have to meet at such a sorrowful occasion. The Professor and his wife have been extremely kind and thoughtful. They've made us feel most welcome."

"How like Father to center the conversation on himself and his feelings," Paul thought. No word or reflection about Evi's death or my loss.

He turned back to Frau Stocker and inquired, "How has Anna been these past four days?"

Frau Stocker's face lit up with a smile. "What a darling and well-brought up girl Anna is. A wonderful child. We first explained her mother was sick. It was only yesterday she was given the news of her death, but that you, her daddy, would be here today. She cried almost continually yesterday but today she seems to have recovered. Outside of asking for her mother a number of times, she seemed to be waiting for you."

Paul noticed that Frau Stocker hardly squinted as she kept on about Anna. Paul was glad that during this time of loss she had managed to gain some measure of happiness through her grandchild. It was not only Anna that occupied Evi's mother; she suddenly remembered that Johan was now in her charge as well and dashed off to give both children a snack before they all left for the church service.

Paul's memory of the day was full of huge holes of amnesia. One minute he was in a room full of chatting guests, talking about small and insignificant matters and aware nonetheless of large, somber wings hovering over them all. The next moment they were silently crowded into the small Evangelical-Reformed church. This time the minister, instead of uniting the couple in holy matrimony, was officiating at death's separation. Though the minister was quiet with understatements, soft with praises, and gentle with family memories, the congregation reacted with a flood of tears. Paul himself did not remember what the minister had said—did not recall a single phrase. However, he did remember how Johan on his right and Anna on his left began to cry and how he himself started to sob, pressing tightly their small hands in his.

After the eulogy and while waiting for a limousine to carry him to the cemetery, Paul managed to have a short conversation with Sally.

"I had to console mother," she said, her eyes red and her voice scratchy. "She's taking it as her own loss. She dearly loved Evi, you know. Though I don't understand German, I felt the loss and Evi's gentle spirit hovering over the service."

The procession to the cemetery took under a half hour, the actual internment not much longer. The minister, having already spoken about Evi at the church, read only a few appropriate prayers from the Bible. The immediate family stood at the grave, friends and colleagues behind them. Mrs. Stocker held on to her husband with one hand and Anna with the other. When the earth started to cover the coffin, Paul took his children's hands, bent down and told them to say good-bye to Mommy. They did, with words and tears.

The next memory had them back in the car once again. This time to the Beau Rivage for the *Leidmahl,* the Swiss repast ritual for the dead. It was a big affair, for Professor Stocker had instructed the minister to invite all their friends and colleagues, not wishing to limit this ritual meal in honor of his departed daughter only to their closest relatives.

The children were taken home. Their day had already been one with too many ceremonies, too many stimuli—a day of death that stretched their fantasies and confused their souls. The maid was instructed to feed them an early dinner and put them to bed as soon as possible.

Paul felt it ironic that once again the buffet was at the Beau Rivage. There were so many reminders of his wedding day: the minister, the church, and now the same hotel. However, this day took place without Evi, without his wife, his companion and friend. His mood was black, his emotions cloudy gray. He looked around the room. People were eating. Many were drinking. Few were sad. With time stretching slowly, the mood of the room became bright, loud, and finally joyous. Jokes were told and people laughed. Paul noticed the Stockers and the Manes were infected with the room's lively atmosphere and happy ambiance. Even they began to smile, began to live without their Evi, experience life without their daughter, without their daughter-in-law.

Paul was not infected by this ritual of life, not taken in by the paradoxical joy of the room. For him, death's scythe could not be sheathed with a ritualized buffet. His grieving heart could be stilled neither by expensive drinks nor by expansive talk.

He did not say good-bye. He just left and boarded the train back to Bern. He rode back to his empty house, leaving his children with one set of parents and leaving the body of his wife lying next to two of her grandparents. His good-byes were left unsaid, his voice too busy answering his own ghostly and icy thoughts.

Here he was, one half year later, once again on a train. Once again he was leaving; this time the city of his last seven years; the city where his children were born; the Swiss capitol city of Bern. Now he was leaving his home, emptied by Evi's death and his children's move to Zurich. Though they had come back these past months for weekends and short holiday visits, the echoes of his former life left Paul aching for his beautiful family.

Why is it that trains mean departures for me? he thought. *Not arrival or adventure, just sadness and loss.* As he headed for Zurich, he yearned for some feeling of joy. His pleasures, however, were tainted with the muddy colors of anguish, his successes hanging listlessly in the heavy still air of bereavement.

He had passed his six months of oral finals with distinction. He had become one of the most respected graduates, both by his fellow students and the faculty. In some ways, his dedication to learning and the long hours of studying had been mourning's escape hatch. He was able to immerse himself into each medical subject with a deep focus that helped split apart the wasteland of his loss. He lost himself in the human body, its functioning and failings, and in man's ability to heal and mend. Each illness understood, each medical advance grasped, helped Paul take a measure of nurturing solace from his own sad and untraveled journey.

In some ways, Zurich was going to be even more painful than Bern. Paul knew that saying good-bye to his children would be a deep hurt to be neither dulled by a tranquilizer nor eliminated with an anesthetic.

Upon arriving in Zurich, Paul's mood remained grim, the joy of seeing Johan and Anna tempered by the time left to spend with them—only two days. In forty-eight hours he would leave them behind and fly back to the United States. No longer would he be a father to his children even on the limited basis of weekends. Now the time for sharing and living together was to be nearly eliminated by the distance of an ocean. Between the cost of transportation, his upcoming impossible schedule at the hospital, and the children's schooling, he knew he would become a father experienced more in his children's memories than in an actual life lived together.

His joyfully scrambling children greeted him immediately at the door. They had not seen Paul for over two weeks, as he had to study hard for his last two exams, ophthalmology and dermatology. In addition, he had to close up the apartment and sell all the furniture. Both Johan and Anna gabbed away, telling him all the news of their happy lives. It was obvious to Paul that both Professor and Mrs. Stocker were doing a wonderful job filling in for their daughter. In the children's eyes and hearts, the grandparents were becoming their emotional parents.

Paul put down his valise and lifted both of them up into his arms. He carried them into the living room and fell into the large easy chair with both still holding on tightly. He kissed Anna and hugged Johan again and again. Catching their mood, he began to giggle and speak as fast as both of them. Frau Stocker, who had let Paul in, saw the love and happiness of the three Manes and quietly slipped out of the room to prepare *Z'vieri*. When she returned with the afternoon tray of cookies, tea, and hot chocolate, the three were still enveloped in their close and intimate world: Anna and Paul laughing as Johan demonstrated the latest successful goal he had kicked at the school game that morning.

Paul was to leave in two days, so the children were permitted to have dinner with the adults both evenings. Professor Stocker made it a point to come home early. He wanted to spend as much time as possible with Paul before he left for his American internship. His relationship to Paul had improved again; this time the closeness had been forged by the tragedy of death on one side and the joyous arrangement of raising his grandchildren on the other. In some ways, they felt closer now, knowing that from now on they were connected in a way that could be torn apart neither by one-sided expectations nor by emotional and age differences.

Paul had tried his best to arrange for his children to live with him. But fate decreed otherwise. His sister, though at first open to the possibility of having them live with her, nevertheless had finally declined. Though she had no children of her own and would have liked to help raise Paul's, Sally explained to Paul that her husband would not countenance Paul and the two children living with them. Their marriage had its share of misunderstandings and could not carry the additional stress of having her brother's children becoming part of her household.

After Sally's refusal, Paul really had no other choice but to yield to the Stockers' strong desire to raise Johan and Anna themselves. Their arguments were heartfelt and correct. They were financially well off, they loved their grandchildren dearly, and, most of all, the children adored them. Most convincing, Paul would not be able to take care of them himself. He did not have any money and for the first four years of training he would be earning very little. His hours would preclude spending much time with them, and a full-time housekeeper was out of the question.

After anguishly deciding it would be best for his children to be raised by their grandparents, Paul had thought hard and long about his own plans. He himself could not remain in Switzerland without Evi. She had made it his home. With her gone, he felt like the foreigner he was. Not having graduated from a Swiss high school meant he would not be able to open his own practice unless he took a grueling equivalency exam.

It really boiled down to his desperately wanting to return to America. Without Evi, he had no life here. He had to pick up the pieces of his life in the United States. Even if it meant he would be separated from his children, he could always visit them here and they could vacation with him there. They would benefit from living in two different cultures and experiencing love on both sides of the Atlantic. He knew by creating a more fulfilling and satisfying life in America it would ensure that his children, in the long run, would feel better about themselves.

At the end his choice had narrowed down to New York or San Diego, the two cities he knew well, the two places where he could live comfortably while slaving through his internship and residency. He had applied to both U.C.S.D. and New York Medical College. He was lucky. Unable to be on the matching internship program, he was notified at the last moment that an opening in a psychiatric rotation was available in New York. One of the previously accepted applicants had to serve his time in the armed forces. This was Paul's only connection to the Vietnam War.

During dinner that night, Paul explained to Professor Stocker the differences between American and Swiss medical training. Paul would be starting his internship on July first. Because he would be on call every third night, he had to find an apartment near the hospital. During his first year he would have at least four months of psychiatry. The residency that followed would last three years. It was only after four years of training that he could and most probably would open his own practice. Without being explicit, Paul made both the professor and his wife understand that they would be able to have Johan and Anna only for that period of time.

After dinner, the children were allowed to join the adults in the living room for one hour. Over coffee and brandy, all the adults' interactions centered on the little boy and girl. Though the children laughed and played with verve and vibrant excitement, even they realized that Paul would be going far, far away. They kept touching and kissing him. The grandparents, who usually got their full attention, sat passively on the sofa, content this time to observe.

When Frau Stocker finally put the children to bed, Paul came into their bedroom to tuck them in and give them their going away presents. He sat down on Anna's bed and gave her a large box.

With large happy eyes and nervously grasping fingers she said, "Daddy, I cannot open it. Please, open it." Paul helped unwrap her gift. "Oh Daddy, she's beautiful."

"What are you going to name her, Schaetzli?" Paul asked.

Anna became still with the complete serious concentration only a four-year-old can muster.

Finally, after about twenty seconds, her face lit up, "She has beautiful hair just like Mommy. I'm going to call her Little Evi, Daddy."

Paul choked up and couldn't talk. Instead, he clasped Anna to himself. When he finally was able to quiet his emotional whirlpool, he said, "Yes, Schaetzli, it is Little Evi. I'm sure you will love her just like Mommy. You and Little Evi can play house and take walks . . ." He paused, his voice breaking, before ending with, "and you can teach her all the wonderful things you learn."

He turned to Johan, who had quietly watched while his younger sister received her present. Paul went over to his bed and gave him a smaller package. Johan deftly tore apart the bow, string, and paper. He also was delighted by Paul's choice.

"Oh Daddy, it's *Max und Moritz*," he cried. "Anna, it's *Max und Moritz*," he said, jumping up and down. "Daddy, please read it to us. Please."

Paul had bought his son the illustrated book of Wilhelm Busch's classical children's story of Max and Moritz, two young boys whose adventures always got them into trouble. He agreed and read to his children the first adventure about Widow Bolte and her four chickens.

After the story he closed the book and told Johan, "You'll soon be able to read the book yourself since you are doing so well in school. Your grandmother, I'm sure, will in the meantime be delighted to read it to both of you," including Anna.

The next evening was the last before Paul's departure for New York. Though the mood was one of music played in the sadness of a minor key, the warmth and goodwill of all concerned permitted a tranquility and calmness belying the family's parting. Paul had spent the whole day with his children. He had taken them shopping and once again bought them presents. At Carl Weber's toy store, he got Anna a simple picture puzzle depicting the Statue of Liberty. Johan, given a choice of a model car or another book, picked the book—intuitively knowing Paul would be pleased. This time Paul chose an English copy of *Tom Sawyer*.

Professor Stocker also gave out presents that night. He had obviously thought deeply about how to express his love for his new family branch. Paul was deeply moved with both presents he received from his father-in-law. The Professor would pay the transatlantic airfares for the children as well as Paul for the duration of Paul's internship and residency. Paul realized it was Professor Stocker's way of telling Paul that he would neither be replaced as father nor would his position be usurped. The antique music box, a Swiss family heirloom in the Stockers' possession for over four generations, proved to Paul that though in the eyes of Swiss society he was an outsider, in the hearts of *this* family he was truly their son.

Professor Stocker said his good-byes to Paul that night, as he would have to be at the hospital at 6:30 the next morning. The following morning, Frau Stocker drove Paul and both children to the Kloten Airport, permitting Johan to miss classes once again.

Over the past two days, good-byes had been said many times, so the emotional parting had already taken place. Frau Stocker worried what to prepare for dinner that evening, the children were enthralled with the planes, and Paul already had one foot in New York. Thus, the actual parting was short in duration and flat in feelings. The kisses, though, were warm and the hugs hard and long. A perfunctory "see-you-very-soon" were their final words.

Dr. Paul Manes left Zurich aboard an American Airline flight, traveling nonstop to New York, at exactly 11 a.m. on June 21, 1970.

Paul—December 1970

The one o'clock lunch shift was the last and smallest of the day but the cafeteria nevertheless hummed with activity. As ever, the almost completely filled dining room reverberated with the garbled hum of table talk intermingled with clanking of dishes and cutlery. The walls were, even here, painted the uninviting light green that coated most New York hospital walls. Only the white islands of Formica tables and empty seats and the gleaming stainless steel structure of the food's showcase relieved the unappetizing color of the room. The employees who ate there every day agreed the meals matched the wall color: insipid and tasteless.

Johan and Anna, though, were enthralled. It was their first visit to Daddy's hospital, their first experience with a cafeteria, and their first taste of American institutional cooking. Johan chose a hamburger, a large order of French fries and a chocolate pudding, while Anna selected fried chicken, corn on the cob, and an Eskimo Pie.

Paul paid for the lunches and eyed an empty table on the left side of the room. He led the three of them toward it. Halfway there, someone else grabbed it. Paul stopped, but then noticed Sophia alone at a table just to the right of him.

"Hi Sophia, do you mind if we join you?"

"Not at all," shaking her head, "and who are these two delightful children?" smiling warmly at them.

"They're mine, and their names are Johan and Anna," he answered, a father's pride bursting through his usual quiet demeanor. Turning to the youngsters, he continued, "Children, this is Sophia. She is a lovely and efficient nurse who works in the emergency room."

"Why thank you." Sophia was pleased with Paul's open compliment. She then turned to the children, "Your daddy is a good doctor and I like working with him when he has patients in the emergency room. And how old are you, Johan?"

"I am six years old," he said proudly with a strong German accent, "and I am going to start school next year and I will a surgeon like Opa become."

"I will become a surgeon like Opa, Johan," correcting his son's syntax.

"And how old are you, young lady?" Sophia questioned the quiet but attentive Anna.

"*Ich, nein,* no . . . four?" Anna first looked down, then up at her father, obviously questioning the language, not her age.

"Yes darling, that's right. You are four years old," Paul agreed and began to stroke her dark hair. "I am four years old," he instructed slowly and clearly.

Johan, not wanting to lose the center of their attention, broke in with, "Pappy, *Sie hat schwartzes Haar wie . . .*"

"No, Johan," Paul interrupted his son, "in America we speak English. What about Sophia?"

Without pausing, his son immediately changed languages. "She has black hair just like Mommy had."

"And just like Little Evi," piped in Anna.

"Yes, children, Sophia does have lovely hair." Paul began to stare at her long and flowing hair, which did indeed remind him of Evi's. He had been aware that the first time he had seen her he had been attracted to her. Aside from her dark hair, though, her features were different from Evi's. Sophia had a Roman nose, narrow but prominent cheekbones, and full lips, each feature in itself irregular, but in totality an exquisitely intriguing face. However, because she displayed a reserve that matched Evi's European upbringing, Paul, for the first time since coming to New York, was willing to navigate the necessary rapids to get to know her.

It was true that he had not made any overtures the several times he had seen her in the ER. He had not taken advantage of an ideal opportunity when just the previous month they had worked long and hard trying to calm down an agitated, delusional, and paranoid patient. The man had believed he was being followed by the Russkies, that the bartender was without question a double agent, and that he had a direct telepathic line to Mary, Mother of God. In the end, Paul had Sophia inject him with a huge dose of Thorazine before they admitted him to a ward. Sophia, following Paul's lead, had always been strictly professional in their interactions. Until this day, Paul had not made any step to change the status quo. Bringing his children to her table was his opening move, pawn to Queen 4, in the game of life and romance.

To deflect Paul's intense stare, Sophia picked up on Johan's remark and echoed, ". . . just like Mommy had?"

"Yes," Paul's mood switched to memory's pain, "she died a year ago. Of cancer."

"Oh, I'm so sorry. I didn't know," Sophia backed off into her normal reserve. After a slight pause, "Do the children live with you?"

"No," Johan broke in, "we live in Zurich with Opa and Oma. We're here visiting Daddy and today is our second day in New York and I took care of Anna on the plane."

"My, what a big boy you are," Sophia voiced her approval of his protective feelings toward his younger sister. Instinctively, she gave him a hug. "I also had a brother who took care of me when I grew up. Tony is also just two years older than me and I love him dearly." The last sentence was directed to Paul.

"Are you aware that I hardly know anything about you?" Paul decided to now move his second pawn. "Would you have some time in the next five days to join us? I want the children to see New York, and I'm sure they'd love for you to come along I know I would."

Hesitatingly, she answered, "Well, the next couple of days are impossible. In fact, I leave this afternoon for Troy to spend Christmas with my family." She paused and closed her eyes for a moment. With a brisk nod of her head, she continued this time in a stronger voice. "But how about Thursday evening? I have an early shift and get off at four. The evening is open and I'd love to spend some sightseeing time with the three of you."

"That's wonderful." Paul smiled with delight. "The kids fly back on Friday. It'll be great. I'll set up something exciting for the four of us." Again he smiled at Sophia, then at Johan, all the while gently squeezing Anna's shoulders.

That was the beginning.

Thanks to Professor Stocker's generosity, his children had been able to come to New York for a short one-week Christmas trip—Paul had to switch three days off in order to have a full six days with them. They had both grown in the half year since he had left Switzerland and in many different ways they had also grown apart from him. It took a lot of patience and unconditional love on his side to recement their nuclear family connection. After finishing lunch at the hospital cafeteria, he first took them to the zoo in Central Park, followed by a visit to F·A·O·Schwartz, where they gawked and marveled at the unending aisles of toys and dolls. The three of them spent the evening, a quiet Christmas Eve, at his apartment.

With luck aiding necessity, he had found the perfect place on his first day in New York: a professional apartment with seven small rooms on the first floor of a staid and solid building on East Eighty-fourth Street. It also was just a fifteen-minute walk to Metropolitan Hospital, the theater of operations where he would spend his working and waking hours for the next four years.

Christmas morning was magical for the three of them. The kids loved their presents: a microscope for Johan and a teddy bear for Anna. Paul took them to see Walt Disney's *Fantasia* and they finished the day at Leo's Coffee Shop. He indulged them once again with hamburgers and ice cream. However, the highlight of their stay with their father took place the following Thursday evening. Sophia came over after work and prepared a delicious home-cooked meal. As Paul had been lucky to get four tickets, they topped off the evening with the *Nutcracker*. The children were enthralled and the two adults fully shared their wonder and laughter.

Friday, Anna cried all the way to the airport. She wanted to remain with Daddy. All of Paul's promises that he would visit them the following June did not alleviate her pain. Johan, on the other hand, was anxious to get back to Opa and relate to him all the adventures of the big city. Paul felt the pain of separation once again but no longer in the fog of grief he had experienced just a brief six months ago.

It was only now that Paul realized he had been living in a cinereous world of hard work, long hours, and little feeling. With his children flying off to Europe, Paul understood the internal mechanisms he had employed for living through his first months of ashen grief. The hellish first year after medical school is, for most interns, twelve months of unrelieved pain. It consists of getting up after four hours of sleep, being on call every second or third night, and doing the scud work as first-year flunkies to the now all-powerful and nonfeeling residents. For Paul, this hypnagogic work schedule was his road to sanity, his path to health.

Evi's death and being separated from his children had narcotized Paul into living in the grayish waters of action and behavior devoid of the vivid colors of emotions. He had left Zurich buffeted by waves of depression and had arrived in New York dulled by the long, uncomfortable trip and a succession of small bottles of airline alcohol. The necessity of work and movement freed Paul from having to feel deeply or look carefully into his weeping soul.

At the start of that intern year Paul had added his own heavy schedule of tasks to the already full calendar of hospital work. He outfitted and decorated his apartment; at first renting, then buying his furniture piece by piece. In addition to acclimatizing himself to American hospital procedures, he had to immediately begin studying for his FLEX exam, the equivalency test for graduates of foreign medical schools. On December 10 he had passed it with a sigh of relief; he was now on par with American graduates and would be able to practice where he pleased.

Finally, to ensure his emotional wolves were kept at bay, he taxed himself to the limit by undertaking the start of his book on impotence, the subject of his Swiss dissertation. He arranged with Dr. Nagel, the expert in behavior modification, to obtain forty impotent male subjects for his study. Paul knew that a specialty in sex therapy and sex research required original work if he were to compete successfully in this up-and-coming area of psychiatry.

What Paul went through his intern year, he would be able to recall only with a vagueness that was entwined in a thick net of confusing details. His mind had been there; he had worked hard and long and had learnt his medicine well. However, having left his heart and soul back in Switzerland, only the tips of events stood out, islands in a sea of forgetfulness.

Most clear were the vivid scenes of the hospital:

His first code 5 and how the doctors and nurses came running. The woman was successfully resuscitated, only to die the following day.

The night he braved down the yells of the screaming naked man in the padded cell, entering alone to inject him with a major tranquilizer.

The eyes of the distraught, hallucinating young woman in 7A, eyes filled with dark horror and fear, induced by inner visions and experienced through a sundered psyche.

There were also the kaleidoscopic scenes of New York:

The lonely and tired midnight dinners sitting alone and silent at Leo's Coffee Shop; the shrill sirens of the ambulances and fire trucks at all hours; the neighborhood bag lady, tall and thin, with cheeks painted bright doll red.

There were also a few scenes in his apartment:

The first small party he had for a couple of fellow interns, getting high on pot and wine and talking shop all evening; crying in bed countless nights, mourning Evi and missing his children; talking to his sister in California once a week.

Of course, it was his trip to Zurich in June 1971 that Paul would remember most clearly. Though the well-ordered city was a dark, somber reminder of his loss, he felt wonderful to be back once more with Johan and Anna. He stayed with the Stockers and reestablished the close connection, a connection forged by the tearing grief of Evi's death. It was a wonderful two weeks and a much-needed change from the harsh emotional exile of his New York internship.

Ten of those days Paul spent alone with his children at the Mürren summer chalet. The hours sped by with a time that galloped to the beat of love. Johan, by now a tall seven-year-old, helped with the chores. For hours, Paul happily watched Anna play in the total absorption of her fantasy world. He lay content, lounging on the patio, recovering his strength, and letting the sun's rays fill and brighten his deeply aching emotional center. If it were not for Sophia, his gray solitude on the other side of the Atlantic would have been totally encompassing. All too soon, the vacation with his small family was over.

Once more, Paul flew back alone to New York, this time to begin his residency.

Metropolitan Hospital did not have well-furnished offices. The walk-in clinic had only four small, metal-partitioned rooms for the twelve residents to share for their regularly scheduled outpatients. These practically bare cubicles also doubled as screening rooms for the myriad of highly upset beings living in the two diverse districts of the wealthy Upper East Side as well as the ghetto's slums of lower Harlem. These emotionally disturbed people wandered in by themselves, were brought in by their pushed-to-the-limit relatives, or were driven to the hospital in police cars. The latter were usually handcuffed, high on drugs or alcohol, and expressed their inner hell by mumbling to themselves or screaming indiscriminately at one and all.

One afternoon in September 1971, Paul, as a first-year resident, had just seen one of his two long-term intensive and supervised patients in one of these badly insulated and poorly lit rooms. He had just spent fifty trying minutes with Marylou, a young woman of twenty-seven, who had been his patient on the ward last June. He had established a good relationship with her as an inpatient and had agreed to her being his first official outpatient.

She had been hospitalized for trying to commit suicide: swallowing more than a handful of semilethal pills. When she was out of danger, she had been transferred from a medical to a psychiatric bed. Paul became her primary physician and spent many hours getting to know her long psychiatric history. With genuine interest and total acceptance, he slowly began to build with her a wholesome therapeutic relationship. She had been the victim of incest for many years. Her father began having sex with her when she turned thirteen and continued to sleep with her until the age of seventeen. To escape, she ran off with a sailor.

Marylou had tried to kill herself at least four previous times. One attempt was serious enough to have caused permanent kidney damage. Her history was littered with the conquests of innumerable men. With a beautiful face; lithe, tall body; and her best feature of long jet-black hair reaching down to her waist, she had no problem attracting men. But once they had been seduced into her bed she threw them overboard to look for the next one, hoping against hope there would be at least one man able to replace her father.

Paul's first outpatient proved to be a most difficult one: Marylou kept trying to seduce him. With an extremely low image of herself, she felt that only through a sexual liaison would she have any chance in establishing any sort of relationship. Her hysterical personality kept pace with his inexperienced therapeutic skills, and he was stretched to the limit trying to help her. Paul at first did not realize the extent of her pathology and therefore had not realized the difficulty she would bring to the therapy hour. His main asset was his genuine liking for her on one hand, while keeping his emotional distance on the other. She was not able to break the therapeutic bond, and in spite of herself was slowly making progress in both insight and behavior.

However, each session was draining. She never let up. She tried time and again to get Paul entangled in her world, as she up to then had not been able to get him sexually involved. He had admitted to her, himself, and his supervisor that he indeed was attracted to her. However, there is an elemental difference between the feeling of sexual arousal and acting on it. For the first time in her life, Marylou found someone who, though genuinely liking her, did not fall into her trap by giving in to her provoking and alluring seductions. Like a young wild mare she brayed and bucked, knowing that to give in to the harness of adulthood meant losing a certain degree of freedom. She would need to give up her dark and magical fantasy of the love of a father interwoven with the powerful spell of lust and sex.

Paul was happy to end the session. It meant that he would be able to leave the hospital, forget Marylou and her problems, and spend a quiet evening with Sophia. As a resident, he was now on call only once every six nights. Sophia and Paul finally managed to see each other on a fairly regular schedule. It had taken them a long time to get intimately close. During his internship, his on-call duty kept him in the hospital every third night while her day and night shifts varied from week to week.

They liked each other right from the start, even though they saw each other only infrequently for the first six months. That evening in

December with the children had built a solid foundation. They had similar professional interests and were attracted to the theater, both having acting experience in their histories. The differences in their backgrounds added a rich complementariness to the time they did manage to see each other. Sophia had come from a large Italian family, the Mansonis. She was the youngest of nine children, had to work her way through nursing school, and at least once a month visited her parents, who had retired to Troy in upstate New York. All her sisters and brothers were married by then. Being single, she felt obligated to spend time with her parents now that all her other siblings had left home. In addition, her father, who was in his late seventies, was beset with the old-age infirmities of a weak heart, arthritis, and impaired vision.

It had taken almost three months for them to have sex. When they finally did, there were problems. Paul had in the past experienced some difficulty with erections from time to time. Not only had Evi been the main love of his life but also, with respect to sex, she had been his best lover. She had been patient with him if he could not become erect as well as loving and tender when he did. At no time did she pressure him to perform. She would usually play with his penis if it decided not to respond. If after a number of minutes it still did not get hard, she would concentrate on other aspects of their lovemaking. With closeness and familiarity, Paul found her touch would invariably bring him erect. After the first month of sexual intimacy, it was rare indeed that they were not able to have intercourse when they so desired.

After Evi's death, he had abstained from sex until one night in late March. Sophia and Paul had seen a romantic film at a local movie house and had slogged through the icy mush back to his place on East Eighty-fourth Street. They warmed up with a couple of drinks, hers sherry, his scotch and soda. They relaxed and permitted their close feelings to unfold, the natural progression of holding, touching, and kissing. This led them easily and with sexual anticipation into his double bed. Sophia, though not completely passive, let Paul take the lead in their steps of love. Though excited by her and sexually ready, he found himself concentrating on his penis, waiting for it to harden. The more he thought about it, the more it shriveled.

Sophia on the other hand was highly excited. Though usually quite reserved, she had made it evident to Paul that she found his lean frame and long swimmer's muscles extremely inviting and desirable. By the time they had finished making love she had climaxed without difficulty. Paul had stimulated her manually, to which she responded with soft groans and hard kisses. She did not mention Paul's lack of erection nor did she seem to miss not having had intercourse. Paul was ambivalent about bringing it up and in the end decided to let sleeping dogs lie.

The following week, after enjoying a quiet home-cooked meal, they eagerly decided to go to bed early and enjoy their newly found physical intimacy. Once again, Paul found that he did not get erect. This time it bothered him to the point of suddenly sitting up and disengaging himself from their tender embrace.

"What's the matter, Paul?" Sophia said, being startled out of her entwined reverie.

"I can't get it up. I thought the first time was a fluke but tonight it's not getting hard again."

"Am I doing something wrong?" she said, putting the fault on her own shoulders.

"No darling," Paul mumbled dejectedly. "I sometimes get into this state where the more I worry about my erection the less likely it follows my inner excitement and desire."

"Is there anything I can do to help?"

Paul was somewhat embarrassed and hesitated for a moment before plunging in with, "Actually, yes, Sophia, there is. I've found that if my penis is touched and fondled, if you play with my genitals, it's a big help in me getting aroused."

"Why, of course, Paul. Why didn't you say so before?" At first she touched him gently on the shoulder. Hesitantly taking the initiative, she embraced him and easily pulled him down next to her. They began kissing. She slowly but smoothly slid her hand down to his penis and began stroking it. "You have such a nice body, Paul, and I like the way this also feels," she murmured.

He began playing with her breasts while embracing her, changing his first gentle kisses into more passionate ones. Though more excited and stimulated than before, his penis would still not extend to its full length and girth. It remained semihard, a state he thought of as rubbery, more hard than soft but too flaccid for entry. Once again he concentrated on his genitals and thereby lost his involvement with the moment. His penis began to shrink.

He took her hand away, slowly sat up, and, leaning on one elbow, said, "No, it's not going to work . . . Sorry." Anticipating her unspoken thoughts, he continued, "No, it's not your fault. I guess I'm just tense."

He told her he was going to put on some water for coffee and asked her if she wanted some. With his mind zoomed in on this second failure, he left without waiting for her answer.

While his hands were busy with the water for the coffee, his mind swam in circles. He knew he was attracted to Sophia—he definitely liked her and felt close to her—but he kept comparing her to Evi and found her wanting. Something was missing; it was not like it had been with Evi. He felt that Evi would be his one grand passion and every other woman would be measured against her. He liked Sophia—in fact there was some love between them—and he was attracted to her, but, but. . . He was stumped. And now this thing with his penis. Why was it so unmanageable? Why?

Sophia let him be by himself for a couple of minutes before joining him in the kitchen. At the small, round, oak table, they sat over the mugs of coffee and nibbled at some Pepperidge Farm Milano cookies. She was quiet but quite interested in his slow, episodic description of his troubled history with erections.

"Even in my first sexual adventure at the age of nineteen, I experienced only a partial erection. My girlfriend, who was more experienced, took my penis in her hand and with a skill I can still recall vividly got me hard. She even helped me enter her."

He continued, "This unreliability of obtaining a desired erection was the reason I became shy with women. I found I had difficulty getting intimate with the women I met and dated. I was always worried about getting it hard, afraid I wouldn't get it up."

After a couple of false starts, he finally broached the subject of Evi. With even more hesitations, he related how he had met Evi and how the problem had finally disappeared. With her, he no longer was plagued with fear or worry. The years of enjoyable sexual relations with his wife had completely erased his performance anxiety. What he did not tell her was that Evi, with a loving instinct, had known exactly how to react, and he had invariably responded to her touch by getting erect.

Sophia finally spoke up during one especially long silent pause, "I like you a lot, you know. I really want us to work. Is there anything I can do to help?"

"The same goes for me. I also want it to work. I really do." He then sat quietly for a couple of moments, lost in his fears and self-doubts. Suddenly he had an idea.

"Sophia, why don't we try the Masters and Johnson technique?"

"You mean *sensate focus?*"

"How come you know about it?" His mood changed. He brightened up and his depressive mien turned to one of joy.

"Having known you for some time, I felt obliged to read up on your area of expertise. I found out that last year, Masters and Johnson published a method for curing impotence based on behavior modification and the principles behind the technique."

"Are you willing to give it a try?" he asked.

Catching his enthusiasm, she heartily agreed. "But first, let's see if I have it straight. By taking away the pressure to perform, your penis will do its thing all by itself. So for the next two weeks we won't have intercourse—just massage each other. Right?"

"Yup." A heavy load was lifted.

"When do we start?" She wanted to know.

"How about right away? I'd love to give you a massage," Paul said, wanting to enjoy himself and not worry about getting an erection. Prohibiting the act of intercourse and permitting only nongenital massages relieved Paul of his impotence anxiety.

Paul and Sophia began their own sex therapy that night. For two weeks they only massaged each other, an activity they both relished and enjoyed. During the third week, they advanced to the next stage.

In addition to full body massages they added genital caresses, with the understanding there would not be any intercourse even if they got extremely excited.

True to expected form, the first time Sophia massaged his penis, Paul immediately got hard. It stayed erect for the full twenty minutes of the massage. It remained at attention though her hands were caressing other parts of his body. He was thankful it was only twenty minutes, otherwise he would have gotten blue balls. The following Thursday, however, he didn't follow the rules they had set up. After a couple of minutes into his massage, he moved without thinking and acted on impulse. Sporting a large erection, he pushed her down and entered her slowly but firmly. Having been sexually aroused by seeing his erect penis and the feel of his body, she was lubricated and ready for him. It was one of the best orgasms of his life. Sophia expressed extreme joy with his actions and achieved a full and sensuous climax as well.

Paul continued to use sensate focus each time he did not get an erection with her. They would begin massaging each other with the understanding that that would be the extent of their intimacy. Most of the time within the first ten minutes, Paul would begin to get hard. On the occasions he didn't, both of them were satisfied with the closeness, sensuousness, and warmth of their embraces. Paul, a fledgling sex therapist, learned on a personal level the enjoyable lesson of sex not always needing to end with orgasm or even intercourse.

Overcoming this problem enabled both of them to get closer to each other. Sophia understood Paul better and felt competent in being able to help him; Paul relaxed with her, knowing that she deeply cared for him. With a higher comfort level, he permitted her to enter and touch his inner emotional spheres and allowed himself to enjoy his activity in the sexual arena.

Though he felt close to a woman once again, though he savored Sophia's sensuous intimacy, he still felt it was different from his former, totally encompassing love of Evi. Maybe it was that she was no longer here and his memories were being prismed through the joyful colors of the past, or perhaps it was she had borne his children. Though Sophia brought out in him the combination of a strong emotional bond and high sexual desire, she still had to compete with the loving ghost of his former wife.

That Christmas, their bond was strengthened with the arrival of Johan and Anna for their second winter's vacation. During the two weeks in the Big Apple, both children fell under Sophia's spell of good cheer and genuine warmth. Toward adults a wall of shyness usually resulted in a reserved mien; however, with the two children Sophia opened the gates of her being. Johan especially loved Daddy's new friend and opened his heart to Sophia in a way he had kept reserved only for Evi. This year the four of them spent Christmas Eve together and shared their presents the next morning.

This visit was similarly patterned to their first trip to New York. Paul was able to get ten days off and Sophia staggered her vacation days so at least one of them would be available for the children all the time.

Paul spoiled his children (movies, TV, pizza, and Burger King) but at the same time made sure they spoke with him only in English. He also arranged for them to experience American culture in all its diverse facets (the Statue of Liberty; a visit filled with gasps and squeals to top of the 102-story Empire State Building; and the highlight of their trip was once again sitting enthralled in the front-row mezzanine while watching the dazzling *Nutcracker*). He was glad his children would not feel completely alien when they moved back with him full-time—as soon as he finished his psychiatric training.

In the one-and-half years since Paul had left them with heavy heart at the Zurich airport, they had grown up loving their life in Switzerland while anticipating each reunion with their father. During these past eighteen months Paul observed that Johan had begun to steer his own course along life's currents. He complained to Paul about Opa doing things differently. In small but decisive ways, he started to disagree with what Paul wanted or directed. Johan seemed to have adopted Professor Stocker as his ideal, as his emotional father.

Thus it was not surprising that Johan opened up emotionally with Sophia and not Paul. Paul had difficulty understanding his son and was delighted when Johan took a sparkling, childish shine to Sophia. He listened to her, cuddled up to her, and tried constantly to get her attention in the typically bravado and bragging manner of a seven-and-half year old. It was also not surprising that this year it was Johan who cried at leaving New York, which included his newly found loving and caring Sophia.

Though extremely painful, the children's parting had the effect of reinforcing Paul's warm feelings toward Sophia. Obviously, she loved the children and they loved her. For the first time, he thought of the possibility of remarriage; for the first time since Evi's death, Paul considered Sophia as a potential life partner.

But it was not to be.

It was not death but a cerebral vascular accident that would separate them. Though it was her father who had been ailing these many years, it was her mother who suffered a stroke. At the beginning of February, Sophia got word that her mother had had to be hospitalized and it was necessary she immediately come up to Troy. Mother had fallen down unconscious. Her father had first called the ambulance and then Sophia. In Troy, it took her a week before she arranged for a temporary homemaker for her father and another week before she was convinced that her mother was recovering satisfactorily. Only then did she return to New York.

With tears in her eyes, she told Paul she would have to move upstate. Nobody was there to take care of her parents. She knew she would be able to get a job at the local hospital. In that way she'd be able to care for her now both invalid parents. Sophia had only ten days to sublet her apartment, sell her furniture, and say good-bye to one and all. Paul knew that even though they had pledged to each other they would travel the short three-hour drive as often as possible, the chances of continuing their intimate relationship was questionable. Their schedules would not permit frequent trips. Her responsibility to her family and his to the hospital would be the actual arbiter and divining rod of their separation.

Her friends threw Sophia a going-away party. The party, with over twenty people already there, was in full swing when the two of them arrived. Over half the people were doctors and nurses at the hospital, the others a mixture of various friends and guests.

"New York will be a desert without you," Paul said to her as they sat alone on the small sofa in the corner. "I'm already feeling lonely knowing I won't be able to see you almost every day," his well-known feelings of sadness once more muddying his life's colors and frame of mind.

Though she looked especially beautiful in a delicately brocaded blouse, she responded through her own curtain of gloom, "I'm not only concerned about us but truly worried about Mother."

Though there was plenty of opportunity and several hints during the past week, Paul did not wish to make a lasting commitment by asking her to marry him. It was not right to push her into a major life decision during this time of stress.

However, contrary to his initial conscious wishes, he said, "We should talk about our future, Sophia," broaching the delicate subject.

"Paul, until I settle down in Troy and first take care of Mother in her illness, I cannot make any plans."

"I do agree," Paul said, relieved. "Let's decide on our future together after that." In some unknown way, he was still ambivalent about Sophia being the right woman for him to marry. Postponing the decision felt correct.

Later in the evening when Sophia was off near the buffet table sharing her future plans with another nurse, Paul, still sitting on the sofa, looked up and saw a thin blonde woman approaching him.

"Paul?" she questioned him.

She looked familiar but he could not place her. "Yes?"

"You don't remember me," she smiled, "but I remember you. I'm Judy."

Paul, still involved with Sophia's leaving, did not attempt to play the social game of, 'let's see where I know you from' and make up the most likely places. Instead, he simply answered, "No, I don't."

"I'm Judy Saroff," still smiling, but by now somewhat more hesitantly.

"Judy Saroff," he was stunned. His former world, a universe he had left behind ages and ages ago, sprang back into the present in the person of Carl's daughter. "Judy Saroff," he repeated. "Judy. Well, it's been a very long time. Yes, a very long time." He continued inanely, "How are you?"

"Fine," she now looked a bit flustered, obviously not having expected this type of response. "How are you?"

"I'm also fine," he continued with the automatic and safe answer. Getting past his initial stunned shock, he looked at her and saw she was ready to disappear if he continued to react to the teenaged Judy of the early sixties and not the woman now standing before him. He brought himself back to the present with, "Judy, I didn't recognize you. You're a grown woman now, and a very beautiful one to boot." He got up with his usual lanky unfolding of legs and arms and embraced her. Looking warmly at her and this time with true feeling, asked again, *"And how are you?"*

"Actually, I'm really okay." Once again poised, her smile had finally surfaced. "What are you doing these days, Paul? Are you still in the theater?" They sat down and without giving him a chance to answer, she continued, "You just vanished. You had been in Daddy's show one day and you simply disappeared the next."

"It's a long story, Judy." He did not want to get into it, especially now. "I've changed professions. I'm now a psychiatric resident at Metropolitan Hospital."

"No kidding, a budding shrink." She touched his arm. "I'm glad, real glad."

He did not know how much she knew of that crazy night at the dress rehearsal and he did not want to discuss it. He switched subjects. "I'm with Sophia. Do you know her?"

"No, I'm with Dr. Phillips, the chief surgical resident. He brought me as his date. Isn't Sophia the nurse who's leaving town?"

Before he had time to answer, Sophia, the subject of their discussion, brought Paul a glass of wine and handed it to him. Introductions were made, and Judy, with both social grace and intuitive clarity, excused herself.

"Who was that?" Sophia asked in a jealous tone that she rarely felt or used.

"Judy Saroff," Paul ignored her intonation, glad that Sophia was with him again. "Remember I told you about Carl Saroff, that megalomaniac and son of a bitch? That's his daughter. God, I haven't seen her for ten years. She used to be a very, and I mean *very*, promiscuous young teenager."

"Well, she has her eyes on you," she said as she looked at Judy's receding figure.

"Come on, darling," Paul said putting his drink down, "It's just that we both were involved with a very difficult man, her father. I'm nothing to her except someone from out of her past." Having had enough socializing and enough of other people, he took Sophia's arm and said, "Let's leave. Okay?" She nodded. They quietly thanked the hostess and snuck out without saying good-bye to anyone else.

Three days later, they parted after an evening of tears and sobs and a night clasped in sweaty, desperate sex. She left with a carload of possessions; he remained with a heart full of memories. They promised each other many phone calls and frequent visits. With a last warm hug on Paul's part and some tears on Sophia's, they separated.

Missing her with an ache that would not leave him, Paul dove into his work once again. This time, however, he was not narcotized to the point of no feelings. In this separation, his other half had not disappeared into the void; Sophia still had a loving and laughing voice he was able to hear on the phone and was still available in person when they saw each other. At first they managed to see each other almost weekly, but then it stretched into every couple of weeks.

By the time May rolled around they both realized that a once-a-month visit would not keep their relationship alive. Both became resigned to the fact that their feelings were not as tight as before; it was difficult to be interested in the other's present life when most of the time spent together was used remembering how close they used to be when they had shared their life together in New York City. The separation had widened; the drift had set in.

When Paul received a phone call from Judy Saroff one evening late in May, he was not particularly surprised. Though he had denied it at the time, he also had received the impression that she was interested in him. She ran on about how she had just broken up with Dr. Phillips and was at loose ends and thought that it might be fun if the two of them would get to know each other and reminisce old times. Paul felt the interest in her voice and found he was intrigued and flattered by her attention. He quickly agreed to a date.

He liked good food and, when with a woman, he savored the right atmosphere. Since Judy lived in one of those large apartments on East Seventy-second Street, he made a reservation for two at one of his favorite restaurants, The Duck Joint, located on First Avenue in the Sixties. The doorman announced him and then, rather than sending him up, said that Miss Saroff would be down in a moment. She was dressed to impress. She had her blond hair done up in a swirl, her dark blue dress was set off by a pearl necklace, and she wore shoes with what must have been at least five-inch heels.

She smiled with an impish grin when she saw him and said, "Where to, my master?"

Her beauty struck Paul. With eyes riveted, he answered, "The Duck Joint, my beautiful princess."

She bowed low, took his arm, and signaled the doorman that a taxi was needed. By the time they arrived at the restaurant five minutes later, she had practically told him her life history. She went on and on without letting him get in a word. Though he picked up many facts, she guarded herself by not imparting her feelings about them. By the time the small salad was served, he had already found out she had left Carl and Jeanette at the age of sixteen to run off with Jamie, a well-known trumpeter. They traveled all over the States, following the band's frenzied schedule of gig after gig in town after town. They had lived together for three years. "Its actually my four-year separation anniversary tonight," she laughed but it contained a harsh and bitter undertone.

The duck, as usual, was prepared to perfection and Paul finished his whole half as well as some of hers when she couldn't finish her portion. Judy wanted to know how he managed to keep his weight down when he ate enough for two. Paul admitted to overeating when the food was great but to keep his weight down he would run an extra mile or two on his three-times-a-week jog around the reservoir in Central Park. After dinner, they continued their conversation by remaining at the table for coffee and brandy. By now, with a healthy amount of liquor in her, Judy relaxed enough to permit Paul his share of talking.

She was surprised at Paul's side of the story with Carl. Her father had maintained that Paul had gotten stage fright, walked off the set without explanation, and simply disappeared from the theater. There had never been any mention of a fight or a struggle between them. If the relationship between her father and Paul had taken her by surprise, his information about Evi's death shocked her to absolute dumbness. She just shook her head and couldn't say a word. Paul had to keep assuring her he was reconciled to the loss by now, that his children gave him a huge amount of pleasure and his life had gone on, as it always does.

"Though two years is a long time and one gets over most things in that time, it's also a very short span in one's life," Paul continued. "I don't grieve anymore. In fact, I've already had a serious affair with another woman."

"From the way you say that, Paul, it seems as if it is finished," she wisely inferred.

"Yes, I think it is. Sophia had to move out of the city and we've been seeing less and less of each other. We've just grown apart. For me, I guess absence does not make my heart grow fonder." Then, in a lighter vein, he continued, "In fact, you're the first woman I've had a date with since she moved out of town."

"Well if that's the case, why don't you come over to my place so you can feel comfortable? I know how lonely it feels when you're used to another person. I've experienced that with Jamie. Suddenly he's gone, and no matter what the reason and no matter whose fault it was, I find I feel lonely without a man."

During dinner Judy made it obvious she was interested in him. She kept touching him, sometimes on the arm, once on his cheek, and several times her foot rubbed his leg under the table. Her hints were not subtle. *Why not?* he thought. *She's pretty and she's interested. Why not?* His half-erect penis agreed.

As soon as the door to Judy's apartment closed behind them, she embraced him and waited for Paul to bend down the few inches to kiss her on the mouth. He did, gently—at first lightly, then with more passion. She immediately responded by moaning, "Oh yes, Paul. I want you. I need you."

He was not used to such quick turns. One moment having small conversation in an elevator, the next, hot passion and lust. He separated from her and found the light switch himself. In the soft light, she looked alluringly inviting, seductively luscious. He let her know his feelings with an intense and lustful look, but with an inner knowledge of himself, he walked over to an easy chair and sat down. He wanted more time before jumping into bed.

"Let's slow down a bit. It'll be more fun that way," he told her. "Can you make me a cup of coffee? I've had too much wine and I won't be any good with all that alcohol in me."

"Anything you want is fine with me," she answered, going into the kitchen. Paul heard the double entendre and wondered, *What is it she wants? Who knows? I'll find out soon enough.*

While waiting for the water to boil, Judy excused herself and went into the bedroom to change. She reappeared wearing a slinky, black-laced gown leaving little to his imagination. Coming over to where he sat, she settled herself on his lap and began nibbling his left earlobe. He delightfully allowed himself to be seduced. She took off his shirt and began playing with his nipples, pinching them to the point of pain. To stop her, he stood up, lifted her in his arms and carried her into the bedroom.

"Oh yes, Paul," she moaned. "You're so strong. Don't hurt me. Don't hurt me like the others, you strong man." He was turned on and quickly tore off his pants and easily removed her negligee. He got on top of her and began to gently kiss her. She was excited and suddenly bit his lip—hard and sudden. Without thinking, he slapped her. Angrily he said, "Now stop that."

"Oh, yes sir, anything you want. But don't hurt me. I'll do whatever you want, no matter how debasing it is. Anything."

With those words, she closed her eyes and laid back, hands over her head, crossed at the wrists. It was at that point Paul noticed the black leather thongs attached to the headboard.

He got off her, moved over on his side, and gently said, "Judy I'm not into S & M. I just like my sex simple and loving. I can't get into this type of sex play."

"All men do," she said, closing her eyes. She covered them with one hand while with the other began to play with his penis. "You're hung and you're huge, so fuck me, big daddy," she both pleaded and demanded. "But don't hurt me with your big cock."

Paul realized that she was playing out a scene she had participated in many, many times, and with many men. He understood she was not in bed with him but was acting out a ritual, a highly erotic fantasy. In no way would Paul be able to function in these rigid conditions. His full erection began to soften. The more she stroked and nudged his penis, the smaller it shrunk, the more it tried to disappear altogether.

After a couple of quiet minutes with neither of them saying a word and the only noise was of her massaging his by now tiny appendage, he removed her hand and said very quietly, "No, it won't work, Judy. I have trouble getting an erection from time to time. I've had too much alcohol. It just won't stand up." He sat up. "Not even for the Queen of England. Not even for the American flag," trying to joke through it.

He started to get up. She pulled him back and with a choking and desperate voice begged, "No, don't go. I'll be good. I'll do whatever you want, anything you want. I just want you to fuck me. Don't leave me. Please don't leave." She embraced him from the back, her hands tightly around his stomach.

He murmured again how he had trouble with women the first time. He tried to calm her by promising her the next time would be better and they would both enjoy it.

"You're lying!"

He knew he was lying. He knew they would never never get together. Ever.

She lashed out, "Don't try to appease me with false reassurances, you bastard. I need you now!"

She wouldn't stop. Her voice got louder and louder. Paul dressed quickly, all the while having to listen to her explosive tirade, her increasing fury.

"Go on Paul. Run. Run away like you always do. When Daddy found out yesterday that I was seeing you, he warned me you might hurt me. And you have, you bastard."

She wouldn't stop. She wouldn't stop yelling and cursing. "You inconsiderate son of a bitch!"

After he tied his shoelaces, he turned around to face her and realized that he had to do something to quiet her down. He walked over to her and, with a sudden movement, slapped her across the cheek. "Now stop that," matching her tone, loud and sharp.

Without waiting for her reaction, he quickly turned and walked out of the apartment. No noise followed him to the door. The yelling had stopped.

It was ironic that he received the following letter in his mail the next morning:

June 2, 1972

Dear Paul,

Delighted to hear that you're back in town. Heard you had met Judy. Hope you don't mind my contacting you after all this time. I trust we can let bygones be bygones.

I have an interesting proposition for you. I know you're working hard as a resident but would you possibly be interested in a showcase production of a great new play? It would only run for three nights. You'll have plenty of time for rehearsals.

Even if you can't, both Jeanette and I would love to resume our friendship. Our love and kisses to Evi.

Looking forward to hearing from you real soon,

Carl

PART III: RANDY

I had not planned on visiting the family, but Mother's attack was sudden and, more to the point, serious. I took the red-eye leaving at 11:15 p.m. I always fly American. They have the most San Diego-to-New York flights and I've already had two free trips thanks to being a member of American AAdvantage. As usual, there were seats available even at the last moment.

"Please fasten your seat belts," the female voice on the intercom commanded. "We are flying through a slight turbulence." A small bell sounded and the buckle symbol lit up.

I buckled up. I swear, the airlines have turned us into sheep. They have us by the short hairs. We comply with their rules and regulations, all in the name of safety, praying they live up to their end of the bargain.

At first, seat 31B did not produce results. The middle seat gave me a double chance for a pickup, namely 31A and 31C. However, this evening's flight with a stopover in Chicago was practically empty. As fate would have it, the window seat next to mine was occupied even though all the seats in the rows around me were clearly vacant. In 31A sat Mrs. Biddle, a seventy-year-old white-haired grandmother, who kept droning on and on about her granddaughter's upcoming marriage (next week in Huntington, Long Island; 3,000 white roses; the groom's bright future in commodities). These unasked-for details finally ended when the movie came on. Luckily, I had bought a headset.

Mrs. Biddle nodded off halfway through the movie and I moved over to the aisle seat. Only then did the stewardess answer my smile as she passed by. I had previously tried to gain her attention but had not been successful. I guess it must have been something to do with sitting in the middle seat next to grandma. I got up and went back to the galley, where she was drinking a cup of coffee.

"How about a scotch and soda?" I began innocently enough, but continued to shine my come-hither smile.

"Sure," she answered with an open friendliness. "When the plane is this empty and all the passengers are asleep, I get bored."

"I'll gladly fix that." I then started the process of getting acquainted with, "My name is Randy," putting out my hand.

"Oh, really?" automatically shaking it.

"No, Gold. Randy Gold."

She laughed. "Well, I guess I asked for that one. Mine's Sandy." This time her smile was the trigger. I felt my cock starting its upward motion.

"No, you haven't asked me for anything as yet," I double entendred. I sat down in the last row, consciously taking the middle seat.

"Here, let me help you," she said, pulling down the plastic tray in front of me and handing me the drink.

I'm sure she noticed my bulge as she sat down next to me. "Is this your regular route?" putting down my drink.

"No, I'm usually on the L.A.-Chicago run, but between the Democratic convention in San Francisco and the crazy schedule changes for the Olympics, I'm on this San Diego flight."

"How lucky for me," I said, hoping the words would actualize the wish.

Sandy was my type: tall, blond, and big-chested. She was animated, buoyantly facile in small talk, and obviously delighted to while away the time with me. I remembered one of Dr. Manes's remarks in our first session and took a chance. I said, apropos of nothing, "You are one hell of a good-looking woman. Is there any way we could get together for some fun and games?"

I thought I detected a faint flush, as she looked straight at me. She smiled broadly and said, "As a matter of fact, I had the same thought in mind." Sandy took my empty glass and raised the tray to its upright position. "And it's been obvious all along," staring down at my bulge. "Are you getting off in Chicago?"

"No. But I have a two-and-a-half hour layover before I fly on to New York."

She put her mouth next to my ear and whispered, "We'll have time to get it on at my friend's place which is right next to the airport. Okay?"

Okay? It was great. Sandy was the cat's meow. For ninety minutes she put New York and Mother out of mind.

We dashed back to the terminal with clothes askew and the aroma of sex still emanating from our pores. She managed to return me to my New York connection a scant five minutes before the door of the jet clicked shut. She had more than fulfilled my long-standing fantasy of making it with an airline stewardess. As a bonus, she also gave me the phone number of her New York friend, Judy, who was always interested in meeting and getting to know "sexy" men.

I drifted off into a needed, but nowhere near long enough, two-hour sleep as the plane took off for La Guardia.

We had to circle and circle the airport before finally landing one hour late—just after 9 a.m. The Big Apple was already stewing in its oven-hot August. By the time I got an air-conditioned cab, I was sweating through both shirt and pants.

"Lenox Hill Hospital," I told the Oriental cab driver, hoping that he knew that it was located in Manhattan, let alone on East Seventy-seventh Street. He nodded and mumbled something. I tried to doze but it finally hit me. Mother's sick. She might die. Why did she pick this time to get a coronary? With respect to me, her timing has always been off. I really can't take time off from the office. Shit!

It really must have been serious for her to tell Dad that I should fly home right away. She had vowed never to set eyes on me that last time four years ago. I closed my eyes, shutting out the present. The past flooded my inner screen.

I had known Betty for almost two years. We had met at the July fourth employees' picnic that Doyle, Dane & Bernbach threw every year. We were on the same softball team and when in the last inning she slid home safely on my two-out single, both of us became D.D.&B.'s heroes. We had beaten our arch-rivals of the advertising world, Young and Rubicam.

The following Monday we were invited to the weekly board of directors' lunch to receive a special company award. As we sat next to each other, I was finally able to speak more than a couple of words to her, and it was there I broke my strict rule.

Though she also worked at D.D.&B., I had three good reasons to ask her out for a date. First, she worked on the thirty-second floor while I occupied a small cubicle on the eighteenth. Second, she researched media for the Polaroid account while I did artwork for Volkswagen. Third, and most important, it was obvious that we liked and were attracted to each other.

We had dinner in a small French restaurant on Fifty-second Street. Between the dark red wine and the flickering dim candlelight, we each saw the possibility of a romantic involvement. Betty was dressed in a simple white blouse and light blue skirt, showing off her well-shaped body. She spoke quietly about her past: the difficulty in growing up as the sixth of eight children; her father, a postman in New Palz, just making ends meet; her mother, always tired, dragging the kids to Mass every Sunday; and how frightened she was when she left home the day after high school graduation to begin a new life in New York City.

I told her of my childhood in Brooklyn: My twin sister, Libby, who was younger by two hours and Father's favorite. I, on the other hand, had been Mother's Dovid'l—her firstborn, her little man. Mom had started our family business. Father used to be a salesman for a wholesale flour mill until Mom began Brooklyn's first freshly baked bagel store on Rogers Avenue. We used to live just one block away on Montgomery Street, right in the heart of the Jewish section of Crown Heights.

Mom, better known as Rivka or Mrs. B., ruled our family with her iron fist. No velvet glove either. What she said was law to all of us, including Father. At first Libby and I helped her out in the store. When we expanded to a second store, then a third, Father quit his job and took over production in the new factory. After that Mom's brother, Max Baum, and his wife, Chava, took over two of the stores, and so on until the whole family worked for mother, a modern-day matriarch.

"So your family owns Baum Bagels," Betty finally broke in on my long monologue. "Why Baum and not Gold? Isn't your name Gold?"

"Yes, but mother's maiden name is Baum," I answered. "She liked the alliteration as well as showing who's the boss of the family. She wanted everyone to know who the leader of our tribe really was."

"You say that proudly," Betty correctly caught the tone of my feeling. "How come you're not working in your family's business anymore?"

"From far away I truly admire her," I admitted, "but if you have to deal with her every day, Mrs. B. is a true bitch. The whole world revolves around her. No one else counts. She gets what she wants no matter how it affects others. She's a master at maneuvering people like chessmen on a board."

"What did she do to you?" Betty gently put her hand on mine.

"She lied. She simply lied." I still felt the hurt. "She had promised me a title, a large raise, and authority as the marketing director. I had done a bang-up job by changing our image with a new logo and new storefronts. I had also insisted that we begin an advertising campaign. She initially resisted. However, one morning, six months later, she marched in and told me she had just come up with a great new idea: we should hire an ad agency and start to advertise.

"Well, the campaign was a huge success, which she of course took credit for. When push came to shove regarding her promises to me, she reneged on all three counts—the title, the money, the authority—everything. I just told her what she could do with her bagels and stormed out."

"What did you do?" Betty wanted to know. The coq au vin arrived at that point, and it wasn't until we were sipping our espressos that I told her how I finished Parsons School of Design and landed a job in the art department of a small advertising agency specializing in food accounts. From there, up the ladder through two other agencies before my present position at D.D.&B., art director for the Volkswagen account.

It was a happy evening for me. I liked Betty and felt comfortable talking to her. Sharing was fun. I was emotionally satisfied and did not try to get her into bed that night. I acted the gentleman and in front of her apartment door sweetly kissed her goodnight.

In fact, we did not have sex for over a month. I began seeing her more and more, and by the time we fell into the sack we both had already fallen into love. Betty was my first and, so far, my only love. I had had loads of sex but never had I combined it with the pleasure of uniting body and spirit, sex and love.

Within six months, she moved in with me. It just did not pay to keep two households going. She had been staying over at my place four nights a week while I stayed over at her smaller studio the other three. We were *Happy*. Deliriously so. Betty was everything I had ever wanted or needed. Life became exciting. I never knew what I was going to do or say. Of course I never ever figured out what *her* next words or actions would be.

And sex! Boy, I just fucked my brains out. I never could get enough. Betty also wanted my *Big-Man* as often as I did. She loved and desired me. I lived in joy.

Day and night we lived on the proverbial ninth cloud. The first storm warning came from Brooklyn, a phone call from Rivka in the form of a plaintive question.

"What I want to know, Dovid'l, is why you've stopped coming over for the Friday night meal?" She didn't buy my excuses of being busy at work. So I finally told her the truth: I was seeing a lot of Betty.

Mrs. B. and I had made peace. More accurately, we had declared a truce. She never did forgive me for leaving her business; however, she had let me know that Libby had taken over my duties so the business was still in the family's hands. Mother implied that my sister was doing a better job, but Libby kept telling me how Mom was constantly putting her down with unfavorable comparisons. She was told in no uncertain terms that she could not do one tenth of what I did. "Dovid'l would have done it better," etcetera.

"So how come I haven't met her?" Rivka said over the phone the following week. "You're ashamed of your Mother? Don't you like my gefilte fish anymore?"

"Okay, okay," I gave in. "I'll ask Betty if she's free this Friday, and we'll both show up. I'm sure you'll love her. She looks just like you and on top of that she loves the new cinnamon-raisin bagels you've just created."

Betty of course had been dying to meet my family but it was not all that simple. I knew that bringing the two of them together would create fireworks at the very least and, what was more probable, a voluble family explosion.

"What you don't understand, Betty, is since you aren't Jewish Rivka will never accept you," I finally admitted to her. "Worse, she'll begin bugging me to get rid of you. It will become an all-out battle, a war between Jew and gentile."

I must have been scared; really frightened. I even tried to get Betty to avoid telling the family that we were living together, which Betty wouldn't accept. She was right of course. But I knew my family. Dad would say whatever Mrs. B wanted him to. True, Libby wouldn't care, though she herself was more religious than the rest of us, including Rivka. However, Libby wouldn't defend me, and Mom could and surely would be nasty.

That Friday the evening went smoothly, but from my point of view it passed with much too much outward calm. My fears were not unfounded but the strategy was obviously new. No direct assault. Mom was delightful that night. In fact, charming. Full of homey stories combined with a focused interest in Betty. Mother's questions brought out a loquaciousness in Betty I never had seen before.

Intuitively, my guard was raised. I did not know when the next word or action would trigger off the dining room's mined terrain. Too much Jewishness was exhibited that night. Every ethnic dish possible, from potato kugel to kasha varnishkes, was paraded out of the kitchen. Talks of synagogues and Israel were bandied about. Never had my family wore their *Yiddishkeit* so broadly on their sleeves. Something was not kosher. And was there an emphasis on Miss Morley when good-byes were said? Why not Betty?

Betty, however, was enchanted. She loved them. "A great family," she said. "If only I would have come from such a home. Such warmth and caring, and the family business keeping everyone together." She was taken with mother: Rivka this and Rivka that.

Betty didn't have an inkling how she had been rejected that night, completely excluded. I suspected but did not realize the depth of prejudice Mrs. B. carried in her Jewish soul.

For three months Rivka kept the lid on her feelings. She did not bring up Betty—for better or worse. However, she also was not asked back for a Friday night meal. Then one day the battle began when Mrs. B. asked when the affair would end. "Is that *Shiksa* out of your place yet?" was the opening salvo. From that point, every conversation began with some critical comment about Betty and myself. A month later, Father joined the fray. I knew the war was fully engaged when even Libby started in. At least she had the decency to preface her criticism with a declaimer that for herself she couldn't care less but Rivka was getting sick from worry.

The pressure increased from prejudicial statements to emotional blackmail. "How can a good Jewish boy, my oldest, my wonderful Dovid'l, live with a *Shiksa?* No, don't answer. I don't want to hear it. You were brought up well. How could you do this to me? To your father?"

I knew what they were after. They wished we would not even begin to think of the possibility of marriage. Of course, Betty and I already had. Our relationship had kept getting better and better. We truly loved each other. Our sex was divine, our time together joyous. We even began to talk of combining our emotional life with our mutual interest in business by opening up our own agency. We agreed if we could line up one medium-sized client, we would take the plunge and open a company that combined public relations with advertising.

On St. Valentine's Day, in the French restaurant where we had our first date, I proposed marriage. It did not come as a surprise and she happily accepted. That night we celebrated with champagne and lots of sex. We finally fell asleep as the sun was beginning to peek over the golden-layered buildings.

One thought kept disturbing the smooth waters of my emotions. I began to worry how to tell my family. No matter what maneuver I came up with, the bottom line was they would not accept my marriage to Betty. I had to tell them soon. The worry increased. I began obsessing even during sex. Too often, in the midst of our lovemaking, my mind would focus on Rivka's face. I remembered one time, just as I was about to come, Rivka appeared and shook her head sadly. I began to cry, coming and sobbing at the same time. Another time, Betty and I had just gone to bed, and I was especially turned on. I was sitting on the bed hungrily watching Betty undress. I was fully aroused. Then just as I . . .

The brakes squealed and I was thrown forward. The cabbie had stopped suddenly. My mind and I were back in the taxi once again, but thanks to my reverie I had an enormous hard-on.

It seemed that the driver knew where Lenox Hill Hospital was. We were just two blocks from it, having just stopped with much noise at the Seventy-ninth and Lexington Avenue intersection. In the two minutes it took him to drive up to the hospital's entrance, I managed to come back to the reality of Rivka's illness. I dreaded what was going to occur in the next couple of hours. Sickness, guilt, family pressure, and fear would be mixed up with my own numerous real and painful problems.

As I stepped out of the cab, I realized it had not gone down. I was still throbbing. I felt crazy. Visiting Rivka in the hospital intermingled with a seething hard-on.

After finding out from the information clerk that Rivka was in room 408, she told me where the men's room was. I entered the stall, put down my small valise, and even before I sat down began to masturbate. I came without a single fantasy. But I just seemed to come and come. The need was great.

On the way to the elevator, I saw a public telephone and remembered I had in my pocket the telephone number the stewardess had given me. I stopped at the pay phone, put down my valise once again, and dialed.

"Judy Saroff?" I asked.

Though my cock did get semihard when she accepted a dinner date for the following evening, I was thankful I was not fully hard again. I waited for the elevator to take me to the fourth floor. To Mother.

I must call Betty. It's only eight o'clock in San Diego. I have to tell Betty.

No thought came after that as I waited for the elevator to reach the eighth floor of the Doral Hotel. The door opened at last. I stepped out into the lobby. Robotlike, I somehow had the key to my room in the keyhole. I clearly remember opening the door, locking it behind me and dropping the small valise on the floor next to the luggage rack. Not only did I notice the decorator colors of the room, mauve-accented cream walls with drapes and bedspreads in cool mint green, but I stared for minutes at a signed original lithograph behind the bed—a calm view of a sailboat gliding lazily along a deserted coast. I memorized that peaceful ocean scene. Mesmerized, I stood there, looking at the breeze-blown and full-rounded white sail, at the dark blue ocean with its spraying and showering foam lapping against the brown and gray barren rocks and the bright blue sky dotted with high cottony clouds.

Suddenly, I shook, a rumbling tremor that began in my throat and quickly traveled down the length of my body, ending where it began, in my throat. However, it was now joined by an added bellow and cry. It stopped as suddenly as it had started. I was now able to turn to the phone and dial Betty.

"Hello?" Betty answered on the first ring.

"Betty, it's me," I said with a voice that felt a thousand miles away.

"Are you alright?" knowing that I wasn't.

"Yes," I continued, trying to keep an even keel; trying to stay calm, in control. "I'm alright. I just got to the Doral. They've done a wonderful job redecorating it. I've been at the hospital till now. . ." I couldn't go on.

"Randy, what is the matter?"

I just held tightly onto the phone. Nothing came in or out. I just sat there. Not moving, not seeing.

"Randy, are you there? Are you alright?" Betty's voice became louder, trying to shake me into talking.

Finally I managed a flat, "Yes." Pause. I took a deep breath and once again said nothing.

"Randy, are you alright? Answer me, what happened?"

"I'm alright." I stopped again, then added, "But mother died," I answered automatously.

"Oh no!" she cried. "When?"

"At 8:49," I answered. "A couple of hours ago."

"What happened?" Betty wanted to know.

"She had a massive heart attack around noon. She stopped breathing and her heart stopped beating. They called a code 5 and jolted her with electricity. It worked and she seemed to come out of it a bit, but she never recovered consciousness again." *There, it was out,* I thought. *I've managed to say it.*

"I'll take the first plane out," Betty said decisively. "I'll be there first thing tomorrow morning."

"No," I shook my head. "You don't understand. My family doesn't want to see you. They won't permit you at the service or at the burial."

"Randy, I'm not coming for them. Don't you understand? I'm coming for you," she said authoritatively. "You need me and I want to be with you. I don't have to go to their funeral but I do have to be with you."

"But they'll cut you dead, and I don't want to see you hurt, darling," I answered. I felt for her.

"I saw them only one time," she continued with strength in her voice. "They do not have the power to hurt me. It's you I'm worried about, not them."

"Okay," I agreed. I needed Betty. I knew it was going to be bad. "However, only on the condition you return to California after a couple of days. I'm going to have sit *Shiva* for one week and we both can't be away for that long of a time. There are too many clients' deadlines to meet."

"When is the burial itself?" Betty wished to know.

"Since tomorrow is Saturday, we cannot bury mother till Sunday morning. *Shiva* starts after the burial."

"Okay, I'll make the late flight tonight and I'll be in New York first thing tomorrow morning. In the meantime, you get some sleep."

"I don't think I can."

"Then take some sleeping pills," she advised. "I know you took them with you."

"I've already had a couple of shots at a bar near the hospital, do you think I should take the pills on top of the alcohol?" I felt lost and couldn't decide even this minor question.

"How much did you drink?" she asked.

"Three or four shots of scotch. Straight."

"Well," Betty explained carefully, "if you cannot fall asleep in the next half hour, take one Dalmane and, if that doesn't do it, take another, since they're only 15 milligrams each. But under no circumstance take more than two. In fact, when you hang up, take two of them out of the vial and put the rest away. Will you?"

"Yes," I agreed, relieved she had taken charge.

"Good. I need to go. Have to order the plane ticket and get to the airport. I love you, darling. Good-bye." She hung up before I had time to answer.

I rummaged through the valise, found the pills, took out two, and put them on the night table. I slowly undressed, brushed my teeth and hair, and remembered at the last moment to bring a glass of water for the pills. Zombielike, I just sat there. Again I looked at the sailboat. How peaceful it seemed. No worries, no problems, just a perfect boat in a calm ocean.

Finally, I slipped under the cool clean sheets. I started to play with my cock. Jerking off always helped me sleep. As it got hard, I thought of Judy. Shit, I can't see her tomorrow night. I knew I'd have to be with the family. Besides, Betty will also be here.

I turned the light back on and called her.

"Hello?" Judy also answered on the first ring.

"Hi," I said in a falsly cheerful voice, "this is Randy. I hope that it's not too late to be calling you."

"Oh, hello," remembering who I was. "No, I was only watching a late movie. How are you?"

"Fine. But I have some bad news. We have to break our date for tomorrow night. Family problems. But how about Wednesday night? I'm staying in New York longer than I thought. By Wednesday everything will have calmed down and I know I'll be able to meet you then."

"Wednesday?" she repeated. "Yes, that'll be fine. Randy, are you sure everything is okay?"

"Yes, yes, sure," I did not want to get into it. "See you at eight o'clock at your place. 'Bye." I hung up fast, turned off the light and slid back under the covers.

Now I can think of her. Let's see. I began to fantasize how she would look: tall, blond, big boobs. She'd answer the doorbell in a slinky black nightgown, showing off her figure. As I continued imagining her, I stroked my cock harder and harder. I got her into bed; I was on top of her, ready to. . .

Thou shalt not kill!

My hand stopped. My mind slowed into numbness. My cock though stayed hard. "Stop that," I commanded. I began to jerk off again.

"Oh, that feels good. Yes, darling, go deeper, yes that's it." Sweating profusely and panting deeply, I climaxed. I felt more relaxed.

First I lay on one side then turned back to the other side. Though feeling exhausted I still couldn't sleep. I kept on turning and twisting. Finally, I sat up and, giving in to insomnia's power, I swallowed down both pills.

Once again I shut off the light, lay down again, and closed my eyes.

Thou shalt honor thy father and thy mother!

"But I did," I answered back. But how could I honor a lying parent? She had lied again and again. Promotion, a lie. Promised me authority, another lie. Told me I'd run things; lies, all of them. She didn't mean it at all. I had to leave to save myself.

"Did you also have to leave the faith?" my sister's voice intruded.

"No, Libby. I didn't leave the faith. You know as well as I do, according to Jewish law, a person who converts to Judaism must be accepted with open arms. You know Betty studied with the rabbi, accepted all the tenets of the faith, and converted. She even went to an orthodox rabbi so no one would be able to point a finger at her and say it wasn't a true conversion.

"Libby, you yourself took her to the *mikvah,* where she submerged herself and became a Jewess. Would it have been so difficult to be in my corner when I actually needed you? I could understand Dad could not stand up to Rivka. But you? Were the position and the money so important you also wrote me off?"

You killed her! You killed her!

"Were you there Libby? How do you know what happened? Were you in the hospital room with me and Mother this morning? I was. And I didn't kill her. She did it all herself. She knew it was time to leave but it had to be on her terms with me being Isaac to her Abraham's swinging sword. Only this time, God did not stop the arm in midair. It hit me, but she's the one who died."

I began to cry anew. After a few minutes I stopped. I lay there wounded in the thigh, the ladder still upright, and the angel sweating but victorious. But I still did not sleep.

"Get out! You ingrate, get out. I never want my eyes to see you ever again. Never! And stay away, you hear? Stay away! Get out!"

The evening started calmly enough. Everything had been prepared with great care. I wanted to make sure that, if there were any possibility of success, I'd have a chance at it.

When I had proposed and Betty accepted, we discussed for many hours the difficulty of my family accepting a *Shiksa* for a daughter-in-law. There was only one possible way out—conversion. At first, Betty would not hear of it. She was ready to write my family off if she needed to, but I convinced her it was important to me and for family peace that we should make every effort.

Betty was not religious but knew all about Catholicism. Learning about the Jewish faith became a fascinating adventure. The Old Testament started to become alive for her. At night, after dinner, she would study the Bible. She even learnt some Hebrew. She was diligent and, in less than a year, knew enough to satisfy the rabbi.

In the meantime, my family kept their distance. They totally disapproved of my living with Betty. They knew the longer we were together the more likely we were to unite officially through a formal marriage. They did not want to see Betty at any family occasion, at any holiday. Of course, Friday-night dinners were out of the question.

The only contact I maintained with my family was with Libby. She played the family's game but really couldn't care one whit whether I married Betty or not. In fact, we had her at the apartment several times and she and Betty hit it off like two sisters. Betty, having two older and two younger ones, instinctively knew what to say and how to act with Libby. Libby, having only me as a sibling, became enamored with a newly acquired sister.

Libby knew all about the conversion. In fact, she was the one who had recommended Rabbi Gershon. She followed Betty's progress with interest and helped with the nuances that the social maze of Judaism demanded. When the time came, she took Betty to the *mikvah,* which as a single woman she had never visited herself. Then, when Betty had completed her studies, she joined us at the rabbi's office and was there when Betty was officially brought into the Jewish fold.

We celebrated that evening, the three of us. To keep in the spirit of the occasion, we opened a bottle of kosher champagne at our place on West Seventy-second Street and then had a sumptuous Jewish meal at Siegel's on West Thirty-eighth Street. The restaurant was the Orthodox community's favorite. We ordered all the Jewish dishes we could think of, from borscht to potato latkes, from gefilte fish to *mandel* cake. We schemed and plotted as to time, place, and what arguments were to be used to change my family's narrow and ethnocentric attitudes.

We finally decided I was to come to next Friday night's dinner. Betty of course was not welcome, while Libby, still living at home, was there every week. After dinner, when everyone was stuffed and relaxed, I would bring up the subject of Betty. I would agree that Rivka and the family were absolutely correct and say I also felt strongly about not marrying outside the faith. With that, Libby would ask if I were willing to stop seeing Betty and I would say no, but I would confuse the folks by saying, "From now on I will never associate with a gentile woman." From that point, we would play it by ear.

Of course, the plan was just a paper-hat fantasy, a flimsy excuse to fulfill my wishes: my Jewish family of Baums and Golds would accept my Betty. Oh yes, the evening started off well enough. Over the boiled carp, the conversation was light and easy. But when the matzoball soup was on the table, Rivka, without warning, began her own campaign and fired off the first salvo.

She turned to me with, "Dovid'l, are you still seeing that *Shiksa?*"

I had not thought she would bring it up. She had not talked about Betty, not even mentioned her for over one year. And tonight of all nights, she broached the subject herself. I was flabbergasted. With that question, our little cabal's strategy was thrown right out the window. Mother had taken the lead and without any difficulty made me feel guilty. I flushed and stammered. Nothing came out, not one word. Mrs. B. took one look and knew her Dovid'l was still living with *that* gentile girl.

She slowly turned to Libby and softly but with real disgust in her voice asked, "And what, if I may be so bold to ask, have you in common with that nothing that you can insult me and your father by socializing with her? What have we done to deserve this from you? David never listened to me anyway, but you? You're a good daughter. What have we done wrong?"

"Nothing, Mama, nothing," Libby backtracked, guilt in her voice and submission in her movements. She seemed to draw back into herself, both physically and mentally.

"Nothing you say," Rivka attacked loudly now. "Sitting with the *Shiksa* at Siegel's, where the whole world saw you, is nothing? You call that nothing?"

"Randy invited me to dinner. I did not know that she would be there," Libby said, stretching the truth past breaking point.

"What?" I yelled at Libby. All thought of taking charge, of creating the right atmosphere were thrown out the door with that lie.

"You're lying, Libby. You were in on it right from the start. Tell Rivka. Tell her the truth."

"And what may I ask is the truth?" Rivka interrupted. "That not only are you living in mortal sin but that you're corrupting my lovely and good child. I just will not permit our family's name to be dragged into the mud. If you cannot keep your sinful filth from spreading into this family we will just have to stop seeing you also."

It was now or never. I looked at Rivka and in a loud and belligerent tone said, "Betty is not filth. She is a wonderful woman. She listens and obeys. She has converted. She is now one of us, a Jewish woman, a member of the Jewish faith. *That* is why we were at Siegel's—to celebrate her conversion."

Rivka anticipated my next statement with, "And now I suppose it is alright for you to marry that *Shiksa?* Am I right? Is that what you have in mind?"

I lowered my voice, my confidence all but gone, "Of course, now that she is Jewish."

"Jewish, she is not. A conversion for the purpose of marriage is not a conversion. Besides, she still is a *Shiksa* and will always be one. You can't make a pig kosher. You can't bless the devil."

"Mother," I countered, "ask Libby. Betty studied with Rabbi Gershon. She went to the *mikvah.* She even took the name of Ruth. Ask Libby."

Libby was silent and dead still. Rivka instead turned to Father, who just shook his head sadly and muttered painfully, "Oy, Oy," after which he also became mute. Rivka turned back to me and with a pointing finger said angrily, "Dovid'l, you will not marry that *Shiksa.* Not while I'm alive. I will not allow you to drag me and the family through the mud. I will not!"

There was no reasoning with her. I simply and very quietly said, "I am going to marry Betty, Mother. I am."

"Then I will simply not have a son," she said. "You will be as if I never gave birth to you. I will have given birth to one child only, a daughter. You will be dead for me, and I will sit *Shiva* for a dead son."

I looked at Father who did not look back. Libby had her eyes closed and was for all purposes not there. Mother had lost the battle but was going to win the war no matter whom it killed.

Again, very quietly but firmly, I said, "Mother I am going to marry Betty. I love her and she loves me. She is a good, kind woman."

"Is that your last word, you . . . you . . ." She turned pale.

"Yes," I said simply.

She suddenly got up, spilling a glass of wine, and began to yell, *"Get out! You ingrate, get out. I never want my eyes to see you ever again. Never! And stay away, you hear? Stay away! Get out!"*

I got out and I did not see the family for almost four years. I did not see mother until today; now she's dead and it's me that is going to have to sit *Shiva*. What did I do to deserve this? Why me? I began to cry again, bawled like a baby. I stopped thinking. I just cried.

I cried for the mother I used to have, a mother who had loved me, a mother devoted to me, her only son. She doted on me; she adored her little Dovid'l. I cried for her not being there.

I suddenly remembered another time I had cried for her not being there. I was only three but I still remember it as clearly as my favorite Bette Davis movie. I was running up and down the hill at the playground and when I turned around and she was not there. She had been sitting quietly reading the newspaper and suddenly she was not there. I was petrified. Where was she? I started to run in circles bawling my head off and crying, "Mommy! Mommy!"

For an eternal minute I had lived in panic and a split second later there she was, holding me to her, soothing me with, "I'm here; I'm here, Dovid'l." I never did know where she went. In later years, I thought maybe she had never disappeared; I had just not seen her.

I kept looking for her after that, making sure she didn't disappear. Ever again. I would go into the kitchen, time after time, making certain she was there. Mother thought I wanted something and would offer me a cookie, milk, or juice. She never understood my fear. I followed her from room to room. It got so bad I would not stay by myself, would not play with Libby for more than ten minutes before checking on Mother.

My need to continually reassure myself of Mother's nearby existence ended when I was six years old. Libby and I were engrossed in some game, and for once I forgot all about time. Suddenly I remembered. I needed to find out if Mother was in the kitchen. Libby, used to my running out of the room at odd times, did not follow me. Mother wasn't in the kitchen. I got scared. I ran to her bedroom which also was empty. I noticed her gray woolen dress and pink slip on her bed. I figured she might be in the bathroom. I quietly went to the door. I peeked in. Yes, Mother was there.

I felt relieved, but only for the first moment, until I noticed her nakedness. She was drying herself with a large white towel, her back toward me. As she bent down, I focused on her buttocks, large compared to the rest of her. Then I saw her peepee hole. It was large with skin around it. Dark wet hair was matted between her thighs. I turned cold with fear and hot with curiosity. I should have snuck away but I was fascinated. It was exciting. So different from Libby's bottom which was pink and smooth, with just a slightly rounded slit to show where she peed.

I remained transfixed, gazing in mother's essence. When she turned slightly, I was able to look at her hanging breasts. Though not huge, they completely filled my eyes and mesmerized my brain. White, smoothly pale, they drew me in. I started to breathe quickly, my mouth open, my tongue and cheeks emitting sounds as I sucked in the air and absorbed the sight.

Mother heard me and quickly twisted toward me. Seeing me in the doorway, she immediately wrapped the towel around herself. She didn't say a word; she just looked at me. We stood there, both of us not moving. I don't know for how long but we kept looking in each other's eyes. I was shaking with fear, guilt, excitement, and the unknown. She was the one who broke the spell. Scowling, she didn't say anything. She just pointed her finger, motioning me to get out, to get away.

I got out. I ran to my room and fell on my bed. I curled up and began to cry and gasp. I didn't understand my feelings. I began to rock back and forth, continued to suck air with an open mouth, all the while crying and mewling.

I cried anew now. Mother was gone forever. I'll never see her again, never ever again. Not in health, not in sickness.

All her life she had been as strong as an ox. She worked from early in the morning till late at night. At first she worked as wife, housekeeper, and mother; then she added the bagel business. At first she managed to keep wearing all the hats, but as Baum Bagels grew, she devoted less and less time to the family. She let Libby run the household and had little time for father, Libby, or myself, except as we intersected in the business page of her life.

When I participated in the business, Rivka had been in the prime of health. She was up at 6 a.m. at least twice a week to supervise the bakers. Many evenings she called meetings that often lasted as late as midnight. It was through Uncle Max I found out that Mother had slowed down these past two years. Father was the one who now had to get up at dawn to make sure the production schedules were being met. Max, who called me at least once a month to keep in touch, let me know the evening conferences now rarely went past nine. As an afterthought though, he let me know the Sunday morning meetings were still obligatory get-togethers accomplishing little but demonstrating to everyone Mrs. B.'s feudal power.

Uncle Max and Aunt Chava were my only family contacts after that disastrous dinner. I did not wish to speak to Libby, Father wasn't strong enough to go against Rivka, and Mother of course had cut me dead. I was thankful it was Chava and Max whom I first met this morning. God, that was eons ago, a lifetime that had contained a living Rivka. *When will the pills begin to work? When?*

I remembered the first view of the hospital's fourth floor was Aunt Chava carrying a vase of roses. She had obviously just come from the nurses' station and was passing the bank of elevators as I stepped out.

"Chava," I yelled after her. "Hold up, Chava."

She turned around, saw me, and came running back to plant a big kiss on my cheek. She did that by standing on her toes, delicately balancing the vase in one hand while hugging me with the other.

"David, my beautiful David," she said as she disengaged herself. "I'm so glad to see you." But from her large and sincere smile, her face shadowed into one of pain and sadness. "Rivka is very sick, Dovid'l; very sick."

"Just how sick is she?" I wanted to know, my mood immediately matching hers.

"Very." Holding on tightly to my hand, she continued, "I don't understand the doctors' language but I've been seeing her going downhill. She just doesn't have the strength she used to have and three days ago she just couldn't breathe in the middle of a meeting. Luckily, the doctor was at the plant and gave her a shot. We took her to the hospital right away."

"Did she have a heart attack?" I needed to know just how sick she actually was.

"I don't know, David," she shook her head. "She had some sort of failure. My Max will know. He's just down the hall in the waiting room." Still holding onto my hand, she led me down the hall.

Max, who was as tall as Chava was short, stood up when he saw us approaching. He also hugged me tightly and kissed me on the cheek. Then, looking at me, he said softly, "She needs you, David. Your mother wants to see you."

"Uncle Max," I still had to know, "just how sick is Rivka? Chava couldn't or wouldn't tell me. Please be honest with me; I want to know exactly."

"Thank God it's not the end." He smiled warmly. "She has congestive heart failure. Her heart is weak and is giving out. She has to rest and take it easy. But you know how she is. Just to keep the doctors quiet, she agreed to everything as long as they would let her out of the hospital as soon as possible. She wants to go right back to running the company. She's told me it's her life; without the business, her life would have no meaning for her."

"So how come she needs me?" I was angry as well as perplexed. "So why did she get Father to call me back here?"

"David, you simply must come back to the business." Max was un-flinchingly honest. Getting directly to the point, he said, "The whole family has finally convinced her she has to cut down on her work. She doesn't trust Libby to run the business. She had always wanted you to head up the company. She had groomed you to eventually take her place, you know."

"Uncle Max," I shook my head sadly. I remembered all too well my frustrating interactions with her. "Her words are the words of Jacob but I'm sorry to say that her skin covers the soul of Esau. Her promises are cheap since she never feels obligated to fulfill them. What makes you think after all these years she has changed?"

Taking my arm, Max sat me down on the orange vinyl chair. Sitting next to me, he thought awhile before he finally said quietly, "She has changed David. She's not as strong. I think she has seen the *malach hamovess* face to face."

"That might be, Max." I was not at all convinced. "She thinks she'll win this battle also. The angel of death doesn't scare her. And you know, she'll never hand over the business to me or anyone else as long as she has one ounce of strength left in her. You know what happened the last time. She just didn't let promises stand in the way of her will."

"My darling David," Chava chimed in, "please listen to your uncle Max."

Max wiped his brow and again sat still for a few moments, his hand remaining on his forehead. Obviously, this quiet and gentle man found his role a difficult one. I knew he did not enjoy fights or angry feelings. As peacemaker, he had to face two strongly emotional beings, Rivka and myself.

He finally tapped into his inner strength and continued, "The whole family met two days ago: Libby, your father, Chava and myself, Uncle Saul, Cousin Naomi and little Eli. We all unanimously agreed Rivka had to slow down. The only way that could be done would be to bring you back to head up the company. Even Libby agreed. She knew Rivka would never transfer the reins over to her.

"So we brought in Rabbi Gershon and he and I saw your mother that evening here in the hospital. It was not very hard to convince her to let you come back, to forgive and forget. It was harder to make her understand she must give over the presidency to you, to let you run the business. But she knows how weak she is; she knows she can't go on like this. David, she wants you back and I know she'll let you be the head of the company."

With the last sentence, his voice broke altogether and he began to quietly sob. Chava followed suit, letting the tears trickle down her cheeks. I knew both of them were very emotional. The Second World War had seen them flee Poland and land in Shanghai for three years. Though they never talked about their experiences, never let anyone know what happened there, it must have been extremely painful. I saw both of them as delicate but beautiful vases; Chinese urns mapped with ancient lines, deep cracks in the glaze that permeated through to their inner souls.

"No." I looked at both of them, feeling deep affection. They loved me and they loved Rivka. "No, it just won't work. Betty and I have a successful and exciting agency. We're doing what we want. It's true that Baum Bagels is also a challenge but it's an impossible situation."

"Why David, tell me why?" Max wanted know, "Exactly why can't it work."

"Because." I knew it couldn't. There wasn't the slightest chance I would be allowed to take over. "First of all, Libby won't work with me; she'll sabotage everything. Second, Rivka hasn't allowed one strong executive in the company. Not one. She's run it alone all these years. So I would have to bring in new blood to get the company moving, to get it to show a profit. You know that for years now Baum Bagels hasn't shown growth or profits. And last but definitely not least, Mrs. B. will not allow me to take over. She'll continue to be the final arbitrator, the final decision maker. I will not wade into that quicksand again. I just won't."

"David," Max, who usually did not stand up to anyone's strong will, did not back down this time. "Give yourself a chance. Just listen to her. Don't make up your mind before you hear her out. I'm telling you she's changed. She wants you back. She's backed down completely. Libby is not a problem anymore. And your mother knows more than anyone else how we need you, your good sense, your drive and knowledge."

"Of course I'll listen to her." I touched his arm and nodded my head. "But Max, please don't count on it. I know my mother. She will not permit this business to be led by anyone but her. Please don't count on it too much. I do not want you to be hurt and disappointed."

"David, if you give your mother half a chance, if you keep an open mind, I know something can be worked out. Something must be worked out or the company will fail and she'll collapse."

"Okay, I'll try." I agreed. "How is she feeling today? And when can I go in?"

Chava answered, "The nurses say that she spent a peaceful night. She isn't in pain anymore and her breathing is much easier. In fact, she's eating her first meal right now. We can go in when she's cleaned up."

We sat there talking for a half hour, catching up on each other's news. Small talk, for we all knew that we were there for one person only, Rivka. Our voices were in the hospital's waiting area but our thoughts were in Mother's sick room.

The nurse came out of Rivka's room. Chava whispered something to the nurse who then reentered the sick room. I felt anxious. Rivka always made me feel nervous. I was awhirl in conflicting emotions, from worry about Mother to anger at her stubbornness; from fear of her sickness to fretting for the future. "What decision can I make without talking it over with Betty? The agency is her business as well as mine. I can't just quit and walk out. I can't simply decide to leave San Diego and move back to New York."

By the time the nurse came out again I was confused, worried, and completely mixed up. She motioned to Chava that it was all right to enter. Chava turned to me and, giving me a warm hug, said, "Be a good boy, David."

I marched in with a false bravado and an envelope of confidence as thin as paper. All my swirling emotions stopped when I saw mother. She had shrunk; her skin had now a gray tone and wrinkles dominated her former strong features. We once again just looked at each other—for the first time in four years. I was young and strong. She was weak, breathing loudly, and obviously in some pain.

"Mother," I ended the silence. "I'm glad to see you." She didn't say anything. To change the heavy and uncomfortable atmosphere, I went to the side of her bed and kissed her.

With that light touch on her cheek, she visibly relaxed and leaned farther back into her two large pillows. "Dovid'l, it's good to see you. I didn't know if I would ever see you again." Her eyes welled up. "You still are my deepest love, Dovid'l."

"And I've always loved you," I admitted to both of us.

"Sit down here," she motioned to the bed, "here, next to me so I can see you, so I can feel you."

I did as she requested and took her left hand in both of mine. It was good touching Mother once again. I was comfortable having her look at me with unquestioning love. I started to relax, but when I took a closer look, I saw she indeed had gone downhill, had grown smaller. She was never a large woman, but with the loss of weight her flesh had dissipated into deeply wrinkled skin that was set off by the now dull and completely gray hair. She had become old and weak. The only strength still remaining was compressed into her eyes. They still held their old power: two dark irises encompassing black pupils, dark staring eyes that penetrated her world.

"So how are you doing on the West Coast?" she said looking at me as if she were trying to either remember her son of former years or memorize how I looked now, here in the hospital room. Without giving me a chance to answer, she continued, "And how is . . ." She stopped, gathered her will and finally went on with, "how is your wife?"

I squeezed Mother's hand, the weight of the unspoken finally off my shoulders. "Betty is fine. She sends you her best wishes for a speedy recovery." Mother always tackled the hard things first. She wanted a clean field to begin the new and a clear path for the coming campaign, the next battle. Obviously, her opposition to my marriage to Betty and her conversion was a thing of the past and not relevant any longer. I had always admired mother's ability to gallop off in one direction, only to stop and swerve to the right or left at a moment's notice. Her strength lay in her focusing on the present and examining the future while permitting the past to take care of itself. I could not do it. My past, stuck to the present, stayed with me and had to be peeled off layer by layer. Once again I appreciated Mother's intuitive and effective tactics, this time as applied to Betty and myself.

But admiration is not the same as trust and I did not trust Mother. I did not know what topics she had on her new agenda. With certainty though, I realized I was one of the major ones.

"Rabbi Gershon made me see I had been wrong," she said, "not only with respect to the Jewish law but in the spirit of it as well. So Dovid'l, from now on Betty will be welcome in my house. But give me time. Not right away. Let me first talk to her on the phone a number of times before I see her. You understand?"

"Of course." I did understand. She had just turned a full one hundred and eighty degrees and I would not be the one to rub her face in it, though part of me was still furious and wished to lash out, to pay her back. However, looking at her sickly mien, I was able to control those angry feelings. What I was not able to control was my anxiety. I began to feel warm. I felt sweat beginning in my armpits and in my crotch. Though I didn't get hard, I could feel the blood flow freely through my genitals.

To bring my anxiety under control, I directly brought up the subject of the business, "I think this hospitalization and attack is a blessing in disguise. You really must slow down and take it easy. You cannot keep putting in all those hours at the office, the plant, and stores."

"That's what everyone keeps telling me," Rivka agreed with a nod of her head. "But the problem is there is no one to take care of all the problems—and as you know, there are many of them. To tell you the truth we have not been doing well lately. The expenses keep going up; it's impossible to find good bagel bakers; and the employees just don't do a good job no matter how much you pay them."

"Well, Rivka," I smiled at her, an external expression for the inner laughter, "I'm glad it's only the same old story. I heard those exact words from you ten years ago."

"But you don't understand, Dovid'l," her voice quivered. I was surprised at that. I had never before heard fear enter her voice. "The creditors are at our neck and sales are down in over half the stores. On top of that, to meet the competition we have to sell the wholesale frozen goods practically at cost. It's such a dog-eat-dog business."

"Yes, I know," I said. I did not continue. I waited for her to bring up what was on her mind.

"Dovid'l, you're the only one who can run the business besides myself. You're the one who knows it inside out and knows what has to be done. I need you to come back, to take over."

"That's difficult, Mother," I answered neutrally. "I now have my own agency and it is finally getting off the ground. In fact this past quarter was the first where we not only made expenses but actually had a healthy profit."

"You see, that's why I need you, why the family needs you. You'll be able to get Baum's Bagels back on the right track, to make it profitable again. Do you know how many people depend on the business? How the whole *mishpacha* lives off the business? What would happen to all of them if the business, God forbid, goes under? You have to come back and take over."

"But Rivka," I flared up, "that's what you said to me the last time and you didn't follow through. You didn't keep your end of the bargain. Don't you remember I already quit once before? I don't want your promises and then need to quit once again."

"Dovid'l," she said quietly, "I'm not in good health. I'm too weak to carry the business all by myself. Things are different now. I have changed. You take charge. I need your help."

"That's it," I jumped up, upset at her last words, words said just in passing. "I know you need my help. But with respect to taking charge, it is just talk. You know you can't let anyone take charge."

"Dovid'l, what do you want me to do to show you I'm serious? Just tell me what you want."

I cooled down a bit. Mrs. B. was a master at getting her way. She was doing it again. I was being slowly drawn into the web of her finely spun arena. To gain time, I pulled over a chair next to her bed and sat down.

"I'm not saying I'm coming back," I began, "but if I do I would have to be president; you would have to transfer the authority to make all the decisions to me and we'd have to agree on a hefty salary as well as stock options."

She didn't say anything.

"In addition, I'd want a five-year contract with all the fine print spelled out." I was surprised at myself for rattling off all these conditions. I had not given it any conscious consideration before this.

"Those are no problem," she said slowly, and thinking out loud she continued, "It's time I step down. As president, of course you will make all the decisions. You've always been a sensible boy and I know you won't take a salary out of line with the rest of the wage structure and what we could afford."

"Rivka," I had to spell out some of the finer but essential details, "Having authority means I hire and fire all personnel and they report to me, not you. We would have to hire a number of top executives to replace the dead wood we now have."

"Yes," she sidestepped the nitty-gritty point, "I'll remain only as chairman of the board. You become president. I'll only advise you while you take the responsibility of running the company."

"Mother, did you hear what I said?" I knew she did not agree. "I need to have the authority to hire anyone I deem necessary at any salary I think is fair." How well I remembered the last time I had signed up with Mother and company. She had been the general, captain, major, as well as the lieutenant. The rest of the army consisted of sergeants, corporals, and privates.

"Of course, of course," she countered, "you will be on the executive committee with Libby and myself. A majority of two out of three will decide on new executive personnel."

"No, Rivka." At last we reached the crux of the matter. "No committee, no two out of three, no divide and conquer. No; absolutely not."

"But Dovid'l, you've been away for so long. Things have changed and you don't know all the facts. I can't just let you make decisions without knowing all the pertinent points. You'll drag the company down the drain if you won't listen to anyone."

"That's what you always say." I now knew that she would not give up control, no matter how ill she was. "That's what you want to believe. No one can make any decision but you. And you are right you know because anyone that could is no longer with the company."

"Don't be such a hothead. After a while when I see that you know what's going on, when you are aware of the myriad of details, you will be able make all the decisions you want. In the meantime, we'll let the committee decide on executive personnel."

"No, Rivka, that is not good enough." In a way I was glad. I did not have to consider all the other points. This was clear and loud. It would be the same all over again and I did not want it. No way.

She got angry, red in the face. "Does it have to be one hundred percent your way? No compromise? Can't you see, I cannot just let you ruin everything I built up over all these years? Isn't it enough I give you the presidency, the money, the stock, and all the authority you will need?"

"Mother," I said gently but firmly, "there is no need to go on. I've just decided not to come back even if you would give me everything I want. You see, I just realized that I don't want it. I want to stay in California with Betty, with my business."

"Dovid'l, please don't say that. Can't you see I'm dying? Don't kill me with a stone of hard heartedness. Can't you see I need you? Don't you understand English? You must come back. I can't do it all alone anymore. I don't have the strength anymore."

"Mother, you have the whole family to help you. Libby is your right hand. You'll manage." I steeled myself for I knew she could not take no for an answer.

"You know what's wrong with you? It's not that your heart is as hard as stone. It is you have no heart at all." Her eyes narrowed to boiling fury. "You're killing me; you have no *rachmonos*. A stranger would have more pity on me than you. Yes, I'll manage. I always have. But if I die, you'll know why and you'll know who drove the last nails into my coffin. That *Shiksa* started it all. You've changed into a cold uncaring person. You're just like a goy. When you married her you became dead for me. You still are dead to me, do you hear? Dead!"

The last was shouted. I didn't know what to do. I did not want to fight with her, to put pressure on her weak heart. I was not interested in who was right or who was wrong. She had to calm down, but how? How?

I sat quietly as she continued to yell. I stopped listening and realized what I must do. I looked down and looked guilty, looked like I had been a bad boy, just like I had done many times before. For the first time in my life though I didn't feel guilty. I finally knew what had to be done in dealing with Mother. I didn't feel guilty but I acted as if I did.

And it worked.

Within two or three minutes of my not arguing with her, of my not defending myself, she did calm down. She stopped yelling. However, when she realized that my guilt and her arguments still would not make me change my mind, she once again began to shout. But this time it was to get the hell out of her sight.

"Get out. I knew I was right the first time. I never want to see you again. Never! Get out!"

Once again I left my mother's room. I left because I wanted her to calm down and halt her extreme agitation. She was still yelling when I entered the waiting room. Libby had arrived at the hospital while I had been with mother. As soon as she saw me leave the room and heard the yelling through the open door, she ran in, closing it behind her.

I sat there, exhausted. What a morning. Mother was her usual self and I was glad to be out of there. Max was quiet; Chava was sobbing silently. We sat unmoving for a long time. Suddenly, the door to mother's room flew open.

"Nurse! Nurse, come quick. Nurse!" Libby was yelling as she came running out.

Two nurses and one doctor ran in to mother's room. Max jumped up, "Libby, what is it? What's happened?"

"It's Mama," she was crying. "She just got all blue, clutched her heart, and lost consciousness. Oh Mama, Mama!"

I put my arm around her. "There, there. It'll be okay. The doctor is there now. It'll be okay. Mother is strong."

Libby pushed me away. She shrank from me.
"You killed her! You killed her!"

Lying in my bed, I relived Libby's horrible voice as she kept utter-ing that awful refrain again and again. I wondered how many years I would have to hear my sister's accusation. I was dead tired. How much more can I take of this awful nightmare?

The doctors had worked on mother for over an hour. She had had a massive heart attack while Libby was with her.

Heart attack. Libby staring off, wrapped into herself. Max and Chava consoling me, each other. Mother—Rivka. Doctors rushing in. Libby rushing out. Mother dead. Libby yelling, "You killed her!" I must have done it. *How do I atone for killing Mother?* Libby pacing up and down. Betty flying out here. *I didn't kill her. Mother knows that. So does Libby.* The hospital bed. A corpse!

Death and life, life and death. Mother dead. I began to sob. I've lost Mother. I'll never see her ever again. No more Mother.

The pills were finally working.

From a white light above me, around me, there appeared a gentle voice. "Dovid'l."

"Mommy, please forgive me."

"Dovid'l, I forgive you."

"Mommy, I love you! With all my heart I love you."

"And I love you."

The phone rang but I did not know where I was. I kept my eyes closed as the phone kept on ringing. I had been dreaming I was at the office in the middle of a meeting. The marketing vice-president of Baltimore Bagel had just told me he was taking his account to D.D.&B. When the phone rang I knew it was Mother calling to gloat over my loss.

The phone kept jangling insistently. With heavy head and still heavier eyelids, I struggled to open my eyes. The dimly lit and close-draped room of the Doral slowly came into focus. I managed to drag my arm to the phone and lift it off the hook. With a raspy whisper, I slowly hacked, "Yesss?"

"Darling," Betty said, obviously in a hurry, "the red-eye was completely booked. I waited as stand-by but there wasn't a single seat. I'm leaving instead from the L.A. airport in ten minutes, just having driven from San Diego. I'm catching the 8 a.m. flight to New York."

"What time is it?" I uttered drowsily.

"It's ten minutes to eleven your time, Saturday morning," Betty slowed down a bit. "I guess the pills must have worked. Go back to sleep. I'll be in New York around 6 p.m. All right?"

"Yes, sure," adding automatically, "Have a good flight."

"'Bye, got to dash." She quickly hung up.

Betty is obviously coming to New York. Good. Why? What am I doing here anyway? From a distant point in space, yesterday's events cometed in and left a trail of craggy meteors in my mind. I closed my eyes, trying to hurl yesterday's thoughts and emotions back out of consciousness. Luckily, the fog of sleep rolled in and helped to gray out the sharp-edged rocks.

Later, I awakened again, but this time to my own, slower rhythm. It was a little after 3 p.m.

I did not jump out of bed, my usual style of waking. I lay there and fully came to grips with Mother's death of yesterday; Betty's flight and loving concern of today; and the expected difficulty of tomorrow's funeral. I remembered Betty's call this morning. She had interrupted some dream. What was it? I couldn't remember the details but it had something to do Baum's Bagels.

I got up to shave and shower. While under the water, I soaped up my cock and got it hard. As I lazily played with it I thought of Betty, fantasized how we'd get it on tonight, and with a sudden sensation, came quickly and spasmodically. Orgasmatically satisfied, I dressed and went down to have a late breakfast.

At the coffee shop, I left the toasted corn muffin half uneaten. I was not hungry. Besides, Betty and I would be eating in a couple of hours. But I did order a second cup of coffee. I was still hung over from the sleeping pills and the traumatic events. As I lolled over the cup, I noticed that the blond young man sitting on the stool beside me was staring in my direction.

"Hi," he began, when he saw I had become aware of him. "You seem very familiar. Haven't I seen you somewhere?"

I did not know if he was making a play for me. If he was gay, he was not obvious. I decided to play the game until I found out. I was ready to trot again and I did have a couple of hours till Betty got here.

"Well," I turned to face him, "I've lived most of my life here in New York. On the other hand, could you possibly be mistaking me for someone else? Possibly someone you've seen in Florence?" I chuckled at the reference, not sharing my joke with him.

He turned his head a bit, lowered one side, and looked at me with a questioning squint. He seemed to be trying to place me. "No, I don't think we've ever met," he finally said. "I'm good at remembering voices and yours doesn't ring a bell." He continued to stare at me.

I still wasn't sure if his interest was of a sexual nature. He had not given me any definite signal. We were neither in a gay bar nor was he giving me a clear physical sign. I decided to take a chance and make the first move myself. I had obviously learned something from Dr. Manes.

It was not my remark, "Maybe you've seen my picture," that propelled our encounter into the pickup-testing orbit. Rather, it was my hand's movement on my crotch and the rearrangement of genitals—a natural gesture that could either be ignored or copied, depending on his orientation and/or intention.

"Possibly." He still looked puzzled. He neither responded with his own hand nor did he look down at my fingers' scratching. He neither smiled nor did he give any sign of a gay man's second language. Reluctantly, I decided he was definitely ensnared by Michelangelo's image—my double's haunting and artistic marble face; he was not on the prowl for a Saturday afternoon's pickup.

Mussing up my dark hair, adding some semblance of curls to my basically straight hair, I looked off in the distance, and said, "Would it help if I told you my name is David?"

The light bulb flashed. "By God," he said with a big smile, "what a likeness. I've been to Florence. Yes, that's where I saw your exact replica." Shaking his head several times, he got up. "Thanks for clearing up the mystery; sorry I interrupted your privacy." And with that remark, he quickly left.

Actually I was glad he had interrupted my thoughts and disturbed my somber feelings. It proved I could take a chance, make a play for someone whom I wasn't sure of and still come out a winner, even if the actual attempt failed. I paid the check and took a walk up Lexington Avenue. Though it was hot and muggy, I did not feel the heat. In some way, I felt cold, alone, and lost.

At Fifty-ninth Street I took a right turn into the crowded, giant, dark, marbled emporium of Bloomingdale's. I worked my way over to the perfume counter and bought Betty her favorite scent, Ma Griffe. I was thankful Betty was flying to New York. I needed her love and support at this time of loss. I had not realized the extent to which Mother had dominated my psychological and subconscious life. Though Mother had been in the background these past years, her influence colored the forms and shapes of all my relationships.

On the way out, I stopped in the candy department. I bought Betty some chocolate-covered strawberries and apricots. We both loved them, and I knew she would appreciate not only the gesture but also the taste. I walked back along Lexington Avenue and got to the hotel in plenty of time to relax before Betty's arrival. I stripped down to my jockey shorts; lay quietly on the bed, listening to my mind's inner chatter; and tried somehow to see my life's movement and direction.

I loved Betty. That much was certain. I was not sure of just how much she loved me. In some very deep part of her, I was sure she truly loved me. However, there were elements of myself she would not accept. I knew she did not mind my fooling around with other women. As long as I did not take away from her the essential feeling of closeness and primacy, she felt secure in herself and in us.

I could not understand her hesitancy with my bisexual side. She knew the gay side of me did not mean all that much. True, I had not shared it. Maybe that was it. It was not so much the homosexual aspect but, by keeping that part of myself secret, I violated her trust. And it was that particular aspect of our relationship she did not want to face. Yes that was it. It was not my bisexuality she avoided; rather it was the question of her trust and my honesty she did not want to look at.

Not only did I still love Betty with a feeling as deep as the one I felt right from the start but I also knew I needed her more than ever. In the three sessions with Dr. Manes it had become obvious that my cock's unruliness was intimately connected with my need for Betty's assurance of love. With our big fight of two years ago on one hand and the undercurrent of mistrust on the other, I was just hanging on. My anxiety level seemed to be directly connected to my having a hard-on. The diary Dr. Manes asked me to keep had made that crystal clear. It had gotten to the point at which I was horny over my insecurity with respect to Betty as well as over my many and varied fears—from business problems to the family fights.

My entry for Monday, July 30, just two weeks ago, suddenly stood out boldly:

Trouble over proposal with Mr. Parker at zoo meeting. Fucked Joanie at Frazee 2X. 2:30pm jerked off in office john. Made it with Betty eleven pm just before falling asleep.

My suggestion for next year's theme, *The Llama Extravaganza,* was received with only lukewarm enthusiasm. The zoo had only two llamas and both were old. Mr. Parker, their marketing director, wanted us to put together a new campaign proposal as an alternative. The bummer was the deadline was just ten days away. We promised we'd have one ready next week. After they left, I became scared we could not possibly have a good campaign ready in seven days.

I had run off to Joanie. As always, she was ready to trot and promptly locked the store. After our first fuck, I remained hard and sweet-talked her into a second time. Coming back to work, I sat alone in my office trying to come up with an idea, a new hook. I used one hand to jot down ideas and with the other began stroking my ever-erect cock. By two-thirty I went to the men's room to release the tension and relieve the pressure so I could concentrate on my work rather than my knob.

Going home with Betty that evening, I told her of the problem with the zoo. We went over the possibilities of what they might like. Over dinner, that's all we talked about. By the time we exhausted the possibilities later that evening, we still had not come up with a solution. But my cock had come up. Betty of course noticed the bulging erection. She got up and sat down on the sofa, saying she wanted to watch TV after a hard day's work.

So I sat next to her, brought her coffee, and though horny and hard did no more than put my arm around her while we watched a comedy on HBO. For what seemed to me the first time in months, Betty made the initial move. She put her hand on my straining prick and began to massage it.

As I recalled the exciting scene, I pulled my cock out of my shorts and began to jack off. I started to get excited once again as I remembered how Betty took my cock out of my pants and went down on it.

Just as I was almost ready to come, there was a noise at the door. Betty came into the room, saw me with cock in hand, and laughed.

"I could have won my bet, Randy," she said as she came over and hugged me. She kissed me warmly on the mouth while taking my cock in her hand. She continued what I had begun.

I didn't say a word. My mouth was covered by hers. My body was hugged, my dick held. Similar to two weeks ago, I lay back and let Betty be the active one. I had been close to coming. Her appearing in person and actualizing my fantasy turned me on even more. She did not have time to undress. I climaxed in her hand.

I showered for the second time that day. Betty declined to join me. I was sure she knew what I had in mind. However, when I was dressed again, she changed her mind and took a quick one while I waited in front of the TV watching the last inning of an exciting 1 to 0 game, with Dwight Gooden of the Mets pitching a three-hit shutout.

She wasn't very hungry, having had two meals on the plane. Between the heat and my mixture of strange moods, I also did not want a fancy restaurant. We settled for Oscar's coffee shop in the Waldorf Astoria just down the block. The light green walls and the cool air conditioning were a good foil for the heat of August; the large fresh fruit salads were light and refreshing.

I was delighted to see and be with Betty. She was as beautiful as the day I met her. Her long blonde hair, still showing that smooth lilt, complemented so well her bright blue eyes. Even sitting at a table, she was majestically tall. Her animated movements and gestures triggered my emotions. Several times during dinner I told her how beautiful she was and how deeply I loved her. Her response was to take my hand and, looking into my eyes, tell me that she, too, loved me completely. That evening my doubts were almost entirely smoothed away. I knew our problems, though large, would not break us apart.

Conversation centered on Betty and San Diego. We spoke at length about the campaign for the zoo. They had accepted our suggestion to borrow as many llamas as possible from the L.A., Phoenix, and San Francisco zoos. The public relations value of such a move would be enormous. Betty told me they had lined up fourteen llamas as of last Thursday and might get as many as twenty-five. Mr. Parker was now the driving force behind *The Llama Extravaganza*. Everyone was delighted with my solution. It had gotten us out of the pickle barrel.

Evidently in a good mood, she continued, "Let's use this success and make hay with it. Our new office space has room for expansion. A couple of new accounts will substantially reduce our overhead and we'll be extremely profitable."

Betty was responsible for finances and the management of our firm. Her down-to-earth, no-nonsense attitude toward expenses had kept us going in the lean times. She now wanted us to cash in our success. These startup years had been hard going.

"How much longer is the computer course going to take?" I replied to her suggestion. "You know we can't handle any more clients without a computer. We've both agreed a state-of-the-art installation is necessary if we're to service our clients properly. In fact, I just can't wait to get my hands on a graphic computer for our brochures and artwork."

"I'm finally finished in two weeks," she said. "I'll be real glad. It's been difficult working full-time as well as putting in four nights a week in class work, but I've learned so much these last months, honey. I'm leaning toward a Hewlett-Packard but I'm still considering an IBM."

I agreed to her suggestion for expansion and we devised a plan, a full-scale campaign to get new clients. After that decision, conversation went from office personnel, to gossip about the rocky marriage of some friends of ours, to a rare night out at The Comedy Store, where Betty and her girl friend went the previous week.

Over coffee, I realized our conversation until then had completely avoided the one subject both of us knew was permeating my every thought and mood. Betty had wisely steered clear from the rocks of my depression and had kept it as light as I wished it to be. I now realized I did not wish to evade or deny the events any longer.

In the middle of a sentence, I stopped. I looked at Betty and said nothing.

"Do you want to talk about it?" Betty immediately sensed my abrupt mood change and took hold of my hand.

I did. I began telling her what happened. At first I spoke hesitantly and slowly. As I continued, I couldn't stop to think out what I wanted to say. The events kept rushing into my mind. My feelings of loss re-emerged, my guilt grew, and sadness swelled. The events gushed out. I let my emotions rule the facts, my mood dictate the story.

The previous night's continual crying had completely dried out my tear ducts. Though I now felt just as bad, if not worse than yesterday,

I managed to only gasp out a couple of dry sobs. However, I was not able to emote with real tears, my normal expression of deep anguish. Betty listened quietly, keeping my hand in hers. She just sat still, being there and sharing my grief. She silently teared up several times, and when they finally overflowed, did not remove her hands from mine to wipe her cheeks.

The waitress was observant and left us alone, not asking us if we wanted anything else. Our booth was isolated from other diners; the noise level was low and our intensity eliminated all distractions. It took over an hour for me to come to some sort of stop and realize that I had just spilled my heart out to Betty. For the first time in our relationship, I had not kept any of my feelings regarding Rivka hidden. Previously I had joked at times or given only parts of the picture. This evening, however, I painted it as it really had been, bright colors of love and respect intermixed with dark shadows of guilt, fear, and hate.

Betty understood. She confided how ambivalent she herself was toward her own mother, a woman who had been so busy raising a family of many children that she had no time to give that special something to any individual child. She comforted me and accepted without reservation my waves of contradictory emotions. Slowly my anguish diminished and my pain lessened. In some way, Mother's loss was countered by Betty's presence and love. I marveled at her intuitiveness. First, she had insisted on flying out here for the funeral; then, when she had gotten here, she jumped right into bed with me; and now she just stayed connected as she quietly listened to my wounds, pain, and maternal loss.

As my mood changed from a sense of loss to one of love, I once again declared my deep-felt love. She continued sitting quietly and let me state my warm and rich feelings without interruption. Once more she was moved to tears. This time wiping them off her face, she told me her emotions for me were just as deep and loving.

"Can we discuss our problem with my bisexuality?" I impulsively brought up the subject that had darkened our vista these past two years.

Her joy immediately disappeared and waves of pain welled up. She shook her head from side to side. Now it was my turn to console her, to lessen her pain. Obviously, she was not ready to discuss it, nor was she able to look at it directly.

I dropped the subject, saying instead, "I love you deeply and the last thing I want is to hurt you. With both of us being sensitive to the other, I am sure we'll work out any and all problems."

I reviewed the various difficulties we had experienced in the past and how we were able to overcome them. However, when I began to discuss my family's resistance to Betty, I once again found I couldn't continue.

Betty, acutely sensitive to my present grief, took charge once more. She became the efficient partner and stopped all conversation. She said it was time to stop talking. She got me to pay the bill. We left the restaurant feeling closer than ever, though we were roiling with internal turmoil. I took her arm in mine and steered her west to Madison Avenue and the Palace Hotel. Betty had not been in the new hotel as yet. I wanted to show her the quiet elegance experienced by the very rich.

We had a drink at the Palace bar before returning to our hotel. My good feelings were again on the rise. My mood had been pulled up by our conversation and I felt warmth from the depth of my sadness to the light of our love. We compared the various hotels in New York and both of us agreed we still preferred the "old majestic lady," The Plaza. By the time we got back to the Doral, I was horny as hell—a combination of love, habit, and lustful emotions. Betty, of course, was fully aware of my hard-on. For the second time that day she made the first move, taking it out of my pants.

Bursting with the need to express my love for her, I did not wait for her to fully get in sync with me but entered her before she had time to come up to my level of excitement. Though I realized it would take some minutes of foreplay for her to join me at my lust's height, I didn't wait and climaxed within a minute of entering her.

With my coming so quickly, Betty's sexual intensity and excitement deepened. For some reason, no matter what I did that evening, she got turned on; she reacted like the Betty I had known at the beginning of our relationship. Ever so gently, she began to rub my back, using her nails to scratch me into a heightened state of desire—not that I had lost my erection. Within moments I was ready to begin my thrusting. This time, Betty was with me all the way and, like the good old times, we came together, loudly and joyfully.

For the first time ever, I lost count that night. Every couple of hours, either I would awaken her, being fully hard and ready to go, or she would awaken me with her hand, mouth, or body. Some time around 6 a.m., as the sun came up, we finally fell into a deep sleep, completely spent, at peace with ourselves and with each other. For the first time in years, I was satiated as well as satisfied.

I awoke a little after ten. I lay quietly thinking of what would probably transpire this day. Rivka is to be buried; Mother is to be put to rest. Before permitting myself to head down into that well of emotions, I looked at Betty. She slept with her mouth slightly open but breathed in and out through her nose. Not a wrinkle in her beautiful face. She was so serene and calm. How wonderful she was. One minute full of life and lust, the next so peacefully asleep.

"I love you Betty," I whispered.

She opened her eyes in response. Smilingly, she simply gave a small nod and cuddled up to me. We quietly held each other and with a gentle stillness enjoyed our closeness. Slowly, she once again began the sexual ritual by rubbing against my cock. Once again we made love. This time slowly, with a passion that built and built, each wave of lust higher than the last. Our powerful orgasms put an exclamation point to this beautiful paragraph in our life, a paragraph written with sentences of love and words of joy.

The day was unbearably hot and humid. All my thoughts and feelings evaporated as we stepped out of the hotel. At first the heat slowly surrounded us, then the fiery sun's midday blast hit us as an aftershock. We had lolled in bed, played and laughed in the shower, and enjoyed a second cup of coffee from room service's full breakfast. Having played with the idea of walking to the synagogue, Betty and I had to hurry the last half hour. We now realized that the weather precluded a slow stroll through Central Park. We had wanted a buffer of time this early Sunday afternoon before joining the congregation of mourners.

I told the cab driver to drive us to the West Side Synagogue on Seventy-sixth Street just off Central Park West. As we crossed the park, I explained to Betty that the feeling I got from the family was she was not welcome. However there was nothing they could do to stop her from joining the service at the synagogue. She reassured me once again that she was here for my sake only and couldn't care less what the family liked or wanted.

When we got out of the cab there were just a few people in front of the synagogue. It was still early as the service was scheduled for two o'clock. Several acquaintances came over and in soft voices offered their sincerest condolences on my loss. From her Jewish studies, Betty knew she would have to sit apart from me. She asked me where the women sat in this orthodox synagogue. I showed her the stairs that led to the upstairs rear section reserved for women, a balcony partially hidden by a wooden trellislike railing. Saying she wanted to get a front-row seat to be as close as possible to me, she pecked me on the cheek and tightly squeezed my hand, slowly releasing her strong grip. Even more slowly, she climbed the steep stairs.

I sensed Betty's loss immediately. Her leaving my side reinforced the loving connection I was feeling as well as my strong need for her. My eyes began watering with the fullness of emotions searing through me. That was how Max, Chava, and Libby found me, alone inside the doorway, slowly wiping away my flowing tears. It had been only Friday that we had left each other at the hospital. In less than two days we became relatives sharing the loss of a true matriarch, our Rivka. Seeing my tears, Chava also began to cry. She hugged me tightly.

"Dovid'l, it's such a loss, such a loss."

"Yes, Chava," I gently stroked her head and back, "we're all going to miss Mother," and with those words, my tears for Betty and myself turned to ones for Rivka. I separated myself from my aunt and hugged Uncle Max who was now also sobbing softly.

"Chava," I turned back to her, "Betty flew in from California yesterday. She's already upstairs, sitting alone, knowing no one. Please sit next to her and make her feel comfortable and wanted."

"Betty is here?" Chava was truly surprised. "Dovid'l, the family will not like it."

Max interposed with a sharp look at his wife and quickly said, "Chava, listen to David. Go up and sit next to Betty. She came here for him, to help him. The least you can do is make it easier for her. Go."

Libby's face also showed surprise and all she said was, "Oh." After a two second pause, she managed another, "Oh."

"Oh," I echoed her. "What's the 'oh' for? What's going on? Chava is unusually secretive, Max is highly uncomfortable, and now you're absolutely mute? Libby, what the hell is going on?"

"We were over at Dad's last night," she looked at me with unreadable, opaque brown eyes and, crossing her arms in front of herself, took a wider stance with her feet. I felt something terribly wrong had taken place. I just knew that it had to do with me.

She continued, "We did not think that Betty would come to New York. You had said she was busy at work and we knew there was no love lost between Mother and Betty."

"Come on, Libby, get to the point."

"We voted." Libby now paused. Then quickly, "It would have been Rivka's wishes Betty should not sit *Shiva* with the family."

"That's all?" I laughed. My anxiety abated. "You're right, she is busy and must fly back. And anyway I'm sure she couldn't care less about sitting *Shiva* for Mother. I know I've lost a mother but I'm certain Betty did not lose a mother-in-law."

Libby sighed. "Well, then there's no problem."

"No, there isn't," I said. "Right after the funeral, I'll take Betty to the airport and come back to the apartment to begin *Shiva* with the rest of the family."

"No," Libby shook her head. "Rivka would not have wanted to have Betty at the funeral. She is not welcome there. Here in the synagogue anyone can enter but at the funeral it's only for invited guests and family."

"What?" I was flabbergasted. "And who do you think is going to keep her out if she comes with me?"

"David, the whole *mishpacha* voted Betty would not be welcome at the funeral as well as at the house. It's a family decision."

"Libby, don't hide behind the family's skirt." I was furious. "It's you who decided it and I'm sure that Dad and all the rest of the tribe just followed your lead. The body isn't cold yet and you've already put on the bloody crown."

With a look that told her what I thought of her, I turned my back on them and went into the synagogue. I took my seat in the row reserved for the immediate family. When Max came in and sat beside me, I gave him a hard and mean stare to let him know I did not take kindly to the family's shenanigans. Then confusion, hurt, and fear foisted itself in my spirit's center. What a day. The day after I lose my mother, the family gangs up on me.

"Did the family actually take a vote to exile Betty?" I asked Max, tightly grasping the back of the blond oak pew in front of us.

"No, David," he answered in a voice so low I had to lean toward him in order to hear his next words. "But there was a consensus: Rivka would neither have wanted her at the funeral nor with us during *Shiva*. Only little Eli thought we had to think of you and wanted us to do whatever you decided was best."

"And how did you vote, my dear understanding uncle?" my voice laced with anger and sarcasm.

"I know how you feel, David," he did not meet my eyes, his voice as low as before. "But I had to take my sister's wishes into consideration and Rivka at the end was not able to really change her mind. She still did not accept your marriage. On top of that, you didn't help her when she needed it most. You rejected her offer of your taking over the presidency." His voice was stronger now and he finally raised his eyes to look directly at me.

"Max, here I thought you were a true friend, and the whole family voted to exclude my wife when none of you even knew if she was going to come." In a louder, angrier voice I continued, "And do you realize you all decided it without consulting me? Without hearing what I might want? Without taking *my* wishes into account?"

"Libby wanted to do what the family thought would be best, and I thought it would be right for everyone if . . ." he did not finish, and once again looked down at the floor.

I did not know what else to say. Instead I just sat immobile, not looking at anything in particular, imagining yesterday's scene in my parents' living room as the family discussed Betty and me. I lost all sense of time. The next thing I knew Rabbi Gershon was leading the congregation in some Hebrew prayers. His eulogy went on and on. Mother was an important member, donated lavishly to the Center, and because of the retail stores was one of the most prominent parishioners.

My emotional storm tuned out his speech. I was brought back to his endless eulogy only when I heard my name mentioned in the context of being the artistic and successful son with his own agency in San Diego. He then continued with my sister. Libby was the daughter following in her mother's footsteps and, just like her religious mother, would continue the policy of keeping this kosher concern closed on the Sabbath—observing the Jewish law even if it meant a loss in sales and profits.

By the time he finished his speech and people were leaving the synagogue, I still had not decided what I would do. Not only was I distraught once again with mother's death, I was hurting with unchecked anger and confused about my family's attitude regarding Betty. It seemed as if Rivka's unsheathed will was being carried over from the grave. Her innate attitudes were now being translated into Libby's actions toward Betty and myself.

I just couldn't understand my sister. She had been in my corner, had shared and enjoyed the conversion process, and had helped Betty with her studies. Then, with Rivka's first direct opposition, she not only backtracked at the time, but also was now leading the opposition and blocking any possible solution or reconciliation. *What gives with you Libby? Is life so scary you can't have your own voice or ideas?*

Getting up from my pew, I still had no idea what the family would insist on or what Betty would want. As we slowly left the synagogue, I felt so alone in this throng. Walking out onto the street I again received numerous consoling murmurs by various acquaintances, distant relatives, and even by Rabbi Gershon and his wife. My response to them was distant and numb. I was searching for Betty, my one emotional and loving contact. I finally saw her next to Chava. Moving quickly through the crowd, I took Betty by the arm and briskly steered her across the street. I wanted to talk to her without being overheard.

Seeing my distraught expression, Betty began to console me with words of support and shared with me the deeply felt emotions she experienced during the services. I stopped her in the middle of a sentence with, "Betty, you don't understand. They don't want you at the funeral."

She looked shocked. "But I want to be with you at this trying time. I flew out here to share this loss, Randy. I love you and want to stand next to you in this hour of need."

"Darling, there is no one more important than you. I just don't want to make a scene. I know if you try to get into the limousine with me, they'd tell you in no uncertain terms you were not welcome at the cemetery. Wait, that's it. Let's take a cab. In that way, they won't know till the last moment you're with me."

"No," Betty responded with her practical logic, "we would only cause those nasty words and thoughts to be uttered at the cemetery itself. I don't know why the other members of your family care that much, but darling if I'm not wanted, I don't want to be there."

Suddenly, I heard the honking of a car horn. I looked across the street and saw the crowd had dissipated and all the mourners who were to go to the burial were already inside the elongated black cars. The limo-line was connected with their bright headlights and were only waiting for me to get into the lead car to join Libby, Father, Max, and Chava. Nobody knew what to do. They couldn't leave without me, the oldest son. However, they did not wish for Betty to join them. No one had the temerity to cross the street, so someone had told the black-capped driver to begin honking his horn.

Telling Betty to wait a moment, I went over to the lead Cadillac and stuck my head in the open door. I looked at my family with a mixture of strong but conflicting emotions. For a minute my anger did not permit me to say a single word, though by then I knew what I had to tell them. Finally, looking at my father, I said, "Dad, since my wife cannot join me at the cemetery, I have to say good-bye to her here and now. So go on ahead and I'll join you when I've taken leave of Betty."

Without waiting for an answer, I recrossed the street to join Betty. I then led her away from the line of cars toward the park. As we got to the corner, I noticed that the long snake of cars had at last begun to move as they slowly headed toward the cemetery. I turned around completely to give one final look at the last of the cars as they disappeared around the corner down Columbus Avenue. I knew I would not join them. The living were more precious than the dead. Betty was more important than Rivka.

I held tightly onto Betty and whispered, "Good-bye Mother. Rest in peace." I started to sob.

Realizing what I had decided, Betty responded with a choked voice, "Oh, Randy. This is so difficult. If I had known I'd be the cause of you having to choose between two people who love and loved you, I'd never have flown here."

"No, Betty, it isn't your doing; it isn't your fault. And I do not have to choose between the two of you. I picked you many years ago, and continue to do so." I turned to look at her directly and continued, "My family will have to bury Mother without her son at the graveside, without having her son say the *Kaddish*. Besides, I want to be with you until you fly back tonight. I'll have more than my fill of my family during the week of *Shiva*. I know this is all for the best."

Squeezing Betty tightly, I kissed her warmly on the mouth. The decision to remain with Betty and not go to the cemetery lifted my mood once more on this emotional-roller-coaster day. On the spur of the moment, I decided we should visit the Metropolitan Museum. We slowly walked across the park and though the heat was still unbearable, I was still chilled from the synagogue's cold air-conditioning and death's icy breath in my being.

The museum was relatively empty on this hot, muggy August Sunday. It was close to four o'clock and the major crush of visitors had already left. After paying our entrance fee and receiving our small, round, yellow entrance buttons, we went to the Lehman Wing showing Ingres's *Princesse de Broglie,* that wonderful lady in blue. She was so majestic, the blue dress so elegant. Both Betty and I found ourselves absorbed by the color and technique. Being able to view true genius calmed us, raised our spirits, and enabled us to share in the joy of experiencing exalted art.

Upon entering the museum I had noticed that the Met was having an exhibition of Henry Moore's wartime drawings and that's where we headed next. The line for this exhibit was moving smoothly. The crowd had thinned and we did not have to view the drawings craning around the back of heads. The hall was uncannily still; no one talked. The only sound was that of shoes shuffling along the marble floors. The subject matter overpowered each viewer.

We stopped in front of *Tube Shelter: Perspective.* The two rows of sleeping figures on the Liverpool Street Extension floor looked like hundreds of concentration camp victims enshrouded in a tunnel of hell. His drawings of sleeping figures gripped my emotional circuitry. This was not peaceful sleep; it was anguished death. Once more I began to cry, not for these Londoners escaping the bombs, but for mankind's inhumanity and for the inevitability of death. For Rivka. Here I was, looking at death, but unable to be at the graveside where Mother's remains were being returned to the earth.

Betty stood in front of these deathlike drawings, sobbing softly. She lightly held on to my arm. I took her hand in mine, drawing strength in our touch. Silently, I once more bid good-bye to Mother. I felt Rivka's presence in these drawings. I saw the start of her heavenly journey from these bomb-shelter tunnels and in these sleeping dead.

As we left the gallery, Betty said, "Randy I felt your mother's presence. I saw the anguish of dying permeating through the fear of the living." No answer was possible, not if I did not want to completely break down. I just nodded. Then nodded again.

We left the museum after that, coming down the seemingly endless white stairs, first from the second floor, then from the front entrance down to the street. I was in mourning's grip of inertia. It was Betty who caught us the cab that took us back to the Doral.

We were both drenched. The heat and emotions had left us wringing wet. I jumped in the shower and lay on the bed while Betty took hers. We still had a number of hours before her flight back to San

Diego. Neither of us were hungry but we needed each other. We lay together on the king-size bed, holding on and lying still.

Without any surprise, my cock started to expand and I began to lust. Betty let me make love to her, long and hard. This time I took the initiative and Betty was the passive one. I kept whispering that I loved her; I wanted and needed her. She responded with mirrored movements and small gasps and groans. I was not finished after my first orgasm but once again brought Betty to a high pitch and with loud groans joined her once more in a second, exploding climax.

That session of lovemaking was our actual good-bye though we still had three hours together until I saw her off at Kennedy airport. I don't remember what we talked about. I don't recall what she looked like as she disappeared behind the security check as she headed for Gate 23. I cannot picture my thoughts as I traveled back alone to the hotel, nor do I know what I said to myself as I fell asleep that evening.

All I knew was I would start sitting *Shiva* for Rivka Monday morning. I would begin a formal mourning ritual for Mother, a mother I buried not at the graveside in a Long Island cemetery but in front of a Moore wartime drawing.

PART IV:
PAUL AND RANDY

He kept staring beatifically at the ceiling, blue irises just thin rims around his large black pupils. Paul's joy had centered in the twin round pools of his light-absorbing eyes. His vision focused on the cracked white ceiling: a plane of forms and shadows containing the truths of eternity as well as the raptures of the moment. He traveled with light speed from galaxy to galaxy, stopping to marvel at the densely invading black holes and pausing to gape at the fiery, ever-exploding supernovas. The universe was encompassed in the fireworks of his mind.

Paul was tripping.

Time measured in microseconds illuminated eons of life; millions of generations existed in the space of a synapse. Sunrise melted the peripheries of universes while dusk inked out the brightest of stars. Cavemen danced with bejeweled queens and sonic booms were whispers in the whirling rings of Uranus.

Paul was peaking, intensely splintered by the chemical forces speeding along the axons of his mind.

Awareness was enmeshed in panoramic visions, beating pulses of infinite lines and gigantic expansions of godly powers. The background music was only a loom to the weave of Paul's mind. *Atom Heart Mother* was just a seed to the rotating discs of heavenly music and Pink Floyd was a concept lost in the cloudless orchestra of life.

Paul was on sunshine, the guru of acid, an orange pill that contained both vision's power as well as psyche's hell. He was transported into an ecstasy that precluded an orientation of time, place, or person.

At that exact moment the well-ordered universe dictated that her mouth cover his with a wet and lingering kiss. Paul accepted her lips with the same delight he had embraced his mind's visual fingers. A tumescence in his groin coincided with the hunger in his mind. Physical lust joined an inner drive to unite, to enter into oneness. Paul, with his heart's pulse, began to thrust. Intuitively, she placed herself in position to receive him. In unison, they seesawed up and down. As one, they rocked together on a floating bed in an unknown room in the center of their internality.

His thrusts increased in intensity; his movements quickened. Exploding universes and white beams of ultimate joy combined with long moans of noisy breaths. She whimpered and groaned her climax. Paul moaned and yelled as his orgasm sped through his loins, his brain, his being.

Applause brought him back to the reality of New York, to West Eighty-eighth Street. His heartbeat had been replaced by the echoes of applause. Paul looked up to see Carl and Jeanette clapping. They were as nude as the two participants on the bed.

"Now that's what I call fucking," Carl said, gleefully.

"How . . . how long have you been watching?" Paul stuttered, still dazed by his ecstatic orgasm, still swimming in the waves of the oceanic trip he was on.

"Long enough to get horny once again," Carl answered by pointing to his erect penis.

"Yes, long enough to want to make it a foursome," Jeanette joined in. Eyeing Virginia's breasts, she began stroking her own nipples.

Paul realized what they were about to start and was repelled by the idea. He jumped out of bed, looked at Carl and Jeanette, and said, "Why don't you begin without me. I'm pooped for now. Besides I need to drink something cold."

Paul watched for a moment as Carl took his place on the bed while Jeanette bent down to kiss Virginia. He did not wait to see the three of them entwine in sexual embrace. He walked a bit unsteadily to the kitchen, gulped down a glass of ice water, then slowly tottered into the living room and plunked himself down on the cushioned daybed. His mind was awash in turmoil.

Virginia was one of Carl's groupies. Paul had seen her a couple of times when he had visited Carl. She was a pretty starlet, petite and cute, and enamored of the theater. Carl had given her a few small roles in some of the tryouts he directed. She returned the favor and was usually available for evenings of fun and games. Paul was not surprised to find her there when he had showed up earlier in the evening to celebrate the signing of the contract.

Two loud chirps from Jeanette's cuckoo clock signified the time to be 2 a.m. They had all swallowed the mind-altering drug around ten. Paul was now definitely past his peak but waves of jagged edges still carried him along the paths of psychedelic distortions. Time was a discontinuous dimension moving through the snapshots of his memory. Carl's letter asking him to participate in a showcase production three years ago was superimposed on Carl's expression when they met the following week. It was their first meeting in almost ten years since that acrimonious and particular bitter parting at *The Iceman Cometh* dress rehearsal.

Paul had taken a booth in the rear of Leo's Coffee Shop. He saw Carl as he slowly trod past the counter where the stools were completely filled up with the steadies. Carl had aged. His hair was now completely gray though still as full and bushy as before. He was heavier and more imposing. His bulbous nose and fleshy lips were still set off by the thick eyebrows and deep furrows of his brow. His gait had slowed down but his stare of awareness was still as sharp as an unsheathed stiletto.

"Hello, Carl." Paul nodded but did not get up. He extended his hand in a formal handshake.

"It's good to see you, Paul." Carl lowered himself slowly into the brown vinyl booth after having successfully looped his black beret onto the coat hook.

"It's been a long time." Paul started the conversation, inanely neutral.

"Yes it has. A lot of water has gone under the bridge." He gave Paul a long stare before continuing, "I was shocked about Evi. I didn't know when I wrote you. I'm sorry. I'm truly sorry. She was a fine person, a wonderful woman."

Paul now stared back. Carl sounded sincere; he probably was sincere. However Paul knew better than to trust Carl's emotions. They were tools in his armament of relations. One moment's sincerity could be replaced by years of casuistry. His remembrance of Carl's behavior toward Evi many years ago did not jibe with the present undefiled warmth. Though spoken in anger and uttered a decade earlier, Carl's words still stuck sharply in Paul's throat. Meanness and a desire to hurt lived side by side with Carl's empathy and largesse.

Too many years had passed, though, and Paul did not want to hold those particular hurts and grudges anymore. The world worked in strange ways. His fight with Carl had enabled him to marry Evi and become a father, as well as study medicine. So with a maturity that shaped hurt into forgiveness, Paul shrugged off his old resentment and answered, "Yes, she was a loving wife and though I've learned to live without her, I don't think there will ever be another woman who can replace her."

A silence ensued. Carl continued to stare deeply. Paul returned the look, his mind and soul reliving Evi.

"I'm also sorry about our fight. It wasn't necessary. In fact it was a shame," Carl finally bringing up the canyon that lay between them.

"I'm also sorry about it." Paul continued to meet Carl's eyes, waiting for an apology.

It appeared on cue with Carl continuing, "I'm sorry I was so stubborn, so bull headed. You know me. I have to get my way."

With a spirit of openness built on a bridge of forgiveness toward his former mentor, Paul buried the months of pain and hurt from an incipient career shattered on the shoals of Carl's uncontrolled ego. "Yes, I know. However, let bygones be bygones."

He brightened the atmosphere with a smile. Carl responded in kind.

Suddenly a wave of acid flung Paul onto the shores of another scene and the smile turned into the laughing and bubbly face of Anna as she ran toward him when he got off the plane in Zurich. He picked her up, kissed her cheeks and mouth, slowly put her down and turned to smile at Johan, who was flanked by his Opa and Oma, Dr. and Frau Stocker.

With another fling of LSD's multiple fragmentations, Paul clearly saw Carl smile in another scene. It had taken place when the final curtain had come down on their first showcase production two years ago. The three performances had been highly successful. The critics had raved and the angels had floated in with money for an off-off-Broadway production. A smiling Carl had hugged Paul and Paul had laughed with glee.

"What's funny?" a voice interrupted his reverie.

Paul opened his eyes to rust-colored pubic hair. Jeanette was standing next to the sofa. She also was smiling. "What's funny? You seem to be having a good time all by yourself."

Slowly Paul came back to this night of acid, this evening of celebration. His memory of his first showcase under Carl's direction dissolved into the reality of Jeanette's sweaty body, her laughing face and satisfied look. She had obviously enjoyed herself in the bedroom while Paul was tripping alone with his smiling thoughts here in the living room. He sat up, pulled her down to him and planted a big wet kiss on her shoulder.

He hugged her and said, "Tonight all the smiles of the world are with me, with Anna, with you and Carl. And I'm laughing all the way to my first Off Broadway play." He continued to hold her tightly, smiling into her eyes. She got into the spirit and returned his kiss, planting her slightly open mouth on his forehead.

"This time Paul, I know it'll go smoothly. Carl is proud of the way you've matured into a fine actor. And you did it even though you had to squeeze rehearsals into your busy schedule."

"Well it's not as if I had a full-time acting career. It's only been two showcases and one off-off-Broadway piece that ran only for one month in the past two years."

"But everything you've done has been divine," Jeanette said with pride. She began to stroke his thigh, slightly scratching his skin.

Paul found himself beginning to think of sex. His penis responded and started to elongate. He had always found Jeanette attractive but as Carl's lover she was out of bounds. Acid, however, rearranged taboos into legitimacy and extended the boundaries of what's possible. He knew Carl and Jeanette had no scruples when it came to swinging with other couples. They bragged about it—claiming sexual freedom, openly sharing the pleasures of new partners, and denying the green dragon of jealousy.

However, Paul knew differently. Twelve years were not enough time for him to forget Carl's insane envy, Carl's violent thrusts of anger at the thought that Evi might have preferred a man other than himself. So Paul, with a caution born on the thorns of painful experience, wisely refrained from starting up with Jeanette. With a slight shake of his head, he took her hand away.

"I'm in a different space, Jeanette. I guess after my wonderful session with Virginia, I'm not interested in that now. Maybe some other time. You do know I find you extremely beautiful and desirable."

Obviously disappointed, but accustomed to giving in to the men in her life, she acquiesced. "All right, some other time." She got up, giving him a peck on the cheek, and went back to the bedroom. Left alone, Paul put on his shirt and pants. He figured it was time to eliminate any unwanted or entangled sexual encounters. He lay down on the cushioned daybed and closed his eyes, enveloping himself in the resonating sounds of The Moody Blues' *Seventh Sojourn* spinning smoothly on the hi-fi.

Either Paul's unspoken message must have registered with the others or the three of them had satisfied their lustful pairings, for when he next opened his eyes, Virginia, nursing a Coke, had on her bra and mini skirt while Jeanette, just going into the kitchen, was wrapped in a blue and white kimono.

Carl, in baggy undershorts, sat down opposite Paul. With a slow sensuousness, he scratched his crotch, murmuring, "Oh boy, oh boy." It was not difficult for Paul to decipher what he was referring to. Not wishing to remain in the sports arena of sex, Paul switched appetites.

"Carl, I'm absolutely starving. Do you have anything that could be prepared? I'm so high that all I'm good for is to put some presliced ham and cheese on a slice of bread."

"No problem, Paul." Carl unconsciously had changed the location of his fingers and was now rubbing his belly. "Jeanette and I have tripped hundreds of times and are able to maintain even while peaking. Since you're just on your second trip you're still out of it." Turning to Virginia, he continued, "Why don't you help Jeanette in the kitchen?"

It was true—Paul was still buffeted by the gales of acid's breath. This trip was just as powerful as his first, which had taken place in his apartment just a couple of months ago. It was Carl who had convinced him to try the drug, maintaining not only would he have a great adventure but also, as a psychiatrist, it would be good for him to test this mind-altering experience. Paul finally agreed, with the proviso that only he would take the drug. In that way Carl would be in a condition to monitor him.

That first trip had gloriously opened up new vistas, shook him into strange prismatic reflections. Carl had done an excellent job in creating the right mood and setting. Paul had listened to music and watched intricate lights and shadows of semiprecious stones. After seven hours into the trip, the two of them sauntered into Central Park. Never had Paul looked at trees and grass with such clarity and intensity. Never had the spring air smelled so fresh.

On the basis of that first experience, Paul had readily agreed to trip again. This time though all of them would drop considering Paul was now an *old-timer*. What had not been spelled out was the others expected the four of them to unite not only in spirit but in body. Early in the trip, the showers, nudity, and uninhibited staring made Paul realize the others were preparing to become sexually active. He had insisted on pairing off with Virginia.

After his orgasm with her, Paul's trip took a detour. Instead of human contacts, he explored by himself the private visions of his emotional and spiritual paths. It was only now he was able to once again join the others in social intercourse.

They ate with gusto and a hunger conceived by the uniting of LSD with sexual activity. Carl as usual led the others in the quantity consumed. He finished off two omelets; slice after slice of toast, each heaped with butter and jam; and topped it all off with several helpings of rice pudding. After several cups of coffee, they were satiated, their acid-induced appetites filled.

It was still a couple of hours before dawn would make its golden appearance on the tops of the city's skyline. Conversation, which had roamed from theater to photography, from sex to gossip, began to wind down. The psychic waves of acid had become gentle ripples.

Sleep was requesting an audience. Paul, after several yawns, finally stood up to look for his shoes.

"I'm going to grab a cab back to my place."

"What's the hurry," Carl asked, wishing to elastically stretch his limit and extend the celebration. "It's still dark out. The kids are still asleep and you don't have to be home till they get up. Besides, it's Saturday and you can sleep all day."

"True, but I'm bushed," Paul argued, continuing to put on his socks and shoes after having located them behind the beanbag chair.

"But that's easily solved." Carl grinned mischievously, a little boy's smile, as he went over to the bookcase. He pulled out a volume from the bottom shelf and removed a glassine envelope filled with white powder. Then from a jewelry box on the top shelf he removed a shiny mother-of-pearl pillbox from which he palmed several white pills. Turning to Paul, he waved the shiny bag and said, "A couple lines of this coke and you'll have the energy to run the marathon. And with one of these Quaaludes you'll be raring to jump in the sack once again. Your pecker will want to be sheathed in some warm hole and give joy to one of these lovely ladies." He broadly swept his arms to include both Jeanette and Virginia.

"No, Carl." Paul shook his head, getting up to locate his windbreaker. "One drug a night is more than enough. It's been great but I'd rather come down slowly from the acid by going home and integrating all that's happened tonight."

"Don't be a spoilsport, Paul." Carl's voice showed the start of a vibration, a hint of annoyance. "The night is young and the party just about to start. Don't you agree?" The last was uttered to the two women.

"Yes," and "Ohh yes," were their affirmative responses. "Don't go Paul," Jeanette continued plaintively, "we haven't had a go at it yet."

Windbreaker now on, Paul went over to her and gave her a big warm hug. "Rain check?" he asked her softly, a white lie to ensure she continued having a good trip. To Carl he gave his hand, and said, "I know my limits. I'm sure you'll have a great time without me. Thanks for a great celebration. I'm sure it'll be a huge success, just like the last one you directed."

He did not give Carl a chance to object. He turned to Virginia and whispered in her ear, "I'll never forget you. It was wonderful. Ecstatic. Thanks." She answered him by kissing him fully on the mouth and saying, "I also want a rain check."

Carl, during these two good-byes, had time to stoke his temper. He began to raise his voice. "Paul, you always have been stubborn." Then cajolingly, "You won't know what you'll be missing. This is the best there is. Come on, join us."

Paul's answer was in his movement rather than in words. He went to the door, opened it, and just shook his head once again. "Some other time, Carl."

As he stomped toward Paul, Carl's voice shook with fury, "Go, spoil it for us and spoil it for yourself. You'll never get a chance to trip with me ever again. Do you hear? Never again." His face red, his arm shaking with rage, he pointed and yelled, "Go, go!"

"I'm sorry you feel that way." Paul turned and closed the door behind him. Waiting for the elevator, he continued to hear Carl yelling. Paul was glad to get out of there. Yes, he thought, "I'll never trip with you again."

In the taxi, while crossing the park, Paul felt he had lived through this once before. Long ago, he remembered, Carl had to get his way and Paul would not give in. It led to the fiasco of the dress rehearsal with Paul giving up his theatrical career. Now here he was involved with Carl once more. They had just signed a contract for an Off Broadway production with Carl directing and Paul having a leading role. He was worried. Will his leaving now and not wishing to continue to party cause a rift again? Will Carl make it impossible for him to remain in the play again?

It was only after he quietly let himself in to his place on East Eighty-fourth Street and looked in on the peacefully sleeping Anna and Johan that Paul finally put out of mind his tense relationship with Carl, an ache that continually and painfully festered just under the surface.

New York reflected its shimmering beauty that early June morning. It was going to be a glorious day: sunny, a slight breeze off the ocean bathing the city with its cooling touch, and the temperature in the upper 70s. Paul was due at the studio at eight. As was his habit, he made the time to walk the distance instead of taking either bus or subway. He needed the exercise as well as see and smell the grass and flowers of Central Park.

Dressed in his gray suit and the required light blue shirt and red tie, he arrived a couple of minutes early at the ABC studios. It was his first TV show. He was slightly nervous, the same type of anxiety he always felt just before the curtain went up before a live audience.

"Miss Collingswood of *Good Morning America* please," Paul inquired of the receptionist in the tall but narrow, white-marbled lobby. His name being on the list of guests for that morning's show permitted him to be cleared and a security guard sitting in front of the elevator directed him to the third floor.

"Dr. Manes, it's so nice to finally meet you," Miss Collingswood gushed as they shook hands.

"The pleasure is all mine. It seems as if we've had weeks of phone conversations. I never thought we would ever agree on a time and date for the interview."

"All's well that ends well, Dr. Manes," she answered blithely. "Sam here will make you up. You'll just need a dab of powder and a smidgeon of red to bring out the lips. Susan Fried will be doing the actual interview, as we want a woman's point of view." With a quick nod and a checkmark on her yellow pad, she disappeared behind the set's wall.

Sam worked on Paul. In a couple of minutes, with an expert's touch, he had Paul ready. He led Paul to Susan Fried and made a quick introduction.

"Dr. Manes, how nice to meet you. I've read parts of your book and found it most interesting," Susan Fried said while taking Paul by the arm. She led him to the set consisting of two easy chairs and a small coffee table upon which were placed two glasses of water and a vase containing a bunch of silk geraniums. "Please sit down on this chair and make yourself comfortable. We still have five minutes. Is there anything you want me to ask you when we're on the air?" She sat in the other chair and attached a microphone to her blouse.

A crewman, hiding a cord under Paul's jacket and clipping a microphone on to his striped red tie, momentarily distracted Paul. "Well yes, there is Miss Fried," Paul said when he was hooked up. "I'd appreciate it if you would ask me about my upcoming role in the next production at the Circle in the Square."

"Call me Susan, Dr. Manes. I did not know you were in the theater as well as being a psychiatrist and author. How interesting. You know it'll help sell your book. Any specific questions regarding the book?"

"No. Just ask what you want. I'm sure I'll be able to answer the questions," he smiled at his attempt at humor. "By the way, how many minutes will we be on the air?"

"We're scheduled for six minutes. That's a lot of time. You'll be able to make many points." Susan Fried then began questioning Paul about his previous hospital work, the research study that was the basis of the book, and his present private psychiatric practice. She made him feel comfortable and relaxed. When the one-minute warning to air time was announced, he was easily in control of his stage fright and raring to begin.

With a wave of the hand, the director motioned to Susan that she was on air. She looked directly into the camera's red eye.

"Sitting in the studio with me this morning is Dr. Paul Manes. He is a psychiatrist practicing here in Manhattan and the author of the new book *Impotence: An Unnecessary Secret.*" Turning to Paul, she continued, "Good morning, Dr. Manes. I'm so glad you were able to come here and share with us some of the findings you discovered in your recent study on impotence."

"Good morning, Susan, it's a pleasure to be here."

"Before we get to the book itself, I understand that you are not only a psychiatrist who does sex therapy and research, but that you act on the stage as well."

"Yes, I find the two careers help each other. I'm better able to know my patients' emotions by being in the theater and I'm a more proficient actor by having shared and alleviated the pains people bring in to my office."

"You'll be appearing in a Circle in the Square production soon. What play is it and when does it open?"

"I'm proud to say I'll be appearing as Hickey in O'Neill's *The Iceman Cometh*. We open on September 17. It'll be directed by Carl Saroff who did such a successful job the last time."

"Well, I for one will be in the audience." Switching then to the book, she continued, "But I want to hear more about what you discovered in your research on impotence."

"Two main points, Susan. The first is, a large number of men live with this condition for many years without doing anything about it. Only their partners know and both are usually too ashamed or fearful to seek help. The second point in our study showed eighty percent of the men with psychological impotence improved significantly within six months."

"Psychological impotence?" she asked. "What other kind is there?"

"Organic impotence. Impotence caused by physiological conditions, such as problems in blood flow to the penis, nerve damage, etcetera. These conditions have to be treated physically."

"I thought impotence was a deep-seated psychological condition that required many years of therapy." From that remark, Paul realized Susan Fried had at least read the first chapter.

"Before behavior modification, before Masters and Johnson, that indeed would have been the professional opinion. Only classical psychoanalysis was used to solve impotency. The trouble was it took many years and the success rate was not much better than chance. One-third of the men got better, one-third worse, and one-third remained the same.

"We now have more tools to aid a man in overcoming his impotence. It takes much less time. One of the main differences is we bring the wife or girlfriend into the therapeutic process. Sexual activity is made up of two partners and each contributes to either maintaining the symptom or alleviating it. The woman is just as important as the man in relieving the sexual difficulty."

"Would you let the audience know what methods Masters and Johnson used and what your results were?"

Paul took a deep breath before answering. It was difficult to summarize half a book in just a couple of sentences. "They established the notion of eliminating the man's pressure to perform. They went back to sensuality and massage, without the need to achieve an erection or have intercourse.

"For over half the men in our study that alone sufficed. However, in a large percentage of cases, I found that was not enough. Other issues needed to be addressed, such as a bad relationship, boredom, childhood traumas, as well as sexual-orientation concerns."

"What was your easiest case?"

"Let's see. Oh yes. A young man came to the clinic one day all bothered and upset. He felt he was impotent. In taking his history I found out the previous evening he had had quite a bit to drink and when he and his girlfriend decided to have sex, he had remained flaccid. I asked him what happened later on. He said he awoke at one and had no difficulty having sex. Upon further questioning, it turned out in the morning the couple had intercourse two more times. It was not difficult to assure the young man that he definitely was not impotent."

Susan Fried chuckled at the story. Paul in turn smiled at her laughter and the remembrance of the young man's relief.

For the remaining two minutes of airtime they discussed the woman's role in helping her male partner overcome his impotence. Before they broke for a commercial, she asked him, "What do you envision will happen in the future?"

"I think in the not-too-distant future the pharmaceutical industry will come up with some drugs that will indeed aid a man in keeping his erection no matter what the cause of impotence."

She thanked him for sharing this most important information. His time slot ended with her holding up his book for a close up and mentioning that it could be found in all major bookstores.

Leaving the studio, Paul mused on the strange workings of modern-day communication. Just ten minutes ago, more people saw and heard him on TV than would ever watch him on stage, even if he were to play to full houses the rest of his life. He was happy to have been able to publicize a number of the major findings as well as promote his book. He was even able to plug the play.

What a glorious day, he reflected as he crossed the park. He knew the interview had gone extremely well. It was a wonderful way to begin his author's tour of twelve cities, squeezing in fourteen TV programs and five radio shows into just fifteen days.

I hope the kids watched it, he thought, his mind returning to the present. He realized that Johan would understand most of it, as he had explained the basic facts of sex to him just a couple of months ago. He wondered what Anna would get out of the interview. Well, he'll deal with it as it comes. He decided to treat the children to a trip to the zoo. His first patient wasn't due until three.

For Paul, the summer began at its highpoint and went downhill from there. After the Susan Fried interview he went on tour—a very tiring experience. The interviews quickly became repetitious, the same questions, the same quick one-minute answers. Only the two one-hour radio call-in shows in Cleveland and Pittsburgh gave him a chance to expand on the short skeletal replies. He was exhausted when he returned to New York after two weeks of lonely hotel rooms and dinners by himself.

If there was a payoff to being seen on so many TV screens, it didn't exhibit itself in the months following the tour. The telephone was unusually quiet that summer. Only one patient came in as a direct result of the publicity. In July, a minister with problems of impotency called. While on vacation in Boston he had seen Paul on TV and he wanted to fix his long-standing erectile difficulty.

In the theater, rehearsals went from bad in July to worse in August. At first Paul did not understand what was happening. He did not fathom how one day a scene would be on its way to being strong and effective while a week later, the same scene would fall apart. He knew that O'Neill was a complex author who needed a strong director to align the many undercurrents and nuances. Carl was strong; if anything, too powerful. So why did the play seem to be flying off in all directions, without unity of viewpoint or action?

During a rehearsal one evening late in August, Paul noticed that Carl was continually sniffling as if he were in the midst of a cold. The scene and action on stage was particularly disjointed. At one point, Carl began to yell. He jumped up and ran to the stage to show one of the actresses how he wanted her, as one of the prostitutes, to play the scene. He directed her to grab two of the men's crotches. He took her hand and held it to his own groin.

"That's the way to feel him up," he said. "Make him want it; make him get hard." He continued to hold her hand there. He closed his eyes and just stood there. The silence in the hall was as strong as the tension on stage. It was bizarre. It was wrong.

A bright light flashed on in his head. Paul finally understood. Carl was high on coke, higher than all the Swiss Alps put together. No wonder the play was in trouble. He realized that he would have to protect himself if he did not wish to sink with the ship that Carl was steering onto the reefs of disaster. After some thought, he knew what he must do. He would acquiesce to whatever Carl demanded of him during the rehearsals. No matter how Carl wished Hickey to be played, he would say yes and follow instructions. But when it came to the actual performance before a live audience, he would act it as he knew it should be and not as Carl, in his intermittently hopped-up state, dictated.

In addition, his relationship with Johan deteriorated that hot and sweltering summer. Now that the two children were living with him, it was Dr. and Frau Stocker who saw them during the children's vacations. However, Anna talked Paul out of her spending time in Switzerland. She wanted to remain with her Daddy. Johan on the other hand couldn't wait to return to Opa. He let Paul know in both small and large, indelicate ways that he was tolerated more than loved, feared more than respected. Johan's true affection was reserved for his grandparents.

When Paul had returned to Zurich three years before for his 1972 summer holiday and had told Johan he and Sophia were not seeing each other anymore, Johan did not forgive him. He blamed Paul for Sophia's disappearance just as he continued to punish Paul for Evi's death. When this year, because of Frau Stocker's ill health, Johan was allowed to be with his Oma and Opa only three weeks, it was Paul again who was blamed.

If it were not for Johan's deep affection for his younger sister, there would have been a continuous family war between father and son. Paul was aware that Anna, though only nine years old, played the role of mediator and referee. However, when Johan returned from Switzerland after his too-short visit, he just would not listen to anything Paul asked of him. In the end, Paul had to send Johan to camp for the rest of the summer. It would relieve him of having to fight with his son every single day.

Though Johan had a good time at camp, their quiet but intense warfare began as soon as he returned at the end of August. Paul was extremely busy. Between his patient load and the last two weeks of rehearsals, he did not have the time or patience to discipline the children. He left most of the decisions to Ursula, the Swiss au-pair who lived with them. Anna did not present any problems and Johan, who liked Ursula and responded to her generous and loving character, listened to her requests more often than not.

On September 16, Paul awoke to an anxiety manifested by an aching headache and a breakfast testiness with the children he had not experienced in a long time.

"What's wrong, Daddy?" Anna felt his unease.

"I don't know darling," he admitted to her.

"Is it anything I've done?" she asked, taking the blame.

"No, Anna, everything here is fine." He then turned to Johan still determined to make peace with his son. "And I'm proud of your work at school. No, it must be the play. Tonight is the dress rehearsal."

With those words, he vividly recalled the disastrous dress rehearsal of 1963. Now, twelve years later, he was thankfully not having any particular misunderstandings with Carl. Carl had not used the argument they had the night of tripping as an excuse to make life difficult for him. It was true they had not socialized since that evening, but as far as rehearsals went, Carl had been pleasant enough to Paul. It was with the rest of the cast that Carl had been an ogre—a bull that veered in all directions, breaking many of the cast's fragile egos.

Jeffrey Katz, the producer, sat down next to Paul during a lengthy intermission that evening. "What's happening? It's not going well. I don't understand why Carl is stopping the performance so often."

"Don't you know what's wrong?" Paul finally exploded. It was truly awful and no one had done anything to stop it. "You've been at most of the rehearsals. Don't you have eyes? It's your production. You should know."

"No, I don't know. What are you getting at? What's wrong?"

"Why do you think we're having this long break? Isn't it a mite unusual to have it in the midst of a dress rehearsal, in the middle of a scene?"

"Yes it is, but Carl must be doing something important," Katz wanted to believe.

"I know where Carl is and it has nothing to do with the play."

"Where is he?"

Paul was furious that his Off Broadway debut was going down the drain. "He is snorting coke somewhere, that's where."

"My God," the producer hit his forehead with a distressful thud. "Why didn't I see it before? It all makes sense now. That son of a bitch." Jeffrey Katz's tardy knowledge was of course much too late to save the play.

The Iceman Cometh opened to scathing reviews in all the newspapers. *The New York Times* in particular was extremely harsh in its verdict. Paul, who had decided to play Hickey as he should be played, disregarded all of Carl's instructions on opening night. Such a maneuver would in normal circumstances ruin a performance, but that night, considering the scattered wishes of the director, nothing could make it worse. In fact Paul was rewarded with being the only actor that received warm and glowing reviews.

The play closed after three performances.

Paul's strategy bore fruit two weeks later. Jeffrey Katz called him to let him know he was going to produce O'Neill's *Long Day's Journey into Night* on Broadway early next spring.

"Would you be interested? I can't promise anything definite but there is an excellent chance you'll get a starring role."

"I'll be anxiously waiting for an audition call," Paul replied, delighted he'd get a crack at Broadway at last.

The same afternoon, he received another phone call. This one was from Carl. They had not spoken since the play closed.

"Paul, it's good to hear your voice," Carl said after the initial hellos. Paul did not answer. "I've some good news. I just got hold of a great new play and there's a perfect role in it for you. It'll only be a showcase but I've been promised monies will be available for a production. What do you say?"

"Sorry, Carl, no," Paul said after a lengthy pause. Then after another long silence, he continued, first with a quick deep breath, then verbally with, "No. For two reasons, Carl. First, I just made a commitment to Katz for a Broadway production early next spring. But second, and more to the point, I just do not want to work with you again."

Paul hesitated but continued before Carl had time to answer. "As a friend, as a psychiatrist, I must tell you you're doing too many drugs and it's beginning to have a deleterious effect on . . ."

"Now you listen to me," Carl interrupted in a harsh and angry voice, "don't you tell me I'm an addict. You're the one who can't handle drugs, who can't enjoy himself. If you had any respect and gratitude you wouldn't try to . . ."

It was Paul who now interrupted. "Carl I don't want to fight with you and I did not say you have a drug addiction, though now that you mention it, I do believe you do. Let's just leave it. I cannot accept a part in your play."

"Well, let me tell you, you are ungrateful and spiteful. Don't you know Katz will never produce anything on Broadway? He spoiled the last production by being too miserly and not giving me enough time for rehearsals. And now you tell me I'm an addict. Is that what psychiatrists learn, to label their betters?" His voice rose in volume and began to spew forth words of red anger.

"Good-bye," Paul said, not in the mood to listen to volcanic invectives fueled by envy's hidden green depths. He calmly and quietly hung up the phone.

It was the last time he ever spoke to Carl.

This *Shiva* was not like the other two. I had experienced the first when I was 16. The rabbi of our family's synagogue had died and my parents dragged us kids along when they went to pay their respects. The crowded and smoky living room was filled with bearded men with long earlocks and women whose hair was hidden by cheap wigs or dull kerchiefs. An alien scene from another century had been displaced into modern New York.

The second one I went to voluntarily. My aunt, a quiet woman, unexpectedly died in her sleep—not of old age but due to a sudden and fatal stroke. I, her favorite nephew, wished to pay my respects to Uncle Joseph and my twin cousins, who were just a few years older than me. That particular *Shiva* also remained etched vividly in my mind for it had been a social gathering, a joyful meeting of the clan, their many friends, and numerous neighbors. There had been no expressions of sadness or loss. It was true my aunt had been a mere shadow in my uncle's life but I had supposed she was deeply loved. I was astounded to see she was not only buried but also already forgotten and out of mind. The paying of respects was an excuse to enjoy the company and partake of the food.

In this, my third *Shiva*, I was not a guest or just part of the crowd. As the oldest son, I was automatically cast into the role of a main protagonist. I played the obedient child on Monday but changed roles on Tuesday and became the prodigal son. This second day of *Shiva*, after a leisurely breakfast, I appeared at Father's place around 10 a.m. I did not wish to arrive early and have to participate once again in the morning prayers. Monday I followed orders and was there at eight sharp: early enough to say the *Kaddish* with the ten men they had easily talked into coming. It was a big mitzvah to be part of a *minyan* of ten men praying for the dead. But for me, the religious zeal my family was parading had little to do with their inner beliefs—it was more a matter of social exhibition and public expectations.

Monday had not gone well. After the morning service, the *minyan* had left and the immediate family sat down to breakfast, a meal that saw me isolated not only at the foot of the table but also in the hearts of my family. Their emotional chill surrounded me like a dense fog. By the time we were into our second cups of coffee, I had had it.

"Father, what is going on?" I addressed the now ostensible head of the family.

"What do you mean David?"

"I'm sitting here as if I were the one in the coffin. No one is talking to me. I feel that at best I'm being tolerated."

"I don't know what you mean. It's just we're all shook up with losing Rivka." I knew he was sincere in his answer. He was not a person to lie or equivocate. His red-rimmed eyes welled up once again. During the *Kaddish,* he had begun crying and had stopped only when Max sat him down and consoled him with whispers and pats on the back.

"Father may not know what we're feeling, but I do David," my sister interjected.

"Yes?"

"We waited over a half hour for you to show up at the cemetery," continued Libby. "We finally had to bury mother without you. Her oldest was not there to throw in the dirt and bid her a final good-bye. You were not there to say the *Kaddish.* I for one was ashamed of you and sorry for all of us."

"Look, Libby, you know very well why I did not appear at the cemetery. You created the score and arranged the music to that scene so don't come off with this holier-than-thou attitude."

"David, haven't you any respect for the dead, for the family, for tradition?" She began to sob; her crying was the only sound in the room. Through her flowing tears, she continued, "I only tried to do what I thought would be mother's wishes and desires. David, why don't you understand I also have lost my mother, that Rivka is gone?"

"Don't you think I'm aware of that fact? Don't you know I'm also grieving? Have you really lost all touch with me? We used to be close enough to read each other's minds. What's come over your sensitivity? Has the sudden mantle of matriarchy gone to your head and made you thick headed?"

Libby shouted, "Enough of that! There'll be no more of that! Do you understand?"

"Children, children," father interjected softly but with an edge of despair in his voice. "Please stop—for your mother's sake if not for mine."

I was touched by the way he phrased that. Even in death, Rivka ruled the family. "Yes, Dad. You're right. This is not the time or place to argue. I'm sorry."

Libby got up from the table, picked up some cups and saucers and left the room without a word.

We did not have words anymore. In fact Libby and I did not talk to each other the rest of the day. We managed to sit on opposite sides of the room, talk to different callers, and even avoid eye contact. I knew sooner or later that week we would have to straighten this out or it would fester into a lifelong antipathy. But not this day. I was too hurt and felt she had become the mastermind behind the family's offensive against Betty and myself.

An uneasy truce continued through the rest of Monday. However, as soon as I showed up Tuesday morning, Libby wanted to see me privately. She led me into her bedroom and shut the door.

"David, I just don't understand you anymore. Aren't you aware the morning service was at eight? You missed the *Kaddish*. You, her only son. Have you no respect for Rivka?"

"And who may I ask has made you into the keeper of the keys? It really isn't any business of yours what I do or don't do. Libby, what's come over you? It's me that doesn't understand you."

"Since you married Betty, you've changed. I used to call you Randy but now I only think of you as David. You seem so distant since you've left the family—a formal name for my distant brother."

"Well, while we're getting things off our chests, let me tell you why there's been a thick concrete wall separating us these past years. You're right; I have become distant and not only by my moving to the other coast. It's because of your action that night when we told mother that Betty had converted. You lied to her. What made you say that you didn't know Betty would be at the restaurant? You were part of the plan right at the start of her lessons with Rabbi Gershon. I thought you two had become friends. You were disloyal to her as well as selling me out at the critical moment. How could you do that to me, your brother, your twin?"

"Don't raise your voice to me!" she responded to my shouting the last sentence. "It's true I lied once I grasped she knew what was going on. No way would she agree to the marriage and someone had to help her with the business if you were going to be stubborn and not listen to her. I had helped you with Betty's conversion, thinking it could change mother's opinion, but when it didn't work, I realized her wishes were just as important as a strict interpretation of the Jewish law."

"I can't believe what I'm hearing." I just looked at her, dumbstruck at my twin's rationalization, at her self-serving logic. "I just don't understand you Libby. At one time I was so close to you I knew what you were thinking and feeling. Now you're the one who is the stranger. No, Mother's mantle does not fit you."

With narrowed eyes and a breath full of anger, she retorted, "David, you're the one without *rachmonos*. You're the one who showed no pity. She was dying and you couldn't respect a last wish to help her with the business. In many ways, you're the one who shortened . . ."

I gave her one last look of disgust and, with a sorrowful sigh combined with a shake of my head, left without waiting to hear the end of that last sentence. In the living room, I took one look at my family and realized I had no friends among this group of relatives. I turned a folding chair around and sat down facing the window, putting them out of my line of vision, if not my mind.

Should I just pick myself up and fly back to San Diego? Obviously my family won't care what I do. My mother is dead, her last words to me still echoing, "I never want to see you again. Never! Get out!" But . . . but there was another part of me that loved her deeply and felt her loss. I realized the week of *Shiva* would give me time for the black cloth of grief to surface and loosen the tangled emotions of hurt and love.

Having reached the decision to stay the entire week made me feel whole. In some way, I knew mother's spirit approved. It was good to act on inner rightness and let the outside social factors dissipate. Let Libby lead the family into battle. I would temper my soul. I got up and faced my hostile kin.

Two events stood out high above the plains and valleys of that day. The first occurred just after lunch. Rabbi Gershon showed up to pay his respects and in my book of accounts his behavior took a whopping loss. For a man of religion, my former teacher's ethical sense of right and wrong was found wanting. He first greeted my father with a warmth matched by the gravity of the occasion. Turning to Libby he spoke to her for ten minutes before proceeding to pay his respects to the other relatives. I did not force myself on him and stayed quietly in my chair. Only upon leaving did he come over to me. With a curt nod, he mumbled some Hebrew words, coldly shook my hand, and departed. There was no doubt as to where his loyalties resided and whom he refused to acknowledge.

However, the second occurrence at four that afternoon was my very own consolation. He appeared in the form of the family lawyer's son. Barry had come along with his parents to pay their respects to the Gold and Baum families. I had met his father many times when I had worked at Baum Bagels and had heard about his son, the artist, but had never met him before this day.

Barry, after introductions, sat down next to me and began chatting away. He was interested in my art background and my PR and advertising firm. However, it did not take me long to realize he was also interested in a physical encounter. Though not outwardly feminine, it was obvious to me his nonverbal language was that of a gay sensibility. When he led the conversation to bars and asked me which ones I liked, I took the first overt risk and mentioned that I liked Uncle Charlie's, a well-known gay locale on Third Avenue.

With that sure sign on the table, he raised the ante higher. "Would you be interested in a roll in the hay?" was the way he phrased it. I laughed in response.

"Now that's what I call chutzpah. You just met me and here I am sitting *Shiva* for my mother. However, you did read me correctly, and to answer your question, sure. If you look carefully you'll see that my body agrees." He followed my eyes and looked down to my lap and the start of a bulge. I continued, "It'll get my mind off the family and be a respite from the grim reaper."

We agreed to meet in my hotel room at eight o'clock when both of us could get away from our families. I stayed hard after he left and couldn't wait until evening to let go of the pressure that had stayed dormant since Betty had left two days ago. To keep my cock from showing, I headed straight to the bathroom as soon as he left. I masturbated silently and quickly just as I used to as a teenager. Meeting Barry showed me death itself could not stay my need for sex and bodily contact.

I did not stay for dinner but bought two slices of pizza and ate them alone in the hotel room. It gave me time to unwind, which I did by taking a steamy hot shower and watching Carol Burnett. I suddenly realized I had almost forgotten my problem since Betty had flown back to San Diego. I noticed that except for Monday night my hard-on had taken an uncustomary vacation. A three-minute hand job last night, a physical release instead of the usual fantasy-induced climax, took care of my tenseness and enabled me to fall asleep right away. Today I had experienced another day of respite from the tyranny of my driving cock. However, with Barry's proposition, it once again came out in full strength. The hovering black cloud of Mother's death had for the moment lost its palliative and benumbing force.

As I waited for Barry's knock, I didn't fantasize about making it with him but thought of Judy, whom I would see the next evening. She was an exciting unknown quantity, a sexy telephone voice embodied in an imagined lusty figure. I got fully hard before I began to think of Barry. He was an open book; the scenario with him was already foretold. He'd make the first move and his mouth would make a beeline for my cock. However, his good looks and self-assurance would predicate his wanting me to reciprocate. I've had enough sex with men to know how to give a decent blow job. Though I had done it often enough, I did not find sucking cock my favorite sexual pastime. If I had to put my lips somewhere other than another mouth, I much preferred a woman's genitals. A man's odor did little for me, but boy did I get turned on by the sweet flowery smell of an attractive female. My mind began anticipating Judy once again.

Switching back to Barry, I anticipated the possibility that he might want to be fucked. I was ready, cock waiting at attention. Though I did not enjoy or permit my being the passive partner in anal sex, I was always delighted to enter a hot, tight asshole, man or woman.

Though his features were clean cut, I had found Barry to be attractive not only in his looks but also in his animated conversation and lively movements. Lying on the bed, with cock bulging in my jockey shorts and hands behind my head, I was ready and willing to do whatever he wanted. I began to anticipate his naked warm body entangled in mine.

By the time his knock interrupted my sexual reveries, my cock, now firmly held in my right hand, was sticking out of my shorts and its head wet with pre-come. I hastily and clumsily tucked it back in as I went to answer the door. I let him in and made sure to lock it. I turned around to face him.

"Hi," he said, his eyes focused on my outlined hard-on, enveloped but not hidden in my shorts.

"Hi, I'm glad you're here," my hand still fumbling with my fly for some semblance of decorum. Giving up, I continued, "As you see, I've been expecting you."

"Yes, so I notice," he said. "How nice." He made no move for immediate contact. Instead, he looked around the room. "They've done a lovely job redecorating the place. It used to be real garish, but this is most pleasant."

Obviously he was not ready to begin "the roll in the hay," so I asked him, "Do you want to drink anything? The hotel has provided us a mini refrigerator full of different alcoholic beverages."

"That is exactly what I want. How about a glass of wine?"

Joining him in a glass of chardonnay, we began talking about our careers and mutual interest in the visual arts. His friendly but distant manner quickly caused a diminution in my level of desire as well as in the size of my cock. When he had arrived, I had given him a perfect opening, which he did not grab at. Now it was his turn to let me know when we were to start the sexual romp as I did not wish to force myself on him.

What we talked about was not important, though my feelings remained clear. The longer we talked, the more attracted I became and wished we would begin the openly stated purpose of the evening. I was not alone with that desire, for Barry also evinced a sharp interest in the sexual part of our encounter. His hand kept returning to his crotch for continual rearrangement while his eyes kept checking on the state of my equipment.

Something held him back however. I knew it was not shyness, not after the forwardness he had exhibited earlier in the day and not after seeing his obvious attraction and desire. No, something else was going on, and I did not have a clue as to what. I decided to respect his hesitation and held back any move on my part, patiently waiting for him to announce what was causing his present inaction. The conversation sputtered; our interest in talk waned into short pauses, then into longer silences.

After a particularly long and by now embarrassing pause, he finally said with a voice full of feeling, "Randy, you know I'm attracted to you and want to get it on with you in the worst way. All day I've imagined what I want to do to your body. But I can't do it, I just can't."

"I don't understand. Either you do or you don't. Obviously you want to. You've come here and your body also wants to." I pointed to his bulge which once risen had never gone down.

"Yes, I do want to. That's for sure. But I can't." He paused before continuing, "My best friend is in the hospital."

"Oh, why didn't you say so? I'd also be hesitant to cheat on my wife or lover if she or he was sick in the hospital."

Barry shook his head from side to side, evidently quite distressed. "No, you don't understand. Bill is not my lover. He is my best friend and they just told him he has Kaposi's sarcoma."

I sat quietly, waiting for him to go on, to release the pain and pressure of his friend getting cancer.

He looked at me. Obviously Barry was waiting for me to say something, do something. "No you still don't understand," he said. "It means Bill has AIDS, that he'll probably die."

"Well, it's not necessary for us to have sex if you're upset about your best friend being so ill," I volunteered to relieve him of the necessity of doing something just to keep his word or just to please me.

"No, you still don't get what I'm driving at. Yes, I am horribly upset about Bill but that wouldn't stop me from living and enjoying life. But it's hit finally me. The AIDS thing has finally hit home." He stopped and just stared vacantly. "I don't want to catch it."

"I don't know what you're afraid of, but I'm quite healthy," I tried to reassure him.

"Well it's plain to see you know nothing about it." He sat forward in the chair. He then explained to me about the newly discovered virus and the method of catching it through intimate sex or blood transfusions. He told me how it's hitting the gay community and how he had not believed the newspapers until Bill came down with it.

"So what's the problem?" I once again attempted to relieve his fears. "I'm not gay. I'm married."

"But don't you see? It's me that might give it to you. Besides, if you fool around on the side like you're doing with me, how do you know you already haven't caught the bug? No, it's up to each and every one of us not to spread it any further."

"Does that mean that you're never going to have sex again?" I asked incredulously.

"No-o," he said slowly. He then paused, silently thinking about it before continuing in a firm voice, "But I've just come to a decision. Until I find a lover and am able to be completely monogamous, I'm just going to have safe sex."

"Safe sex?"

"Yes, safe sex. As they phrase it: no exchange of body fluids," he explained to me. "In plain English it means, no fucking, no sucking."

"So what's left?"

He finally smiled. "Well, we can't catch anything by watching someone jack off, can we?" putting his hand on his cock. He quickly unzipped his pants, took it out and began to slowly jerk off.

I did not move to join him. I was caught off balance. One minute we were getting ready to have a ball, now new rules regulated what we do. Maybe AIDS had a meaning to him because his friend had come down with it, but it had nothing to do with me. I had Betty. I only fucked women and just played around with guys to get my rocks off. But if it's catching, I thought, maybe I ought to cut down on making it with the easy-to-have gay men.

But just jerking off? I could do that by myself. Who needs to do it with someone else in the room? For me it was just a simple physical release if I couldn't hold and caress someone while fucking. I just kept looking at him, not making a move to follow suit.

Barry must have realized watching him stroke his cock did not turn me on, for he got up and began to undress. As he took off his shorts he said, "Come on, take yours off and let me see you stroke that nice dick of yours."

I followed his orders, feeling I would give him what he wants and jerk off with him. That way, he'll leave and let me be. I began to play with my cock, getting myself hard.

He was excited and kept mumbling encouragement and instructions as to how I should spread my legs, play with my balls, and the like. Looking at him getting more and more turned on finally did have an effect on me and I did get somewhat into it. But not like him. He finally couldn't keep his hands off of me and began fondling my cock. He came furiously and loudly. I followed with my own orgasm a few moments later.

Who needs this? I thought, as I lay in the dark after he left. If sex with men is so dangerous, if all gay men can safely do is jerk off, I'll take a rain check. There are enough beautiful women in the world. On top of that, I have Betty who'll be more available and loving once she finds out I've stopped fooling around with men. My straying into another's woman's bed had never been a problem with her.

Once again I began to wonder what Judy would look like. She sounded like one hot woman. Again I began stroking my cock as I began to see myself fucking her. For the second time that night I came by jerking off.

This was no piss hard-on. I had just dreamed a hot scene and when I opened my eyes I stared at a hefty boner. Though the room was cool and the air-conditioning on, the sheet under my body was drenched, as was most of my body. What had woken me that early Wednesday morning was a beam of sun moving slowly over my face. The dream had faded almost immediately. Two white thighs surrounding a V-shaped patch of ash blond hair, black shiny sheets, and a videotape of some guy jerking off were the only remnants of my exciting sexual dream.

It did not take me long to get my rocks off. I used the reality of a masturbatory climax as an overlay for the images of my erotically powerful dream. A long shower, a lazy breakfast, and minutes spent looking down at the hypnotic wave of traffic along Lexington Avenue left me calm enough to face my jousting family. However, the tar-baked sidewalks of August's sun and the nonexistent shock absorbers of my taxi left me hankering to charge at any family member who so much as looked at me sideways. And Libby did.

"Why didn't you return our call? We needed some things at the supermarket. We've been eaten out of everything and needed to stock up for today's crowd of visitors. Where were you?"

Though I had heard the phone ring last night, I had not picked it up because Barry and I were in the midst of negotiating our safe-sex session. This morning, I needed time for myself and did not reply to the flashing red light on the telephone. I then forgot about it until I stopped at the front desk on the way out of the hotel where I picked up last night's telephone message from Libby. I knew I'd find out soon enough what she wanted and sure enough here she was giving me no chance to get in the door before going on a tear.

"Look Libby, I don't answer to you. I was busy last night and just found out not fifteen minutes ago you had called me."

"Were you by any chance with that sissy-boy, Barry?" His father was looking for him high and low.

"After your reactions to me this week, let me tell you who I'm with and what I do is none of your damn business. Can't you understand that?" and I stomped angrily into the living room.

"What's wrong?" my father asked softly when he saw the mood I was in.

"It's your daughter who, I'm sorry to say, is also my twin sister. She knows how to push my buttons," I answered, more upset at her drawing near my bisexual secret than at what she actually said or meant.

"She loves you and respects you," Dad tried to keep the peace.

"Yes Father, I know." I lied, not wanting to upset him.

For the next couple of hours, Libby did try to make me feel at home. I couldn't understand it, for it did not fit into her past week's behavior pattern. After lunch I found out why. She had not only assumed the role of head of the family, but the previous evening had convinced Father to make a new will for himself. Everything was to be shared equally between the two of us, his two children. However, all the shares of the business as well as all the real estate he had just inherited from Mother would be put into a trust, with Libby getting the right to vote my shares.

"In other words, you'll do what you want with my share of father's estate. I might as well kiss it good-bye," I said slowly and dejectedly. "My, what a week this is turning out to be."

"David, you don't understand. It's necessary to do it this way so the business will continue to grow and prosper. When father dies after a hundred and twenty years, we can't have us fight and ruin what Rivka built up and what I'll try to keep on a steady course."

"Yeah, I know," defeated before the fight had begun. My eyes welled up, and ran into the bathroom to let go of the tears in private. I felt stepped on and battered not only by death's left-handed jabs but also by the family's right-handed uppercuts.

Father must have overheard or noticed, for he came over to me a half hour later and began gently, "David, this is a difficult time for you, in some ways even more difficult than for the rest of us. We at least continued to receive Rivka's love until the end. Did Libby tell you I want to make a new will now that all the wealth of the family is in my name? You know, she left everything to me."

"Dad, you have every right to do with your money and shares as you wish. It's not for me to interfere," I said with honest conviction.

"No, Dovid'l, you're not interfering. I'm asking what you think. I want everything to be fifty-fifty between the two of you. But I do think it is right for Libby to vote your shares in the business since she is now the one who is responsible to see it continues to grow and prosper."

"Yes, Dad, I do understand that." I paused. Then "But . . ."

"But what?"

"But why is it necessary for her to vote my shares in this co-op? It has nothing to do with the business."

"Yes, Dovid'l, it doesn't, but Libby is the one who lives here with me. Where will she go if you would want to or need to sell the place?"

"That's exactly the point. For all practical purposes, I don't inherit a penny until Libby decides to sell the business or the apartment."

"I've also thought of that; do you have any ideas how to make it come out even?"

I was quiet for a while. At least father was aware that, with Libby voting my half, I had nothing to look forward to. "Have you thought of taking out a life insurance policy in my name? I know it's very expensive but you can take the premiums off my share of the business and real estate."

"That's a fine idea, Dovid'l. Yes, why didn't I think of that? The co-op is worth close to half a million and you know there's no mortgage on it. I'll take out a five hundred thousand dollar policy in your name. In that way, when the time comes for me to join your mother, you'll at least get that amount of money right away.

"And while we're talking openly, I want to tell you I'm proud of you. You've always been a good son. I know it was difficult working with your mother but I know you tried for a long time. Also, I want you to know from my point of view, you did well by having your wife convert to Judaism and using an orthodox rabbi to sanction it. In the future, when you come to New York, bring her along. I want to see her."

I started to cry. I did not expect father to show this type of strength. He had now put himself on my side of the fence, disagreeing with both his strong-willed wife and his equally assertive daughter. He took me in his arms and also began to sob.

My clean feeling and the family's good mood lasted for less than an hour. Father told Libby what new wrinkle had been added to the financial arrangements. She became furious and I knew why. She would never be able to control me in any way whatsoever. It was not equality she wanted but control; not love, just power.

For the rest of the afternoon, she did not speak a single word to me. Max and Chava, who saw the all-too-clear battle lines, took her side as they had done all week. Father, by his action and his one great effort to right some wrongs, did not have any more strength to oppose Libby's unspoken command to have me silently pummeled, if not excommunicated.

My resolve to stick out the prescribed week of *Shiva* evaporated with these new and tortuous conditions. I decided to call it quits and fly out early the next morning, back to Betty and a return to some sanity.

My only leave-taking was a whisper in father's ear, "I'm going back to San Diego tomorrow. I have business I must take care of."

He was not fooled. "I understand," he answered softly, gazing at me with that sad expression he had developed these funereal days. "Have a good flight and let me hear from you. Please call and keep in touch. Let's hope we see each other at happier occasions." He hugged me tightly and kissed me on the lips. I hurried out.

My horniness had returned. I couldn't wait till my date with Judy later that evening and once again jerked off in the hotel room. The orgasm helped me push the anxiety and my hostile family into the background and my making reservations for a flight the next day relit my desire to see Betty. My cock stayed semihard all evening anticipating the sexual rendezvous with Judy. A lazy shower, a light dinner at the coffee shop, and a leisurely walk up Third Avenue brought me to the front of 320 East Seventy-second Street just a couple of minutes after eight o'clock.

"Miss Saroff. I'm Randy Gold," I announced to the uniformed doorman.

"Go right up, Mr. Gold. She's expecting you. Take the elevator on the right for apartment 7B," he smiled. Or was it a leer? I guessed I was not the first nor would I be the last man expected for an evening or night. Riding up the elevator, my sexually oriented imagination had me lusting. The cock followed suit and did its expanding number. I was fully hard by the time she opened the door.

"Come on in," she swept me in, the full kimono sleeve following gracefully her arm's wide arc. I followed her down the two steps into the living room. Her blonde hair, spread across the shoulders of the blue gown, almost grazed the silky white Japanese sash. I was immediately attracted to this lovely and lilting woman.

"What's your poison? Mine's martini," she said as she scooted behind the highly polished mahogany bar.

"Do you have any white wine?" I didn't want hard liquor to dull my throbbing senses.

"Sure, whatever you want. Make yourself comfortable while I fix them up," directing me over to the white leather sofa with another sleeve-waving motion of her arm. My drink was poured from a gallon jug, hers from a previously prepared concoction. I sat down, carefully pushing my hard-on down and under, trying with little success to minimize its bulge. I was sorry I had not put on a jock strap. Dummy!

She put my wine down on the shiny teak coffee table and then melted into the black leather easy chair just to my left.

Holding tightly onto her olived martini, she said, "Well, that's done. I'm glad we're finally meeting. Sandy really liked you. I go by her opinion, as she's hardly wrong in judging people. We've known each other for many years. In fact we went to high school together. On top of being friends, we're like family. I'm sorry she's away so much of the time though I'm glad for her. She's having a ball flying all over the country. She has so many adventures."

She did not give me a chance to utter a single word and, except for the occasional pause to swallow her drink, she kept on and on. What's she so nervous about? I'm certainly not the first man her friend had fixed her up with. Sandy told me they swapped men all the time. So what gives? I decided to let her continue until she either ran out of topics or her anxiety leveled off.

She kept running on. I slowly sipped the cheap wine, squeezing in an occasional "yeah" or "really?" Her anxiety spilled into me and I needed another drink. This time something stronger. In the middle of a story about her traveling days with the band, I got up for that drink. My movement stopped her. She must have realized I was not listening.

"Where are you . . . Oh, I'm sorry. I didn't notice you needed another drink." She hurriedly followed me to the bar to give me the drink she had not previously offered. I got to the scotch bottle just before she did. In her newly found zeal to play the proper hostess, she tried to take it from me.

It slipped out of my hands while she never got hold of it. Both of us tried to catch it. We bumped heads and upset a half a dozen glasses. Finally giving up, we both stood still, letting the glasses clang on the bar. We bumped our foreheads again when we tried to pick up the bottle and the glasses that had thumped onto the thick white carpet.

The second bump finally broke the tension. She put her hands on her hips, looked straight at me for the first time, and began to laugh.

"Now that's what I needed," she gasped into her guffaw. "What a bore I've been. Do forgive me, Randy, but I've been nervous all day. Here, sit down, let me clean this up and get you a scotch. How do you like it?"

"If you're talking about scotch, on the rocks. If about other things, any way I can . . . and as often as I can."

"Well, I'm sure we can satisfy your thirst as well as your other appetites," following my innuendo. Bringing over my drink, she sat down next to me on the couch.

I picked up on the change in her mood. Her hiding behind nervous chatter had now changed into trying to please an obviously aroused man. I therefore initiated the next step with, "I sure hope so," eyeing my rounded and full crotch. Rather than try to hide it, I now slid down the sofa to better exhibit my ever-patient, erect-and-waiting cock. She took it in with a long look.

"I'll do whatever you want, but don't hurt me," she said slowly, staring down at my straining sex.

"Well, for starters, why don't we take our drinks in to the bedroom and make ourselves more comfortable?"

"Yes, Randy, why don't we?" echoing me as she stood up and led me into the softly lit room.

She was out of her kimono and onto the black sheets before I had time to unbutton my shirt. By the time I was fully undressed, she was lying on her back, arms over her head, and whispering, "Yes, I'll do whatever you want. Anything you want, anything."

"Anything?" I stood by the bed, cock pulsing close to her face.

"Yes, anything, no matter how debasing. But don't hurt me. You're so large. Don't hurt me big daddy."

"Suck it good and wet it so I can fuck you long and hard," I uttered huskily, excited by her attitude.

"Oh yes, big daddy, I'll lick it and suck it. Just don't hurt me." She leaned over and began to give me a wonderful blow job. She obviously knew what to do, for she managed to deep throat me without any difficulty.

"Oh yes, baby. That's a good girl. Make me feel real good and I'll give you what you want."

She took her mouth off my cock. "Don't hurt me big daddy," she said, scratching my ass cheeks with her long nails.

I reacted to the sudden pain. My cock got harder, and I jumped on her. Spreading her legs, I entered her quickly with a deep thrust.

"Oh daddy, you're so big. Don't hurt me," she kept moaning while moving her body in rhythm to my furious and deep plunges. I came quickly. Keeping my still-hard cock in her, I moaned, gasped, and slowly came back to the world of people and language.

"Did I please you big daddy? Did I make you feel good?"

I laughed with pleasure. "Yes you did but not as much as I'm going to please you, my little kitten," and I began to slowly thrust once again. This time, though, I kept my eyes open and followed her motions and twists. Having come once, I was now ready to please her and get her off.

"Oh, don't hurt me," she murmured again and again. This time her nails bit deeply into my back. I reacted by twisting her hands up over her head, and away from my body.

"Now you're going to get it baby, you're really going to get it." I began to thrust long and deep while holding her hands tightly. I kept on and on. Her cries grew louder, "Don't hurt me big daddy." Suddenly she changed to, "No, I don't want to. I can't, I can't."

"Oh yes you can. You'll do what I tell you to do. You're going to come; you're going to go over the top. You want to please me; you know you do. Please your big daddy by being a good girl and doing what he wants. Come, come."

Her movements began to take on a life of their own, her hips moved up and down, up and down.

"Oh daddy, I'm going to come, daddy I'm coming. Ahh!" she screamed.

After she stopped shaking, her moans turned to whimpers. Her whimpers then became deep and mournful sobs. I sat up and held her close to me.

"What's the matter, Judy? Wasn't it good for you, didn't you enjoy it?"

She just continued to sob and cry.

"From my point of view, it looked liked a humdinger of an orgasm. What's wrong?"

It took many minutes before she was able to finally say, "You don't understand. It was great. It was my first orgasm in three years."

"Three years?" I was surprised, stunned. "Three years?"

"Yes, its the first time I've been able to climax since my father died."

"Tell me about it." I stroked her hair gently and held her tightly.

I was the first and only person she ever told.

No cloud adulterated the clear blue sky. The sun shone bright yellow and the day itself was luminously white. The bright and pure colors of that morning blended into a palette of smooth pearliness. What a wonderful day to get married, Paul thought as he stepped out of the elongated and highly polished white limousine.

The chauffeur helped his mother out of the limo, his father disdained any aid, and the two children scampered out by themselves. Johan and Anna ran up the church steps, free at last to move their bodies, having had to sit quietly this past half hour as the car smoothly wended its way from Paul's apartment in the Upper East Side of Manhattan to St. Anthony's Church in Great Neck, Long Island.

Though he had been brought up Episcopalian, Paul had always been impressed by the power of the Catholic hierarchy as well as awed by the Church's imposing architecture. Paul had lost his belief in formal religion many years ago and had only agreed to a church wedding to please Mary. She had wanted to be married in her family's church and to be united in holy matrimony by Father O'Flannigan, a close friend of her family, the Haggertys. St. Anthony reminded Paul of Rome's San Paolo Cathedral, in style and feeling if not in size. The same massive columns in front, the delicately etched stained glass, and the unending height of its dome all contributed to the seriousness of the day and the solemnity of the occasion.

The purity of that June day was carried into the church by the large white gladioli bouquets on either side of the altar; the two candelabra, each holding a dozen white burning candles; and the white hanging banners depicting the risen Christ.

When Paul and Father O'Flannigan entered the church from the side vestibule, the two families were already seated. The Manes family's side of the church contained less than a dozen occupied seats. Though the Haggerty half had narrowed down the list to their closest relatives and friends, they could count over a hundred people on their side.

Inwardly at peace, outwardly calm, Paul waited patiently for Mary to appear. First came the two bridesmaids: Mary's younger sister, Grace; and Paul's sister, Sally. Both were dressed in similar pink gowns. Then followed the two out-of-step but brightly laughing ring bearers, Mary's three- and four-year-old niece and nephew. When the organ finally and grandly echoed the Bridal Chorus, Mary appeared on the arm of her father. Her beauty and innocence changed Paul's tranquil mien to feelings of love and joy, expressed in the welling up of tears, which needed to be wiped away when they trickled down his cheeks.

Mary had told Paul that Father O'Flannigan had agreed to officiate because of his long and warm relationship with her family. He had not been pleased that she was marrying outside the faith, just as he had been upset when Mary had left the convent four years earlier. However, he took into consideration the facts that Mr. and Mrs. Haggerty were devout churchgoers, their seven children were good Catholic pupils, and that Paul had acquiesced in putting on paper his agreement to raise any children they might have as Catholic.

Though the reception was held next door in the parish hall—the floral decorations sparse and the food merely adequate—the festivity and good cheer was more evident here than had been displayed at the previous night's lavish dinner at The Four Seasons. Paul's father had gone all out to impress one and all with the munificence of the rehearsal dinner. Though delicious and exorbitantly expensive, the Haggerty's nuclear family was much too uncomfortable to enjoy it, let alone talk and mingle with the upper and preeminent class of the Manes family.

However, here in the parish hall, with the groom's relatives in the minority, the Haggerty's and their friends celebrated Mary's nuptials with a freedom that was aided by alcoholic boisterousness.

Mr. Haggerty, sporting a broad grin and a glass of champagne in hand, walked over to Johan who was sitting between his grandfather and sister at the solitary Manes table and asked him, "Well young man, are you having a good time?"

"Yes I am, thank you, and I'm glad that my father married Miss Haggerty," he answered politely.

"Johan, now that she is your new mother, you may either call her Mary or, if you would rather, Mother," Steven Manes instructed his grandson in the difficult task of relating to his new stepmother. He stood up to chat with Mary's father.

"I'm going to call her Mary," Anna whispered to Johan. "She's not our real mother."

"I like her, so I'm probably going to call her Mother," he whispered back.

"I'll only call her Mother if Daddy wants me to," she wavered.

"I'm proud of the way you spoke to Mr. Haggerty," Mr. Manes complimented his grandson as he sat down again, emphasizing his pleasure with a slight playful tap on the boy's shoulder. "He's more friendly today, and much more loquacious now that he's belted down a few."

"What's loquacious?"

"That's right, Johan. If you don't understand a word, ask. That's the only way you'll learn new things. Your father used to ask me many questions when he was a young man like you," he said wistfully, stressing the words, "used to." "Loquacious means talkative or effusive," he finally answered the thirteen-year-old's question.

"Grandpa, when we move to San Diego, will you take me to the soccer games like Opa used to in Zurich?"

"If you want to go, I'll definitely find time to go with you. I'm sure we can have a great time. You know, the San Diego Sockers is the best team in the United States, so you'll see some real good games."

"Will you also take me to a baseball game? Daddy is too busy rehearsing or seeing patients," letting his grandfather know of his dissatisfaction.

"Of course, Johan. I'll make sure I'll have time for you." He patted his only grandson on the back. "Now that you'll be living on the West Coast you'll get the benefit of all the years of my experience. Have you ever been in a courtroom and seen a trial?"

"No, Grandpa."

"Me, neither," piped in Anna.

"Well, Sally, I guess we'll have our hands full showing off these two lovely children to the judges and our fellow attorneys," bringing his daughter into the sphere of their future activities.

"I guess we can let Paul and Mary bring the children and let them all witness your Perry Mason style," Sally expanded his initial suggestion.

"If I know my son, he'll want nothing to do with a courtroom or his father's activities," his voice showing more anger than sadness. "However, your idea to let Mary bring them is a good one."

"Whom am I supposed to bring where?" asked Mary, who had just come up with Paul to make a table-hopping circuit and had only heard the last part of her father-in-law's sentence.

"Daddy, Grandpa is going to take us in to a courtroom with a real judge." Anna jumped up and tugged at Paul's arm, asking, "Will you take us? Please. I want to go with you."

"Of course, my darling. Mary and I will love to take both of you. We'll arrange it as soon as we get settled."

"Grandpa is taking me to see the Sockers," said Johan, a hostile current in his voice and a show of bravado in the shake of his head.

"That's nice of you. I know how busy you are," Paul first addressed his father. Then to Johan, "You see, you aren't losing Opa, you're getting a second grandfather."

"Speaking of Opa, how is Mrs. Stocker?" Sally asked her brother.

"The last letter was not encouraging. Her last stroke left her partially paralyzed. But she is making some progress."

"When are you going on your honeymoon, Daddy?" Anna asked, still holding on to her father.

"In a little while, *Schaetzli,* but we'll be back in less than two weeks," he said as he hugged her tightly. "I'm going to miss you a lot."

"I'll take care of her, Father. You don't have to worry. We'll be alright," Johan said with a happiness that was probably fueled by his father's imminent absence.

"Are you sure you can leave the children alone?" Mr. Manes asked of his son.

"Don't worry, Father. Ursula has taken care of them for years. I've managed all these years very well, thank you." His tone expressed annoyance at his father's interference. "Isn't it a bit late in the day for a show of concern?"

Mrs. Manes, who was sitting next to Sally, had kept quiet throughout the conversation. Now she spoke up, "Paul, your father is genuinely interested in his grandchildren, especially now that you're moving out to San Diego."

Mary put her arm through his and unobtrusively squeezed his forearm.

"I'm sorry father," he gingerly backed off, paying heed to her signal. However, he continued with, "I know you mean well and I know the children will be delighted to visit a courtroom to see how justice is served." He uttered the last phrase in a low tone and somewhat ambiguously.

"Come, Paul, we must visit the other tables if we ever want to catch our plane," Mary nudged her brand-new husband.

"Yes we must," he agreed.

Paul shook hands with his father, embraced his mother and sister, and then shook hands with Johan, giving him last-minute instructions and encouragement to keep a sharp eye on Anna. Last, as Mary was saying her good-byes to her in-laws, he bent down and gave Anna a warm kiss and a teddy-bear hug.

They moved on to the bride's family and friends. A half hour later, the bridal bouquet was thrown backward to the eligible single women and Paul threw Mary's garter to the group of single men. The same white limousine that had transported them to the church now whisked the newlyweds to Kennedy Airport for a two-week Bermuda honeymoon.

The consummation of their marriage first took place on the third night of their honeymoon. They had caught their plane in plenty of time. Mary had changed into a bright yellow outfit, complete with a wide-brimmed straw hat she planned to use as a fashionable sun-screen. Paul had rarely flown first class and made use of the occasion to sit stretched out comfortably next to Mary in the ample leg space of seats 2A and 2B. The stewardess, who immediately recognized the pair as newlyweds, made sure to keep their champagne glasses full.

By the time they settled into the bridal suite the first evening, they had eaten another small meal in the dining room and had more cham-pagne—this time compliments of the hotel. They both became tipsy. Mary was only used to a rare glass of white wine with dinner while Paul, who did drink in moderate amounts, definitely was not accus-tomed to the two full bottles of champagne that he had managed to consume over the past twelve hours.

Mary, who had been quite nervous and who had lain awake the previous night with a fear borne of the unknown, now lay next to Paul giggling at the way Paul was having trouble getting out of his pants. When he finally tripped and fell on top of her, they both convulsed into a bubbling and hiccuping laughter. He gave her a big sloppy kiss, turned on his back, and, with socks and shirt still on, fell into a deep and sonorous sleep. Mary looked at him fondly, glanced shyly at the slight opening of his undershorts, and finally covered him with the blanket before she herself joined him in a benumbed and satisfying slumber.

Though Paul woke up early the next morning with a hefty erection, he knew Mary, who was still asleep, would not want them to make love for the first time in the brightness of the morning sun. Early on she had confided her fear of having sex and had asked him to be gentle with her both physically and psychologically. With an inner certitude, he real-ized the first time would have to be under the covers with the lights out. He looked forward to having sex with her this coming night. He would leave the window and curtains open, permitting the calm sound of the waves as well as the dim rays of the moon to filter in.

The newlyweds spent a leisurely and delightful day. However, there was an unspoken tension between them, the pressure of their unfulfilled intimacy. The second night it was not the alcohol that stopped them from joining as man and wife; it was her fear and his diffidence.

When Paul had met her, Mary's inexperience in the sexual arena was absolute. She had never gone beyond kissing her two previous boyfriends and knew none of the pleasures of simple sensual touching, let alone the delights of erotic sensations. The nuns had been extremely successful in damping her sexual curiosity, let alone her urges. The ten years out of the convent and the six years of analysis had not as yet altered Mary's lifelong obeisance to her religion's sexual proscriptions. Hell in the hereafter still had more reality than the painful aridity of her life's repression.

Ever aware of others' weaknesses, Paul had been most reluctant to push the issue. He had originally met her during a PTA visit. As Johan's teacher, she had been concerned about his classroom behavior. Their initial interactions dealt only with Johan and his problems. At first their meetings took place in the school office. Having coffee in the school cafeteria followed naturally. When they started to see each other regularly, they usually met, at his suggestion, in dimly lit restaurants.

During this courtship, Paul became enamored of her innocence, her love of the children, and her gentleness of manner. She was touched by his interest in her, cheerfully enjoyed his desire to hang on to her every sentence, and breathed in deeply the maturity of his life's experiences.

He made attempts to expand their intimacy to include sexuality. However, she resisted each step forward. One night, she reluctantly allowed him to sleep over at her apartment. From the sofa in the living room that first time, he slowly managed to break her steel-like resolve layer by layer, until at last they slept comfortably naked next to each other in her double bed. However, there was one line she would not cross: she would not permit intercourse unless it was done in the sanctity of a marriage bed.

During their courtship, she was extremely passive. Her developing love for him permitted her to break taboos and cross into the world of sexual sin but not to the extent of conscious pleasure. His erections were not fondled; his orgasmic needs were not fulfilled in her presence. She permitted him to touch only her breasts; her genitals were off limits. His mouth could kiss only her as far as the back of her neck. With silent but intuitive movements, she held in check his desire to suckle her firm and inviting bosom.

His attraction grew. His frustration mounted. They saw each other practically every night. He now slept over at least three times a week and they became friends, if not lovers. For the first time in his life Paul was unable to have the woman he loved satisfy his physical needs. Masturbation was never so lonely, so meaningless.

While ironically cognizant of his sexual frustrations, he was also aware of his emotional captivation and love. And so, one night at the end of a romantic dinner, he proposed to her. Mary accepted gladly, her assent given with a love felt deeply and with a pledge to him of unending commitment.

On this second night of their honeymoon, she was ready to fulfill her wifely duties and determined to put into effect her marital obligations. However, decades of erotic denial could not easily be dismissed, even if there now existed a sacred marriage vow performed by Father O'Flannigan. Though she now permitted Paul to place his mouth on her breasts and though she, with inbred reluctance, let his hands wander over her thighs and explore her private parts, she made no move to make his advances more enjoyable for either of them.

At first Paul welcomed the unspoken resistance, the silent inhibitions. It lowered his fear of performance and the need to worry about his erection. He concentrated on her reactions and her need for touching assurances. It required all his skills as well as timeless patience. At first she clenched so tightly that for the longest of times he could not even put his finger into her vagina. After a couple of hours of murmurs and gentle fondling he managed to relax her vaginal spasms. But by the time she might have been ready for entry, his penis would not become erect. While concentrating on the task at hand, he had completely lost his own sexual desire.

So he stopped vaginal play and halted bodily stroking. Instead, Paul began to kiss his virginal bride with love and affection. Instead of sexual advances he began a sensual stroking, to which she finally began to respond in kind. For the first time that night, she felt safe enough to show physical affection. They fell asleep in each other's arms; he tired and unsuccessful, she relaxed and full of love.

Sunning himself beside the pool early the next morning, Paul lay with his eyes closed, his mind running on fast-forward and his emotions in circles. On one level he knew they were getting closer and their intimacy more intense. His half erection, however, would not let him forget his inability to consummate his second marriage. Doubt and insecurity entered his psyche, closeness and joy drifted away. He was glad that Mary was still asleep. He did not wish to communicate these thoughts and feelings.

Luckily he fell asleep. When Mary woke him with a playful peck on the cheek, he was thankful that his mood had changed. He was able to respond to her happiness and they took a long walk and chatted about everything and nothing. She was carefree. He still carried the sexual agenda for both of them. After dinner, they watched a Carmen Miranda movie on TV before retiring for the night.

This time, Paul decided to begin with sensuality and let the sex take care of itself. It worked to the extent that Mary continued to respond with her own caresses. Though these lacked sexual intensity, they communicated to him her gentle and intense affection. Not having to worry about the sexual aspect of the love play, Paul became erect. Though she felt his erection on her thigh, Mary gave no indication she was aware of it. Paul, however, felt it was time to move the action into the genital arena. He began to stroke her inner thighs and gently touch her vulva. Once again, she became still. Once more she withdrew and tightened up.

At first the previous night's activity repeated itself. By the time Paul managed to calm his wife and have her relaxed enough for entry, he again had become flaccid. He knew all he needed was her touch to kindle his penis into action. However, Mary's fears and inexperience ruled that out. The result was this third night of marriage again ended up in sleep rather than in sexual fulfillment.

The difference, however, was one hour later Paul woke up with his penis turgid and ready. Mary, asleep, did not put up any resistance. She permitted his genital explorations, first the slight strokes of his fingers then the gentle probing of his penis. When he finally penetrated, she was only partially awake, not fully aware. She allowed his entry and accepted his member. She was physically ready with a lubricated and relaxed vagina. With each stroke, she awoke more fully. By the time he achieved his orgasm she had once again put up her inhibitory guard and tightened up. Though partially flaccid after his climax, Paul had some difficulty in withdrawing his penis from her clasping inhibitions.

A honeymoon is the ideal time to work out these sexual and intimate concerns. However, in the case of these newlyweds, their Bermuda trip was cut short the very next day.

Paul received a phone call from Dr. Stocker telling them his wife had died the previous night. Paul immediately made plans to fly to Zurich. He remembered vividly how his in-laws had consoled him when Evi had died and now wanted to repay Dr. Stocker for his years of support and concern. That evening they flew back to New York where Mary disembarked. He continued on to Switzerland to attend the funeral of his former mother-in-law.

The aborted honeymoon, the unfulfilled closeness that had begun but was not completed, left an indelible mark on their marriage. Mary was not able to achieve an orgasm, while Paul's bouts with impotency became more and more frequent. Though their emotional bond remained secure, their sexual life never did reach a level of satisfaction.

⟨───⟩

Temperature can be measured as easily as reading the gradations of a thermometer. Lunch at the quiet restaurant was consumed in a room that read a normal 70 degrees. Considering that Paul would have to walk four blocks to Dr. Erickson's house through the summer's sweltering 103° heat, it was not surprising that he dawdled over dessert. Besides, Paul was not fully alert and time moved in an unusual rhythm, the minutes ticking not to the steady beat of a clock but rather to a nonsynchronous wave of his altered psyche. He did not remember clearly what had happened that morning, but Paul did know when he finally got up from the table he was late.

"Come in Paul, come in," Dr. Erickson waved him to the empty seat. "I was just telling the others about my youngest daughter splashing about in the backyard pool when she was only three years old. She could not swim but the heat drove her into the cool water. Nature did the rest and by the end of the summer she had mastered the art of floating, dog paddling, and even an awkward imitation of the butterfly stroke."

Coming in late made Paul feel awkward. Why did he linger so long in the dining room? Paul did not understand his behavior. It was unusual for him to be late, especially as he was learning so much. Neither was he prone to forego the advantage of being in Milton Erickson's presence every possible moment. The man was inexorably going downhill. He was weaker and obviously in much more pain this summer.

Returning to Dr. Erickson's voice, he picked up the thread, ". . . carefully for hours on end. At first she always stayed near the steps, making sure that the water was never higher than her waist. With confidence and time she ventured to the depth of her shoulders. One day she enjoyed her daydreaming so much she was not aware she had floated into deeper water. When she opened her eyes and saw she was in a depth way over her head, she wisely closed her eyes again and with small movements, making certain that she remained buoyed on her back, navigated back to the shallow end of the pool.

"She had found out for herself how delightful it is to be able to close your eyes and drift into the deep part of your mind. That's right. Though floating on the surface of the water, it's possible to go down to the depth; and just as the water is cool and the air is warm, the ability to remain cool when it is hot around you is as easy as learning how to swim—how to maneuver in a manner that speaks to you and you . . ."

When Paul opened his eyes, he noticed he was now sitting next to Dr. Erickson and the other six therapists were all watching him. He had no idea of how long he had been under, how long he had been in a trance. Neither did Paul have any memory of what had transpired. At dinner that evening with one of the other therapists, he learned he had been out for over two hours. Milton Erickson had put Paul into a deep trance within two minutes of his entering the room. As to what had occurred during his trance, Paul felt more comfortable not knowing. He did not ask his colleague what had taken place.

Paul never did find out. The two weeks he spent in Santa Fe learning the art of trance induction were lost in the haze of being in an altered state. Most of what he learned remained in his unconscious and never was called back to conscious memory.

This was the second two-week summer seminar in Santa Fe away from his family and San Diego. He spent the mornings and afternoons in the cool study of Dr. Erickson's adobe house. Once again he stayed at La Fonda, the old but grand hotel in the center of the city. It was just fifteen minutes to the master hypnotist's home, to which Paul walked every morning and evening. Paul was in awe of the city's beauty and took advantage of these walks to let his eyes drink in the multicolored browns and greens of the surrounding hills which rose even higher than the seven thousand feet of the city itself. The air was clear and thin at this height and the daily cloud formations brought forth a continuous wonder of form and movement.

These walks were also a time of reflection, especially the late afternoon ones, when Paul was still half immersed in the deep and inward-focused trances of the day. He felt fortunate in being able to get to know Dr. Erickson, to study hypnosis with the leading expert in the world, and to improve his skills as a psychiatrist while delving into and examining his own personal problems. Paul felt confident as well as satisfied in the professional areas of his life. Both of his careers were going well.

The move back to San Diego had taken place three years ago. He could not and did not refuse a chance to join The Old Globe Theatre company. Jack O'Brien's unexpected invitation for him to become an associate member of the cast was a direct result of his performance as Hickey in *The Iceman Cometh*. The San Diego director had been in the audience on opening night and witnessed Carl's disastrous handling of the O'Neill play, but had been excited by Paul's acting skills. The timing was perfect. Both Paul and Mary agreed to relocate. They moved in August, and by September 15, he was already rehearsing six days a week for the November opening of George Bernard Shaw's *Too True to Be Good*.

Paul's acting skill blossomed with steady work and under the high standards of the talented directors of The Old Globe. He was in two plays that winter season and two more on the Festival stage the next summer, where he excelled in both Shakespeare plays, *Henry V* and *The Winter's Tale*. He became one of San Diego's leading actors, recognized not only by his peers but also by the public. He was known and acclaimed as the talented "psychiatrist actor."

The first patients after his move to San Diego did not come through the normal channels of the medical profession. His referrals at the start were theater people: other actors and actresses, producers and directors, and even a couple of opera singers, all of whom he met at formal functions and informal parties. San Diego, though already the tenth largest city in America, was still a small town in many ways. The acting community was a closely woven group, not at all like the multitude of cliques in Los Angeles or New York.

Hillcrest's Fourth Avenue, known by one and all as "Pill Hill," was where he rented an office. By the time he was able to make himself known in the psychiatric and sex-therapy communities, his practice was already full. He had very quickly decided not to practice full-time. Fifteen, up to a maximum of twenty patients, were all he would see in any week. As in New York, he continued to give lectures on impotence, sex therapy in general, and the relationship between theatrical and therapeutic skills. His caseload was varied and interesting. A waiting list developed. As Paul did not like to refuse anyone who wanted to see him, he began to hone his skills to shorten even further the length of treatment time. Believing in short-term therapy, it took an average of less than six months before his patients had their problems solved and were able to be discharged.

California was much more liberal than the East Coast in permitting and accepting all types of therapies. People were into rebirthing, primal therapy, and acupuncture, as well as making use of the more established treatments, such as Jungian psychoanalysis, bioenergetics, and Rogerian client-oriented therapy. It was not long before Paul had heard of Bandler and Grinder's neurolinguistic programming, a new concept that had the ability to shorten the time of therapy even further. After a number of workshops with them and their trainers, he found himself being drawn to hypnosis, one of its prime building blocks.

Milton Erickson, who had moved from Phoenix to New Mexico, was mentioned again and again as the man who looked at therapy in a new light and who was able to achieve cures time after time. When other therapists gave up, it was to Erickson they sent their "failures." Paul decided to personally study with him and after a lengthy correspondence had arranged a two-week stay in Santa Fe with the master.

In many ways, Dr. Erickson stood therapy on its head. The basic premises were different and the treatment plans more unorthodox. Paul, in the short, two-week interaction with Milton Erickson, began to refocus and question anew the underlying assumptions of therapy. He learned that he needed to spend even more time in improving his skills to be able to pick up the slightest clues his patients were constantly emitting. He had to sharpen his skills in the nuances of language and minimal body movements in order to facilitate in his subjects ever-deeper levels of hypnosis. Paul learned deeply by experiencing Dr. Erickson not on an intellectual level but by being put into altered and trance states.

Paul signed up for the following summer. Once again he learned hypnosis by spending the two weeks in Dr. Erickson's seminar in amnesiac trances. Paul realized in some odd way he was not only improving his professional skills but was also working on his personal life, in which problems were hiding just under the surface of his consciousness, waiting for either a gust of externality to bring them into the open or an internal spark to ignite his self-hidden emotional universe, exposing it as a flame of feelings and knowledge.

Paul never discussed his personal concerns with Dr. Erickson. He asked only professional questions that dealt with the theories and techniques of hypnosis. Never did Paul mention Mary and the problems they experienced in bed. Not once did he address her lack of orgasms, his difficulty with erections, or the slow but sure diminution of sexual activity between them. Neither did he raise the subject of Johan and the increasing emotional gulf that divided father and son, nor did he bring up his lifelong feelings of separation between his own father and himself.

No, Paul wanted to keep his instructions on a professional level, his gain of knowledge in the domain of psychotherapy. Dr. Erickson, the master of utilizing what anyone brought in, respected Paul's desire not to consciously stir up the personal stew. Paul, being adept right from the start at going into deep trance, was instructed by Dr. Erickson to remain in a profound hypnotic state each time he went under. Amnesia was strongly built into Paul's trance work, with the result that he had no conscious awareness of what had transpired during the previous as well as this year's hypnotic seminars.

After the first summer in Santa Fe, Paul knew that he had somehow changed. In inexplicable ways, he felt different about himself and his family. His personal life somehow stabilized even though the eddies of problems remained; they did not greatly improve but neither did they get any worse. Mary and he somehow managed to have sex a couple of times a month. Though she still did not have any orgasms, he managed to elicit from her some minimal cooperation, enabling him to remain erect and ejaculate most of the time.

During that year Paul's father requested that he be permitted to take Johan to Hawaii during Easter vacation. Because he extended this invitation only to Johan and not both children, he consolidated Johan's magical view of his grandfather while strengthening in Paul the chill he harbored toward both Steven, his father, and Johan, his son.

The second year's fortnight was over on Saturday. Paul was once again dawdling over lunch. This time he was sitting alone on the second-floor patio of the Ore House overlooking Santa Fe's main plaza. He was wide awake but the heat of the day and the effect of two glasses of white wine created a lethargy that countermanded his mind's alertness. He reviewed the morning's happenings. He had gotten up early, had room service send up breakfast while he showered and packed, then set off on the fifteen minutes' walk to Dr. Erickson's home for a last morning of stories, oblique instructions, and the easily induced trance.

His plane back to San Diego did not leave till 6 p.m. As Santa Fe did not have an airport, he would have to start his drive to Albuquerque around four o'clock. Sitting in the shade, he took in the throng of tourists milling around in the square. Some were bent over the Indians' silver-and-turquoise jewelry, all neatly displayed on row upon row of outdoor sidewalk blankets; some were gathered around a bearded guitarist; others were meandering slowly, licking their just-bought Häagen-Dazs cones. The tourist dance, he thought. He realized that he had not bought Mary or the children any mementos of the town and decided he would do so this afternoon.

He had no other plans. *Yes,* he decided, *I'll do some shopping.* He would buy Mary a necklace, a Pueblo Indian doll for Anna, and for Johan he'd get . . . he did not know what. *I'll find something appropriate.* He was set to start on this shopping trip when he realized he must do something else first. But what? Perplexed, he was benumbed into inaction. He ordered another coffee to put off his indecision. What must he do? He had already paid his bill at the hotel. There was something, he knew, but what? That morning he had exchanged phone numbers with the two therapists from Southern California, the ones with whom he hoped to keep in touch. What else?

Dr. Erickson; something to do with him. He had already said good-bye and had wished him a speedy recovery. What else? He must see him again. But why? Paul just knew he had to go back there again. He looked at his watch. Twenty to two. He had just enough time. He quickly paid his bill. Somehow he should be there exactly at two.

As the cathedral bell rang the hour, Paul knocked at Dr. Erickson's door.

When Mrs. Erickson showed him into the study, Paul said to the doctor, "I've come to thank you for the kindness you've shown. Not only to myself but to the others who like me wish to learn from you."

From his wheelchair, looking directly into Paul's eyes, Dr. Erickson answered in his low gravelly tone, "Thank you for being so prompt. I wanted to see you one more time and I shortly have to take my afternoon nap."

"Prompt?"

"Oh, forgive me. I forget so easily these days, what with these drugs that are supposed to arrest the spread." Dr. Erickson shook his head as if to clear his thoughts while motioning for Paul to sit down opposite him. "Yes, of course you wouldn't remember my suggestion. You were deep in trance though you did have your eyes open."

"What suggestion?"

"That's right. Make yourself comfortable. The suggestion to come back at two o'clock, to enter the room and return to the morning's trance. Yes, that's right."

With glazed, open eyes that stared straight ahead, and in a monotone and flat voice, Paul very slowly said, "I . . . do . . . not . . . remember."

"That's right. You do not remember what happened this morning just as you do not remember what took place when you were in trance these past two weeks. You're a very good subject, Paul. Go deeper still. Yes, while I'm waiting for the next minute, go deep, deeper." He waited and closely watched Paul. "Now that you're in the middle of nowhere, you feel relaxed, you feel comfortable. But this time as you listen to my words, I want you to pay close attention, for you'll remember clearly each and every word I say this afternoon. Your memory will be sharp, the thoughts and sayings etched strongly, the future will carry this afternoon's words along your stream of consciousness while still keeping hidden in your unconscious the previous ones."

He paused. Paul sat absolutely still, waiting for him to continue.

"As you have seen, I have a garden in the back of the house. I've always liked to grow things with my own hands. I love to see the seeds turn into shoots, which then turn into plants that flower and bear fruit. My favorite plant is the tomato. I've always had good luck with them. From the very first time I planted one, they've always borne me large and good fruits.

"I always grew the large red variety. One summer, one of the seeds gave fruit to an unusual tomato, a yellow tomato. I had expected my usual red crop and instead I was given a plant of bright yellow ones. At first I was disappointed for it was not what I had expected. I did not know if the mutation had taken place before the seed had been planted or if the change had occurred in the ground itself. If I wished for more yellow ones, I knew that the fruit itself carried in its genes the new genetic information. But what about the stock of seeds from the original red ones? Were they also changed?

"I therefore, as a good scientist, decided to experiment. The next spring I planted the original seeds in one bed while in a second bed I put in the seeds of the offspring, the yellow tomatoes. As expected from the second bed I received only yellow fruit but from the parent seeds I was delighted to see some plants bore red tomatoes while other seeds gave rise to yellow ones. However, the bigger surprise was that a third variety surfaced: an orange tomato. My experiment to seed again the original stock gave rise to the best tomato of all, a golden orange tomato that not only was beautiful but also was sweeter than the others."

Dr. Erickson stopped talking. Paul sat catatonically still as the hypnotist sipped some water.

He continued, "My wife loves to cook with the herbs and vegetables grown in our garden. In the section next to the tomatoes I had planted several beds of basil. They did fairly well in the spring and fall but in the heat of the summer they wilted and did poorly in the sun's heat. One day, during an especially hot day a couple of summers ago, as I was tending to the badly seared green herb, I thought of a possible solution. Basil plants, like some delicate people, need a sheltered environment, a temperate condition. I decided to plant the basil in the same bed with the tomato. The tomato, as you know, grows tall and bushy. In fact one has to tie them straight to stakes so they do not fall over when heavily laden with their ripe fruit. They would cast their cooling shadow onto the smaller and more delicate basil plants.

"The basil prospered under the tomatoes. And, by planting both plants in one bed, I now had room to plant some other herbs in the rows where the basil used to be.

"Paul, I want you to remember the strength of the large plant casting its cool protection. The basil reaching its potential under the patient and loving shade of its partner in the one bed. The ability of the tomato to change its seed and fruit into new varieties, different colors, and changing tastes. The original seed did not need to remain pure and perfect. Its imperfections and mutable inclinations gave rise to the sweet golden tomato.

"You can in the next few minutes think about this. Take two minutes, all the time in the world, to integrate and learn. When you are ready, come back to this room and time, fully alert and wide awake, remembering what you need to remember."

They both sat still for two minutes. Paul then blinked several times, stretched his arms and legs, and looked at Dr. Erickson with seeing eyes. They smiled at each other.

Propelled with a newfound energy, Paul got up. For the second time that day, he bade good-bye and gave his thanks to the man who not only taught Paul an innate knowledge of hypnosis, a wonderful new tool to use in his professional life, but also bestowed upon him the ability to alter his personal relationships in a manner appropriate to Paul—changes that sprang from his unconscious core and did not disturb his conscious awareness until after the fact.

He peacefully and quietly left the house. Dr. Erickson died six weeks later.

I arrived ten minutes before my scheduled appointment. It was early in the day, so I had no trouble finding an empty parking space. The air was cool. My blue Hawaiian short-sleeved shirt barely protected me from the moist morning haze, a fog that still cast its lazy tendrils over Hillcrest and environs before it would dissipate sometime around noon. I quickly slipped two quarters in the meter and hurried through the black and spire-gated fence into the calm warmth of the doctor's waiting room.

The blonde receptionist had me sign another Blue Cross form, took my check for the twenty percent that was not covered by the insurance policy, and said, "Dr. Manes should be out of session by nine. Make yourself comfortable," pointing to the couch and giving me a big California smile.

The violet and white impatiens were still in bloom, showily hugging the atrium's palm tree. I had not been to his office in over three weeks. First I had to fly to New York when the telephone call reported Mother's final illness, then I had to wait for Dr. Manes's return from his summer vacation. Staring off beyond the moss-covered tree trunk, my mind meandered along its own inner branches. With Mother's death, my external world as well as something inside me had changed. In some way my problem with my unruly cock was not as acute. How come? I did not understand what was different about me. What had altered?

Before I could sort it out, I heard his door open and saw a tall and very good-looking woman stride out. Her blue eyes focused straight ahead and she quickly headed to the front door without looking at me or anything else. Dr. Manes came out a minute later and motioned me into his office. I sat in my usual chair. He easily settled into his Morris chair after taking my file from his desk.

He began with, "I was sorry to hear about your mother's death."

"So much has happened since our last session. I had desperately wanted to see you the moment I got back to San Diego but you were away. I didn't want to see your replacement so I waited until you returned from your holidays."

He caught my tonal pique and replied, "It's natural for all of us to be upset when the people to whom we look for support are not there when needed. I'm glad my secretary was able to juggle the schedule to get you in here today." He paused, then continued, "Do you want to tell me about it?"

"There's so much. I don't know where to begin," I said plaintively.

"It doesn't matter where you begin. Just tell me what you see as the important events and how you view your life as of right now."

"It started with a call from Uncle Max telling me Mother was in the hospital. I caught the first flight to New York and managed to get there before she died. But it wasn't a peaceful . . ." I stopped.

"Yes?"

"We had another one of our famous fights. Even at the end, she demanded that I kowtow to her. She wanted me to return and head up the business but . . . but with her continuing to manipulate the strings. When I refused, she told me to get out. She yelled that she never, ever wanted to set eyes on me. I obeyed her and left the sick room. While I sat in the hospital's waiting lounge, she had another massive coronary ten minutes later—a final attack from which she never recovered."

I sat there reliving the scene at the hospital, my heart once again in turmoil. I started to cry. Through the tears, I managed to finally utter, "She never wanted to set eyes on me ever again. She got her last wish." Now I really began to sob.

Sitting quietly, Dr. Manes let me be.

When at last I came back from my grieving maelstrom, back to the room and the present, I looked up and saw that he had tears in his eyes.

"You loved her deeply," he said softly. Once again my tears started to flow, this time in explosive heaves. It was a full five minutes before I calmed down to the point where I was able to relate the rest of the story.

In that session, he did not interrupt my nonstop emotional out-pouring. It was only when the hour was over that I understood just how important it was for me to have been able to verbalize my still overflowing grief. Though I had cried and cried with Betty and had been able to empty the black, enveloping shadows of bitter memories with her, it was not until that morning in Dr. Manes's office that I finally managed to inter them.

The following session, however, was quite different.

Very quickly, he put me into a deep trance. He used that special soft tone, that hypnotic cadence. I drifted off and stopped paying attention to his voice; I became aware of my inner secure spot, my middle-of-nowhere lagoon. I entered into my vibrating stillness, listened to the voices of my past and present, and experienced again the images and scenes of yesterday and yesteryear.

It was impossible for me to gauge how long I had been under. The myriad emotions and the scenes of my trance dreams seemed to last for a very, very long time.

The first thing I remembered upon coming out of the hypnotic trance were his last words and instructions: ". . . that's right. Let your unconscious integrate and sense all you've seen and felt. Feel free to float deep and through your inner self yourself at the speed and depth comfortable to you and you. Take a minute of clock time, all the time in the world to see and learn to learn to see. When you are ready, come back to the present time and place, to this office feeling fully refreshed, wide awake, and alert, remembering every thought and sentence, each image and voice clearly and in all detail. Though you have been deep inside yourself you can remember all that transpired here in this session, each question asked by me, every answer you uttered and thought. So take a minute or two, as long as you need. Nowwwwww . . ."

Dr. Manes had previously hypnotized me three or four times. Never had I been so deep but never had I so clearly recalled the trance and its dreamlike material. The previous times he had somehow gotten me to forget what went on while being under. Intuitively, I understood why this time he wanted me to remember.

And remember I did.

Dr. Manes had me go over in detail all my New York sexual escapades, all my erotic feelings. At his suggestion I had my eyes open. Unable to focus properly, I had, in a slow trancelike voice related to him my sexual adventures from Sandy, the luscious stewardess in Chicago, to Barry's frightened safe-sex masturbation; from Betty's loving sexual devotion at the hotel to Judy's need for a continual reenactment of her lustful *Daddy*.

When I had fully returned and was fully alert, Dr. Manes made sure I remembered everything I had told him while being under. "And what was Judy's last name?" he wanted to know.

"Let's see. It was Saroff. Yes, Judy Saroff."

He hesitated. He looked at me with intensity—a look I had never before seen on his face. After a couple of moments, he asked, "Was her father the director, Carl Saroff?"

With furrowed incomprehension, I slowly answered, "I don't know his first name, but yes, he was a director, the dirty bastard." I paused before continuing, "He fucked her and really fucked her up."

"How did you feel with her? How was sex for you?"

At first with hesitation, then with inner certitude, I said, "I quickly realized she needed me to be her *Daddy;* she needed to be loved by him in the only way she knew love from him. Sexually." I paused and then continued, "So I obliged. I became her father and took his place. At first she didn't want to believe me, but I completely gave of myself and in my mind I loved her as a daughter. Though older than me, she became my daughter. It obviously worked. She was able to reach a climax for the first time in three years."

"That was intuitive and generous," Dr. Manes commented when I stopped talking. "Is that all she represented to you? Was she only your daughter?"

"No. She represented all women."

"Anyone in particular?"

"You mean my mother," I uttered after thinking it through. With that remark, I shut my eyes. A shudder ran through me. I was flooded with anxiety and began to shake. My hands first started to tremble, then slowly the tremors spread throughout my body.

After an eternity, he softly asked, "Did you ever want to have sex with your mother?"

"No," I cried. "No."

"Were you ever aroused by your mother?" He would not let go.

"No." An eternal pause. Finally I admitted, "Yes. When I was very young.

"When?"

"When she was taking a bath and I saw her naked. Yes, she was beautiful. I wanted, I needed her love."

"Every boy loves his mother, needs his mother's love," he gently confirmed. "It's not wrong. In many ways it's beautiful; the purest of loves.

I began to cry. "Why didn't she love me?"

"She did, Randy. She did, David. She loved her Dovid'l. With all her heart she did. But she had difficulty in showing it, in demonstrating it. It's not your fault that she didn't have the skills to show it."

"Why? Why?" I didn't know what I wanted to know. "Why?"

"You know. Deep inside you know," he played it back to me.

I nodded. I did know. I became calm. Peaceful at last, I again thought of Judy and her physical need for her *Daddy*. I began to cry for her, for her insatiable need. It hit me suddenly I was lucky in being able to get love, to fulfill my innermost needs through Betty.

I smiled through my tears.

For some reason he did not let go of that scene with Judy in New York. He continued with, "What did Judy tell you about her sexual relationship with her father?"

I closed my eyes to recall the scene more vividly. We had just finished sex. We were both drenched in sweat. Her hair was pillow-spread. She was lying quite still next to me, her eyes closed. She kept holding my hand in a tight grip.

"She was still tense though much looser than before we had made love. I began to gently hold her and whisper that everything was all right. She began to cry and utter over and over, 'Daddy I love you, Daddy, I love you.' I don't know what made me ask her how it had all begun but it opened up the dam and a flood of words and feelings came tumbling forth."

"What did she say? Can you remember what she said?" Dr. Manes wanted to know.

"I don't understand what her relationship with her crazy father has to do with me." I paused. He said nothing. "But I remember vividly what she said."

"Yes?" he was insistent.

"She said it had begun very early on. The first time she remembered something went on between them was when she was eight years old. She had walked into the bedroom one day and he was jerking himself off. Her mother had gone out shopping and the two of them were alone in the apartment.

"He told her it was perfectly alright to see how a man gives pleasure to himself when he doesn't have a woman to please him. She had been fascinated with the big cock sticking out of his enclosed fist. She watched in trance as he played with his balls with one hand while pumping his cock faster and faster with the other until with a loud groan he shot off.

"He made her promise not to tell her mother and promised her that if she were a good girl he would allow her to feel his cock and let her give him pleasure with it. That's how it began. She was mesmerized with his cock. She loved touching it, loved to see it get bigger, to watch it shoot its load.

"From jerking him off, it was not long before she was talked into blowing him. At first she could hardly get the head in her mouth. With practice and his encouragement she became adept at it and that became the favorite pastime between them. She wanted his cum in her mouth as much as he wanted her to suck him off." I stopped talking and did not go on.

"And how old was she when he began to have intercourse with her?" Dr. Manes wished to know.

"I thought it was weird. For years he had prepared her for it. He told her she could have his cock in her when she began to menstruate. So she kept thinking about the time when her father would begin fucking her. Year after year, that's all she thought about.

"And at the age of twelve, two months after her first period, he slipped it in and began having a steady diet of daughterly sex."

"Did her mother know?" Dr. Manes inquired.

"Not for years. Judy and Carl were in cahoots. He told her she was a much better lay than her mother—a better woman. But eventually he got careless and when the shit hit the fan, Judy's mother packed her bags, moved back to Chicago, and was never heard from again." I shook my head, not understanding how a father could fuck up a child in that way. "But why is it necessary for me to go over these details? What does it have to do with me?"

Dr. Manes shook his head as if in sorrow. "It does not have much to do with you. You see, Randy, I knew both of them when I lived in New York. I suspected something of the sort might have occurred. I'm sorry to hear that it did."

"You knew Judy?" I couldn't believe it.

"Yes, when she was around fifteen or sixteen," he said sadly. I just looked at him, too stunned to say anything. He finally continued, "Actually I knew her father quite well in those days, but that's water over the dam and you're right, it does not relate to you or your problems."

I looked at him, trying to conceive of him as a young man, imagine him with a Judy who was fifteen years old. Suddenly, I asked without forethought but with a certainty of its importance, "Was that the last time you saw them?"

He did not answer right away and when he did it was not to the point. "How did you feel when all that spilled out?"

I felt that he was using a therapist's technique on me. He wished me to go back to my feelings, my life. However, I did not follow his lead. "Come on, Dr. Manes. Tell me the last time you saw Judy or her father."

Again he hesitated before he answered. "It was quite a while ago. Must be around twelve years, I would say."

"I thought so."

We never did get back to my problems that session. The time was almost up anyway and, rather than go back to Judy and myself, I filled him in on Judy's life since he last had seen her. I knew he wanted to know. It was obviously important to him.

Assisting him in this way made me glow on the inside. He had helped me a lot. Giving him information about these people from his past was the least I could do to repay his kindness and concern.

The following Friday evening Betty and I took the northern route to Palm Springs. We had missed the heavy rush hour traffic, as both of us could not leave the office before seven. Having just finished dinner in a family restaurant just outside of Hemet, we tackled the last fifty or so miles to our desert weekend and a respite from the day-to-day business pressures.

At first our move into the new space had gone smoothly. We both had finally agreed to get out of our tiny cubbyhole of an office. As an initial set-up it had been ideal: small and cheap. This past year, however, we picked up three new accounts. When we installed a new Macintosh to relieve Betty and the clerk of the mountainous stack of paperwork, the quarters became too constricting. We therefore rented a lovely downtown office on Seventh Avenue right off Broadway in a well-kept older building. Rather than pay top dollar in one of the new high-rises, this move permitted us to have a couple of extra rooms for future expansion as well as a private art studio for my own use.

The future looked rosy though Betty was up to her ears in trying to get our computer to work. It had been months since we bought it but it still was not up and running. Just yesterday she had discovered a major glitch in the accounts receivable software and had to return it for a new program.

At first luck was with us. Two weeks after we moved into the more expensive space we landed a small new account for a prestigious toy store in Pacific Beach. This past week, however, we lost two of our larger accounts. Baltimore Bagels was having expansion trouble— two of their new outlets were losing money. They gave us one month's notice: all PR would from now on be done in-house and their advertising would be cut back to the bone. Our services were no longer needed. Piret's restaurant, on the other hand, was too successful. They sold out to a large food conglomerate who notified us that all marketing would be handled from their main headquarters in Los Angeles as of the first of December.

The loss of business was not my only headache. With my having been so long in New York, I had two other accounts whose deadlines were past due. On top of that, we lost out on a bid for a potentially lucrative account, the Century 21 real estate firm and most of its San Diego branches. Whereas we had previously been showing a small net surplus, we were now once again running in the red.

My mind kept mulling over these business headaches. When Betty turned onto the Ten from the Seventy-nine I closed my eyes hoping to blot out furniture campaigns and escape cash crunches.

Was it only two days ago I had heard from Clara? She had called me at the end of a long, hard day.

"We haven't heard from you in a long, long time. Everything okay?"

"Oh, Clara, it has been ages. Much has happened in the past couple of months but the proverbial dust is finally beginning to settle."

"Randy, how about coming up for an evening of fun and games? Both of us have missed you, you horny hunk."

My cock responded to the invitation in its usual manner—it began to expand. "And I've missed the two of you. Remember when I was up in your neck of the woods this past June?"

"Do I ever. You just couldn't get enough."

"Well, I'd love a repeat but I'll have to call you early next week. I have to work late the next two nights. Then on Friday Betty and I are taking the weekend off and driving to the desert."

"Are you sure you can't break free tomorrow evening?" Clara knew me well enough to put just that extra bit of pressure on my cock.

"I don't see how. But I'll tell you what. I'll give you a call tomorrow at lunchtime if I can see myself able to jump up to Cardiff. Okay?"

"Well, you do know what's waiting for you with open arms. Hope to hear from you."

Though I wanted to call her, she did not hear from me. I made much too little headway on the in-basket that Thursday morning. I was not able to keep my hard-on from knowing its loss, however, and by the time I left the office yesterday I had jerked off two times.

In a way, I was glad that I had not given in to Clara's invitation. Clara would have to wait until I was able to achieve a closer and more satisfying relationship with Betty.

We arrived in Palm Springs after eleven and had to ask a gas station attendant before finding the Sheraton Oasis, which turned out to be only one block from the main drag. It was a motel type of building, encompassing almost one whole block. While the parking lot abutted the open end of the two storied U-shaped structure, the center of the 'U' enclosed Southern California's obligatory kidney-shaped pool, a three-foot-deep Jacuzzi, and a perfectly kept lawn encumbered with cheap plastic deck chairs.

We had taken advantage of their two-day special of $60 a night. We did not care that the hotel had already seen better days; what we wanted was a reasonably priced bed. Bone tired, we quickly undressed. Betty showered. I did not bother. I was asleep before she finished her night's toilette.

Saturday morning I opened my eyes to a warm, clear, blue sky. A family of three was lolling around the pool just on the other side of our mini alcove, which had been described in the hotel's brochure as a private balcony. I turned back to look at Betty; I still marveled at her beauty. After all these years, she still made me feel like a boy in a candy store, all these goodies not only to look at but to have just for the asking.

Betty had changed her attitude toward me ever since Mother's death. In New York while at the Doral she had been more loving, more accepting. Since I had come back to San Diego, she was even more devoted. In the past few months she seemed to have forgiven as well as forgotten my bisexuality. She never brought it up. As she had done at the start of our marriage, she was once again ready to open her arms to me, ready to have sex—always wet, always ready.

Betty had changed these past months and it definitely had something to do with my mother's death. In some way, I think she felt that her main competitor for my affection had left the battlefield. It seemed it was neither other women nor even other men that had threatened her as much as my ties to my family, to my mother. For her, the umbilical cord's tug had been much more important than the pull of the sexual tension I always exhibited. She instinctively knew that though I had my own company—had consciously given up on my family's business and moved clear across the continent—I still was not free from Rivka's grasping reach.

With mother's death, Betty finally became secure in our relationship. We both now knew that it would be Libby and not "Dovid'l" that would continue the Baum legacy. We both realized that I had finally, with Mrs. B.'s passing, been set free. No more would I have to worry what Mother would think. I would no longer find it necessary to anxiously do the things that either pleased or spited the mother who lived inside my every cell.

As Betty's love intensified, I had to rearrange my feelings from the expectation of rejection to once again anticipating unquestioning warmth and affection. Betty did not refuse a single sexual advance ever since we had made love in New York. Whenever I was horny she was glad to oblige me and participate in my lusty drives. Once I realized she wouldn't deny my overtures, I began to consciously test its boundaries.

At first I tried to find the limit in terms of frequency. The first week back, I went at it with her a minimum of three times a day. One evening I fucked her four times. I started it by rubbing against her while she was in the kitchen preparing dinner. She willingly stopped cutting the vegetables, put down the knife and joined me in a quickie. After dinner I went at her once again. She responded in kind. We fucked twice more that night before both of us finally got a well-needed sleep. She kept pace with me and climaxed a multitude of times. In many ways she wanted my affection and sexual attention as much as I needed to make love to her.

My anxiety began to abate and my nervousness diminished. I don't exactly know when I became aware of it, but when I did I was amazed to realize my anxiety could now be taken care of in Betty's loving embrace. I did not know how much longer it would be necessary to see Dr. Manes. Events had conspired to lessen my problems. Maybe one or two more times just to tie up some loose ends. Besides, we were running tight with respect to money and here was as good a place as any to cut back.

Morning erections are delightfully playful. There isn't the deep and driving need to fuck, just an extended cock that wants something warm and soft around its cool skin. As I looked at Betty who was still asleep, I decided to enter her gently and slowly. She opened herself to me and before I really began to stroke in earnest, she was wide awake, whispering, "Oh yes, Randy, oh yes." I began concentrating on her reactions and kept increasing the speed and pressure until she began groaning. She came in her usual high-pitched "oh, oh, ohhh," quickly followed by several deep moans. It did not take me long to follow suit and I came with my own spasms and yells.

"Let's get some breakfast." I was the first to come down to the point of being able to talk. "I noticed a coffee shop just down the street," I suggested to her.

"I want to shower first," she leisurely climbed out of bed, stretched a couple of times, and slowly walked to the bathroom. After the water had been on a couple of minutes, she yelled through the steam, "Randy, come here, will you?"

I obeyed, reluctantly getting out of the lazy, comfortable bed. "Will you scrub my back please?" she asked. I climbed in with her. At first I soaped her back as she wished, then I let my hands wander to her breasts. I began to get erect. She felt my cock as it pushed against her. She bent over and I entered her from behind and once again we were at it. She climaxed quickly but it took me somewhat longer to come this second time.

With light steps and spirits, we strolled to the restaurant. It was a glorious day. After breakfast we spent time sunning next to the pool, splashing playfully in the Jacuzzi before lunch, and in the afternoon we walked and window shopped the length of Palm Canyon Road. We especially enjoyed visiting most of the galleries along the way. There were only two in the whole strip that attempted to exhibit good art; the rest just sold the typical touristy, high-priced, tasteless canvasses.

We had dinner three blocks from our hotel at the highly recommended Melvyn Restaurant. We had had to wend our way through a driveway of parked Jaguars, Mercedes, as well as one or two Rollses and Bentleys. Betty, in her sedate pink chiffon dress and her white cashmere sweater loosely draped over her shoulders, fit in with the quietly murmuring diners. My beige jacket just barely made the grade but the well-worn jeans blew it. Our table was halfway into the hallway and the waiter instinctively knew that we were neither old money nor even a couple of the nouveau riche.

The meal, however, made up for the waiter's upturned nose and lukewarm service. We both drank more than we were wont to do: drinks before dinner, a bottle of an expensive 1983 chardonnay during the meal and brandy in our coffee afterward. I was still tipsy when I played with the key to our door. After a few unsuccessful attempts, I finally managed to connect and let us in. Betty giggled and giggled at my klutzy ineptitude.

"Now this is an all-time first," she laughed. "I've never known you not to be able to get what you want into any hole. Losing your touch?"

"None of your lip, young woman," I said, interrupting myself with two hiccups. "In your state you'd not even see the hole, let alone find your keys in that jumble you call your purse."

"Okay, honey, let's not fight over who's more tipsy." She came close and held me tightly as she began to nip my left ear lobe.

Closing my eyes, I concentrated on her smell. I held her and leaned my head on her shoulder, eyes still closed.

"I'm dizzy," I broke from her and lay down on the bed. My head spun and I felt myself falling backwards. "Please get me some coffee, darling. I'm not feeling good."

She quickly lifted the telephone and ordered some from room service. I kept my eyes closed, trying to stop the spinning. Betty must have a stronger constitution, for she began to strip and head once more into the shower. As she emerged with a towel draped around her, there was a knock on the door. The young waiter, a boy just out of his teens, brought in the coffee. He ogled Betty and forgot what he was about. I don't think he was aware I was on the bed. Betty noticed the look and played it up to the hilt: first rearranging the towel around her breasts, then bending low to sign the chit he had dropped on the table.

"Wasn't he cute the way he looked at me?" she asked after he had slowly closed the door behind him. "I think he must be a virgin."

Sipping my black coffee, I answered with a jealousy that was both unusual and intense, "I'm too dizzy to have noticed."

"Come on, Randy, I know you well enough. When it comes to sex your antenna's always in place as well as pointed in the right direction." She was quiet a moment before continuing in a slightly slower tempo and with a lower pitch, "You know our agreement always has been it was okay to make it with others as long it didn't interfere with us. But what we've never tried is a three-way."

"I'm shocked at you Betty. What's gotten into you? Lately, I thought we've begun to get closer, just the way it was at the start." I put down the cup, took off my jacket, and walked slowly to the closet. I hung it up. "A three-way?"

"Yes. He's cute. And did you see bulge in his pants?"

"Betty, you're drunk. Aren't you getting enough sex? Am I not meeting your needs?" expressing a new thought, one that I had never before felt with Betty.

"Oh, Randy, of course you are, you gorgeous hunk. Is it the thought of another man together with us two that's making you so uptight?"

"I thought that was behind us, something in our past. I've tried to never bring it up in your presence. So how come you're doing it now?"

"I'm not doing anything of the sort. I just thought it would be delightful for us to put the make on the obviously big-eyed kid. I did not mean to bring up your bisexuality, darling. I'm sorry." She came up behind me and snuggled against me.

I didn't know what to say. I was stunned. This was the first time she brought up the subject when she didn't feel in a one-down position. As it was, I was the one who felt somewhat uptight. I had thought that it was truly behind us and here, while tipsy, she was suggesting a threesome with another man.

Though I didn't answer her, she continued to hold me. After a couple of moments she started to unbutton my shirt with one hand while with the other began unbuckling my belt. "Why don't you take a hot shower? It'll extract some of that alcohol out of your skin and you'll feel better." As she lowered my shorts she continued, "And I'll make you feel *much* better."

My cock knew what she alluded to and began its escalation. Before it had time to fully extend, I slipped out of her hold and headed to the shower. "Yup, I like that idea." I disappeared into the bathroom.

Under the steady beat of hot water, I tried to clear my confused head. Something was wrong. I felt anxiety in my stomach and a tight, dully aching band enclosed my chest. My temples continued to throb. I began to soap myself and tried to think about how we would get it on as soon as I stepped out of the shower and into Betty's arms. As I began to lather my genitals, I found my cock did not want to stand up. "It'll come to life," I thought. "As soon as Betty starts to fondle it, it'll grow. She likes and wants my Big Man." I tried to convince my reluctant member.

After drying off, I walked naked into the bedroom. She was already under the covers. One small light on her side of the bed showed the contour of her lovely breasts through the white sheet. I noticed that her legs were spread apart, a clear sign of her readiness to have sex. I got in but made no move to touch her. I did not understand what was going on; all I knew was part of me did not want to have sex. A side of me I did not know existed was telling me now was not the time for sex; not with Betty, not with anyone.

She nuzzled against me and kissed me gently but warmly on the lips. She moved closer and held me tighter. When she became aware I was not returning her embrace, she began the one maneuver she knew would bring me to attention. She started to gently scratch my balls. Sure enough, my cock began to harden. Her fingers began to play a clarinet melody on my member while her mouth hummed a happy tune on my nipples.

Though she had been an active and most willing sex partner in the past few months, this was new. Betty was into it again with a zest and drive I remember we both had exhibited the first few months of our frenzied lovemaking. Not only was she busy making love to me, her own body shook with desire, her legs twitched and moved to the rhythm of her hands.

Suddenly, I took her head and pulled it off my nipple. I then swept her hand away from my cock. Thinking I wanted to take charge, she lay back, ready to receive any ministration I wished to make. I, however, swung my legs off the bed, the bedcover tenting my hard-on.

"Where are you going, Randy? I'm ready whenever you want it."

"Betty," I answered slowly, "I'm not in the mood."

"Not in the mood?" she echoed.

"No, I'm really not into it."

"Randy, what do you mean you're not into it?" She pointed to the blanket's bulge, not comprehending my words. "Just look at that and tell me you're not in the mood."

"Sure my cock's ready and willing. It's just I'm not. I'm not in the mood."

"Is it the alcohol? Do you feel alright?"

"No, it isn't the booze. It's just that I'm . . . I'm . . . I don't what's wrong but I don't want to have sex."

"Is it something I've done or said?" She was confused.

"No, Betty. It has nothing to do with you or your actions. You've been, you are lovely, and more to the point, quite sexy. It's me. I just don't want to have sex right now. I want to lay here by myself and be inside my head."

"What's wrong, Randy?" a tremor in her voice.

"Nothing's wrong. I just don't want to have sex."

"Nothing's wrong," she repeated, then began to cry. "You don't want to have sex and you say nothing's wrong. Oh, Randy, don't you love me anymore?"

"Hush, Betty," I said quietly as I began to gently hug her. I began to stroke her hair. "No, Betty, there is nothing wrong between us." She began to sob quietly but permitted me to lightly and softly stroke her face, eyes, and hair.

"I don't understand," she whispered through her sobs.

"I don't fully understand it myself but I know it's correct. You see, even my cock agrees," I said, putting her hand on my flaccid cock.

"You've changed, Randy. I've never known you to lose your hard-on once we started to play around."

"Maybe. I think *we've* changed. Our relationship has gotten better and I love you more than ever."

"What a way to show it," she said, but no longer with a tremor in her voice.

"Let me show you another way how much I love you," I responded. "Let's just hold each other without sex."

I quietly slid down next to her and held her. I kissed her gently, with warmth rather than passion.

I don't remember when I fell asleep.

Paul was drenched. Several large sweat spots showed through his white shirt. The perspiration also manifested itself in two small oval stains just under the armpits of his light blue seersucker suit. Without looking, he knew his pants must be sweat darkened around the belt as well as his inner thighs, he felt a cool moistness in his groin. Though he enjoyed walking, he knew he had made a mistake. He should have taken his Nissan Maxima. Mister A's was just a short fifteen- to twenty-minute walk from his office but in today's heat it might as well have been five miles away. The Santa Ana had hit San Diego during his morning sessions and Paul had not realized the temperature had climbed above ninety degrees when he began his stroll to the restaurant.

It had taken Paul over thirty minutes to get to Laurel and Fifth. He had started out briskly but with each succeeding block he had slowed up; the brisk step quickly turned into a leisurely stroll, which ultimately ended up as an enervated trudge. Looking at his watch he saw it was eight after one. He was late for his luncheon appointment. Steering his world on the standard of promptness, Paul felt somewhat anxious at his tardiness. Waiting for the elevator to take him up to the top of the building, time seemed to crawl and his anxiety increased with each second.

It was their first get-together since the July Fourth family barbecue, where they had hardly exchanged more than two sentences. By the time the elevator arrived, Paul was unusually tense. Four jovial men got in ahead of him. Bankers, he judged by their banter. One of them pushed twelve, the square button that, in elegant gold script on a deep red background, advertised the restaurant, Mister A's. Paul quickly approached the maître d'.

"I believe there's a reservation for Manes."

"Ah *oui*. Mr. Manes is already at his table," said the polished but overweight headwaiter. "Follow me, *s'il vous plait*," and led him to a corner table overlooking the downtown skyline.

Steven Manes got up slowly and, shaking Paul's hand, said, "It's not like you to be late. Anything wrong?"

"No, it's just the heat. I decided to walk here from the office. What a mistake!" Paul took a long look at his father. He noticed that in the past couple of years the man had visibly aged. Though obviously still in good health, his seventy-plus years stood out: a number of brown spots on his forehead, a fine tremor calling attention to prominently veined hands, and a subtle but distinct rounding of his once straight-held shoulders.

The bar hostess, a tall blonde wearing an off-the-shoulder bright orange dress, took Paul's order of a cup of coffee, not following his father's lead of scotch and soda.

"I have three more patients after lunch," Paul said, needing to explain his abstinence to his father.

"There's no need to answer to me," came the laconic reply.

Paul got angry. *A put-down already,* he thought. *I should not have accepted the old man's invitation. What's the use? We'll never bury the hatchet. Our sparring habits are too ingrained, our distrust too deep.*

Trying to calm down, Paul looked out over the city. He noticed a jet making its approach landing at Lindbergh Field. "I can see why you've kept this table ever since Mister A's opened. It's a gorgeous view."

"Yes it is. I also love to see the planes land, skimming the tops of the buildings. You know, in the past five years we've had more new construction downtown than in the past fifteen."

"You must be doing very well. Sally tells me that you're now more in real estate than in law."

"There's much more money to be made."

Paul did not answer. He always thought his father had been governed more by the dollar than by the intrinsic workings of the law.

"How are you doing financially?" asked his father.

"I can't complain. I have a full practice. Or to be more precise, I have as many patients as I want to see. On top of that, I get extra income from the theater."

"What's the next play you're going to be in?"

"Simon Gray's *Quartermaine's Terms.*"

"Do you have a good part?" Mr. Manes continued his questioning.

"God yes. I play St. John Quartermaine." Paul paused. Then asked his father, "How come all these questions about my acting? You never showed the slightest interest in either of my professions before this."

"That's not true, Paul. Your mother and I have always taken great interest and pride in your careers."

"Father, that's a lot of crock. When was the last time you went to see me on the stage? Tell me truthfully, when?"

"Let's see. It must have been *The Importance of Being Ernest.* Sometime in August of '82 wasn't it? True, it has been a couple of years, but not because I'm not interested in or proud of you. You know how busy I am and how many dinner obligations we have."

"Yes I know," the sarcasm was mixed with hurt. Even in middle age, the years of his father's indifferent attention still left a paternal void in the depth of his being.

"Did you know that your mother has kept a scrapbook of every production you've been in since you moved back to San Diego in 1977? She has cut out every review in *The San Diego Union* as well as the ones from the *L.A. Times.*"

"No, I didn't," Paul said in surprise. "Mother never mentioned it."

"Well, you know how your mother is. Proud of her son but reserved in how she shows it. Many an evening, she pores over them and interrupts what I'm doing to read me a particularly fine sentence or phrase."

"Yes, Father I do know how Mother feels about me." He paused, not knowing exactly how to continue without insulting his father. "Yes," he finally said, "Mother does truly care. I have always felt that and, in her own way, she has demonstrated it over the years in a manner I was able to see."

The elder Manes did not answer this attacking thrust. He just sat quietly and looked at his son. Paul stared back at his father, looking at the two steel gray irises, not glancing away. They sat silently looking at each other. It was the father who finally dropped his gaze.

Paul felt his father's sadness in that glance toward the dark blue and red carpet. Paul's first impulse was to be protective and assuage his father's depressed feelings, but then the years of anger and frustration at his father's coldness tempered his own. He said nothing.

"Paul . . ." Steven Manes began, but stopped. He began again, "Paul, one of the reasons that . . ." The red-jacketed waiter had approached their table. Mr. Manes changed his tone and in a lighter timber turned to the waiter with, "John, I will have the usual."

Paul in his turn said, "I'll have the same." He knew it would be clam chowder to be followed by a patty melt. His father's habits were ingrained through years of unwavering repetitions, a life dictated by resolute principles and persevering actions. "Are you still smoking your three cigars a day?"

"No, Paul. The doctor put his foot down and I've cut it down to one after dinner. The same with coffee. I'm down to two cups a day. Would you believe it? I miss the coffee much more than the cigars." He said it slowly and as he shook his head, he again looked old and sad as he glanced down to the floor.

"What did you begin to tell me when the waiter interrupted you?"

"Oh, it can wait till we're finished eating. Let's not spoil a good lunch." The elder Mr. Manes braced his shoulders and took a couple of deep breaths. He continued, "Well, what type of part is this John Quarter or whatever his name is?"

Aware that Steven Manes was a master of timing, Paul, unable to influence his father's actions, accepted and allowed the old man to determine when he would bring up what was on his mind. He answered, "St. John Quartermaine is an English instructor at a school for foreign students. Slowly but surely he is losing himself, becoming more and more disconnected from the others. As in Gray's other play, *Butley,* the main character falls apart, but the final fall is such a quiet one that true tragedy is felt."

"Real men do not fall apart. There must be a major flaw in the man."

"I beg to differ with you father. Under appropriate circumstances everyone, and that includes men as well as women, have the human capacity to fail, to break."

"Not the men I have looked up to in my life. My father did not break though he lost every penny in the depression."

"That's not what I'm talking about," Paul didn't know if he could explain what he meant. He continued, "True manliness contains in its center a capability of weakness, softness, and even failure. Success is not the only characteristic of the male, nor is it limited to him."

"Don't preach to me," the older man spoke sharply.

Sadly Paul shook his head, "I know. I've tried for years but we still cannot speak to each other ten minutes before that undercurrent of wrath comes to the surface. Too bad this river of anger has spawned a lake of mistrust on my side and a sea of disappointment on yours."

"Paul, why do you insist on interpreting my actions with motives I do not possess? How often must I tell you that both your mother and I are proud of you, proud of your accomplishments."

"Could it be because for years I heard nothing from you, neither good nor bad? What you did say usually got back to me in the form of a criticism given secondhand either through mother or Sally."

"Paul, my dear Paul, you just do not understand," he answered with a sigh.

The chowder arrived and before the soup was put in front of them Paul managed to get in, "Maybe I never will." Mr. Manes did not permit conversation to dilute his pleasure of eating.

After the main course, Steven Manes pushed back his chair, added a half spoon of sugar to his black coffee, and lit up his two-dollar cigar.

"I thought you cut down."

"Today is an exception, Paul. I have some big news and it deserves a token of celebration. That is one of the reasons we are having lunch. I wanted to tell you myself, son."

Not having heard the word, son, from his father's lips for many years, Paul knew something unusual must have taken place. "Yes?" he waited patiently.

Steven Manes, a master of theatrical effect, paused before answering. "I am retiring as of November first. The law firm of Manes,

Manes, Walsh, and Wolfe will have only Sally as an active Manes partner. As you are quite aware, I have been spending less and less time with law. When my partners found out I was turning seventy-five this year, they sent Sally as messenger to find out if I was willing to retire."

He sighed once again and looked out at the city's enlarged downtown before continuing, "I am hardly meeting my draw these days. I am too busy putting together real estate parcels and overseeing limited partnerships for me to really practice law anymore. Your mother and I have agreed we are going to sell our house in Bird Rock and move to the Palm Springs condo."

Paul was not surprised. The man looked tired in spirit as well as in body. "I'm glad that you've decided that, Father. You have been most successful in whatever you decided to do. I know you will retire with zest and verve, just as you've always done in law and real estate. How does Mother feel about it?"

"She is glad for my sake. She always thought that I worked too hard. It will give us more time together. Besides, over the years she built up quite a large social circle down in the desert and is looking forward to playing bridge on a steady basis."

Though the words were right, Paul knew his father was not really taking this proposed diminution of activity well. His looks and posture gave lie to his verbal assurances. "I assume your pension and past capital gains will cushion any possible loss of income."

"Of course. Money is not a worry and I will finally have time to improve my golf game," said Mr. Manes.

"Well, from my point of view, I'm delighted. Since you've lived a productive and full life you'll now have the ability to reap its rewards. Of course both of you will visit us as often as you wish. Mary, I know, will love to have you over. She thinks the world of mother and looks up to you with an awe that I thought went out in the nineteenth century."

He smiled for the first time. "Sally extended her invitation with the same gusto. I guess we must have done something right if both of our children want us to visit them regularly."

He motioned the waiter over and paid the bill. "Let us take a short constitutional in the park," he suggested. Paul knew there was still something else on his father's mind. He acquiesced by saying nothing. As was customary, they permitted the silence to both separate and unite them. Neither spoke to the other as they slowly walked the one short but scorching block into Balboa Park. Mr. Manes sat down on the first available shaded bench.

"I would like to bring up a subject that might not be pleasant for you." Paul turned away from his father, steeling himself for some sort of blow. As far back as he could remember his father had had the capacity to hurt him. He waited, jaws tight and muscles tense. He did not permit himself to hear the soft tone and the tentative quality of his father's voice.

Extending his legs, Steven Manes looked at his son and, without waiting for Paul to return his gaze, said, "I would like to talk to you about Johan."

"Is he in trouble?"

"No, in fact it is just the opposite. He is excelling. Are you not cognizant of what he is doing?"

"Johan and I do not communicate too well. He keeps his thoughts to himself no matter how hard I try to break through."

"So Johan has not told you as yet."

"Told me what, Father?"

"That he has been accepted to Yale Law School."

"Yale Law School?" Paul was dumbfounded. He had not known that his son had applied. "Yale?"

"Yes. My alma mater. We discussed his career six months ago and he wished to go to Yale. Follow in the footsteps of his grandfather and his aunt Sally." There was a broad pride in his voice. Mr. Manes's sadness was replaced with the satisfaction of generational continuity.

"I had no idea," Paul was speechless. He knew his son was doing well at U.C.S.D. but Johan hardly ever confided in him. Years ago Paul had given up trying to make contact or get close to him.

"But you have not failed with him, you know. Johan also wants to follow your lead. He wishes to combine medicine and law and go into medical jurisprudence."

"That is not my influence. It's because of his other grandfather, Dr. Stocker. Johan loved him dearly," Paul uttered his honest but painful conviction. They once again sat quietly for a few minutes. Finally Paul shrugged his shoulders as if to say, "What will be will be." He said, "I did not expect Johan to go to graduate school, let alone law school. I just bought Anna a convertible for her birthday. It'll be tight but I'll manage somehow. I always have."

"Part of my conversation with Johan was I would foot his bill. I have more than enough to see him through Yale."

"No, Father, I can manage to send my own children through school."

"Now do not be stubborn, son. Johan told me he did not want to put an extra financial burden on you so I volunteered. Besides, why did I earn so much money if it were not to be able to give it to my children and grandchildren?"

Paul knew he would accept his father's largess. It would ease the financial strain. One cannot ever become wealthy being a part-time psychiatrist and a half-time actor. With mixed emotions, he said, "Thank you father. It's very generous of you. Thanks."

"Paul."

"Yes," finally looking at his father.

"I have not interfered in how you raised Johan and Anna, as it was not my business. Besides, you have done a wonderful job in a most difficult situation—what with Evi and everything. I have just one word of advice with respect to Johan. Keep trying to get through to him. It is never too late. As the maxim puts it so well: Better late than never. That is all I want to say."

Paul was deeply moved. A solitary tear fell down his cheek. He responded to the gentle advice by squeezing his father's hand for several seconds. They got up without speaking.

⌒≈⌒

A bedroom for some people means sleep. For others it connotes sex. Mary loved to go to bed early, sometimes as early as nine, in order to escape from the pressures and anxieties of the day. Years of convent living had imbedded in her the value of peaceful solitude. She found their waterbed's padded warmth a comfortable nest. In bed, when not catching up on the latest educational journals, she loved to lose herself in the desperate lives that "Catholic" novels depicted so familiarly. She was enjoying Father Greeley's *Thy Brother's Wife* that evening when Paul came into the room. He also found reading in bed gave him pleasure. Touching Mary from time to time, it permitted him to be in quiet proximity to her while at the same time allowing him to catch up on his *must* list of professional journals.

"Hi love," he said as he settled in on his side of the king-sized bed.

"How is the memorizing coming along?"

"The first act is down pat and the second is almost there," he answered. As he opened the latest hypnosis journal to the first article, he asked her if she had read an article by Dr. Gilligan. He was proud of her learning and using hypnosis as a teaching tool. Accepting his suggestion to learn hypnosis, she had easily mastered the theories and techniques as they applied to children. She was considered one of the best teachers in her school.

"Not yet, so please save it for me. But before you get lost in your reading, I'd like your opinion regarding Johan," Mary resolutely brought up the subject. "I did not wish to decide this by myself without first checking with you."

"Yes?" he answered, a pique in his tone.

"He wants to spend Christmas Day in Palm Springs with your parents. He'll be here Christmas Eve but wants to drive out to them early in the morning. I told him you would be hurt since he'll be leaving for the East Coast so soon. But he has his heart set on spending part of the holidays with his grandparents."

Paul sighed and said, "Of course he can go. I don't want him to stay here if he doesn't wish to. No, Mary, I'm not hurt." And in a lighter tone, "In fact I'm delighted he wishes to spend Christmas Eve with us. It'll be a lovely holiday, I promise you." He leaned over and pecked her on the cheek.

She went back to her potboiler and he began the fascinating article on the use of metaphor in hypnotherapy written by one of Erickson's most prominent students, Steven Gilligan. They became absorbed in their respective readings, aware of each other only through unconscious receptors and years of quiet ease together. Paul read through several articles, skimmed the rest, and after a half hour of reading was ready for his regular evening session of self-hypnosis.

Paul shut off the light on his side of the bed. Lying flat on his back, he shut his eyes and immediately began his automatic inward focus, quickly losing himself in hypnotic dreams. He considered this extremely rewarding and deeply expanding state as the high point of his day.

When he first learned self-hypnosis he concentrated on the relaxation of various muscle groups, attended to any sounds in the room, and any images behind his closed eyes. Finally, he would focus on his breathing.

This process of deepening his trance would take around five minutes. However, with years of practice, he was now able to get into that altered state by just shutting his eyes, feeling how his left hand felt, becoming aware of his rhythmic breathing, and within thirty seconds be deep in trance.

Paul never knew where his hypnotic trance would take him or what symbols would come up from his unconscious, that unknown part of himself that controlled all his actions and feelings. He had learned that his conscious mind was not in the driver's seat in his trip through life. As a psychiatrist and hypnotist, he respected and was awed by the power of the unconscious mind. He obeisance was expressed in the ritual of his daily trance, a time he devoted in uniting the various parts of his psyche.

If his day had been hectic or trying, he would let himself drift into his favorite peaceful scene of lying quietly on the beach, relaxed and calm under a warm and bright sun. Paul had developed the ability to completely lose himself in that scene, staring at the rhythmic motion of the white-topped gentle waves as they lapped up to the sandy shore and then calmly recede back to the blue expanse of the Pacific Ocean.

That night as he became one with the peaceful water of the Pacific, his trance transported him back to last month's scene with Johan, a conversation held just one day after the Balboa Park talk with his father.

". . . and is it so difficult to confide in your father?"

"I know you care, Dad. I'm sorry. I thought you knew I had applied to Yale Law School," Johan said with a vehemence that belied the statement's truth.

"Son, I not only care, but I love you deeply."

The trance dream changed with that thought and Johan turned into his other child, Anna. Dark haired, opened armed, and beaming a wide smile, she came running toward him, "Oh Daddy! It's beautiful. The black seats go just great against the white body. Oh Daddy, I love you so. You're so wonderful." She hugged him and in the strength of her joy, turned her tall father around several times before kissing him warmly on his cheek.

"Anna, my wonderful Anna. You'll always be my *Schaetzli*. I love you so much."

Paul went into a part of himself that had neither memories nor images. Time was not part of that space though if counted by a clock it lasted less than one second. He moved through time and space and landed in Algernon's brocaded divan in the morning room where he was facing the formidable Lady Bracknell.

"Now to minor matters. Are your parents living?" she asked him.

He, as Jack Worthing, had just proposed to Gwendolen and was now being interrogated by her mother. "I have lost both my parents."

"Both?" She paused, staring down at him. "That seems like carelessness."

Before she was able to continue, Paul became aware of the audience's laughter. He looked out into the theater.

When he glanced back onto the stage, it had changed into Harry Hope's dim-lit saloon and the clock had advanced to 1912. Larry had just told him to remember the old times when he had brought kindness and laughter with him instead of death.

Instead of continuing with the next line, Paul, as Hickey, skipped right into the middle of his long soliloquy. ". . . There's a limit to the guilt you can feel and the forgiveness and the pity you can take! You have to begin blaming someone else, too."

There was a momentary memory flash to his office, where he is sitting opposite Randy, who had just told Paul about Judy's guilty life under Carl's lust. "And what has happened since?" he asked his patient.

"Three years ago they were found by the police one morning."

Rather than hearing the remainder of Randy's answer, Paul found himself in Carl's apartment on West Eighty-eighth Street, in the dusty and cluttered bedroom. The desk in the comer is covered with dozens of manuscripts. He is sitting as an invisible spectator on the black beanbag chair. They are drunk in addition to being stoned and drugged.

"Let's try some of that new smack. It's time to get a bit high," Carl slurps his words. Without waiting for Jeanette to answer, he wobbles to the kitchen to get the wanted drug.

Shocked, Paul is amazed at Carl's transformation since the last time he had seen him. His large features seem to hang from loose skin. His bulbous lips surround wrinkled, unshaven cheeks, while his still-prominent gut hangs loosely over his gray-washed jockey shorts. Jeanette also has aged, her hair now more gray than red, her features wasted, dissipated. She is lying naked, half comatose, wearing only her brassiere and the gold necklace that Evi had given her one Christmas years ago.

It is obvious that the room had not been cleaned in weeks or months. Dirty dishes and smelly bedclothes complement the thick and settled layer of dust. Jeanette's eyes are closed waiting for the next shot of euphoria. Her arm is outstretched, anticipating the tourniquet to heaven. Carl comes back with the glassine envelope containing the awaited white powder. From under the bed he pulls out the rubber tubing and syringe. He empties the powder into a spoon and heats it in the candle's flame which he finally manages to light after wasting three matches. Sucking up the liquid into the syringe, he is ready to give Jeanette her needed fix. With some difficulty he ties the tube around her arm. The first stab misses her vein and he must stick it in again before succeeding in drawing back a little bit of blood. He shoots the stuff into her arm.

"I'll wait a bit. I want to see you enjoy it. They swore that it's great shit."

He watches her for a couple of minutes, goes back into the kitchen, and reappears with another envelope. He goes over to the bed and looks at her. Suddenly he is aware that something is wrong. She is neither nodding nor breathing. He tries for a pulse and finds none.

"Jeanette, wake up! Say something!" he yells.

In his drugged state, it takes him several minutes before it fully sinks in. She is dead.

"Oh no. I've killed her. I killed her," he first yells, then moans. He looks around the room, first at the desk, then back to the bed, and quickly away to the dirty window. He mutters, "I need a drink."

Once more he goes back into the kitchen. This time though, his shoulders are bent. His gait is unsteady, a reaction to both fear and drugs.

Paul is dazed. He sits and watches his former mentor come back with a bottle of Jack Daniels in one hand and a bottle of pills in the other.

Without looking at Jeanette, Carl spills all the red capsules on top of the TV and begins to swallow them. He washes down each Seconal with a swig of bourbon. When they are gone, he sits on the edge of the bed staring out the window but seeing nothing.

Paul waits an eternity. Finally Carl sags forward and falls down, banging his head on the floor and bruising his arm on the base of the floor lamp.

Paul closes his eyes, attempting to shut out the image and distance himself from that grotesque finality. When he opens them up, he finds himself once again in his office with Randy sitting opposite him. "So Carl had been dead three years the night you were with Judy?" Paul wished to confirm the time frame.

"Yes. All the police knew was that both had died of an overdose, the woman of heroin and Carl of barbiturates. They did not know if it was murder and suicide or two ODs or what."

Suddenly the time changes; it is a couple of minutes earlier but still in the same session with Randy. His patient is in the midst of describing his sexual encounter with Judy.

". . . At first she didn't want to believe me, but I completely gave of myself and in my mind I loved her as a daughter. Though older than me, she became my daughter. It obviously worked. She was able to reach a climax for the first time in three years."

"That was intuitive and generous," Paul interjected when Randy had stopped talking.

Paul's trance lightened and he floated up to a semihypnogic state. He began an internal dialogue in his mind. Intuitive and generous, Paul thought. Yes, Randy had always been intuitive and generous when it came to sex. Not like me. Why can't I be like him? Why not take on some of his better traits? Let me learn. Let me be he.

Down down he sped with that internal command. He easily traveled down the steps of his unconscious to the golden place where he was safe to take on another's mantle. He entered Randy's psyche and completely fused the two beings into one. Paul was back in 1972. After having had dinner at The Duck Joint, he was back in Judy's apartment on East Seventy-second Street. Sitting next to Judy, he found himself aroused and erect once again. This time though he merged into Randy's mind and took on the mantle of his persona. Hundreds of cases had prepared the way while years of acting had honed the skill.

She settled herself on his lap and began nibbling his ear. He delightfully allowed himself to be seduced. Later, in the bedroom, in the midst of a passionate kiss, she suddenly bit his lip. Without thinking he slapped her. Angrily he said, "Now stop that."

"Oh, yes sir, anything you want. But don't hurt me. I'll do whatever you want, no matter how debasing it is. Anything."

Paul did not get off her, did not lose his erection. Instead, Randy's driving psyche and sexual momentum thrust him forward, spreading her willing legs. As his mouth surrounded hers, his penis got harder. He began to feel a lustful warmth spreading from his groin. His body glowed; his head throbbed. With a deep, quick thrust he entered her.

"Oh daddy, you're so big. Don't hurt me," she kept moaning while moving her body in rhythm to his furious and deep plunges. He climaxed quickly.

"Did I please you, big daddy? Did I make you feel good?" Paul laughed with pleasure. Rarely had he experienced such a satisfying and lustful orgasm. "Yes you did, but not as much as I'm going to please you, my little kitten." He began to lazily thrust once again. When her nails bit deeply into his back he twisted her hands up over her head and said, "Now you're really going to get it," and began to thrust long and deep.

"No, I don't want to. I can't big daddy. I can't."

"Oh yes you can. Please your big daddy by being a good girl and do what he wants."

"Oh daddy, I'm going to come, daddy, ahh," she screamed.

"So am I, so am I," he gasped as he ejaculated a second time.

Again the scene shifts. It is late at night. Paul had just finished some insurance reports and locks up his office. He notices his secretary is about ready to leave. He feels her attraction. He reacts and that warmth in his groin begins to radiate once again. He moves with the sureness of Randy and begins kissing her passionately. They are naked on the floor of his office when they both climax simultaneously.

Three beautiful actresses surround him. The redhead begins to massage his thigh. He comes to quick erection. With a movement of his hips, he begins to concentrate on that heat emanating from his groin. He moans in desire. The lights suddenly go out.

Immediately, Paul's trance is lightened and he quickly opens his eyes.

He reasons Mary must have just shut her light out, his usual cue to come back. What was not usual though was that his sexual reverie was pulsating throughout his body and the warm trance-induced glow still surrounded him. His strong erection connected him to his hypnotic experience. He moved closer to Mary, spooning himself comfortably in the crook of her back. His erect penis firmly pressed the insides of her thighs. He began to kiss the back of her neck and both hands gently played with her nipples.

"Wait a minute, Paul. Let me take off my nightgown," she said without enthusiasm. She sat up and clumsily took it off. She lay down on her back and was absolutely passive.

This time her lack of movement did not deter him. Still lying on his side next to her, he placed his face over her ear and whispered, "My darling Mary. My wonderful Mary." He kissed her fully on the mouth and began once again to gently play with her nipples.

"I love you, Mary."

"And I love you," she answered when his mouth left hers. "My, aren't you excited," she referred to his hard penis still throbbing against her thigh.

"You turn me on you know," he murmured in her ear. He began to nibble on her lobe while continuing to massage her breasts. He was playing a different melody, for he neither needed her to play with his penis for it to get erect nor did he find it necessary to enter her quickly in order to consummate their lovemaking. He wanted to please her, to make certain she enjoyed their lovemaking rather than suffer her wifely duty.

He was patient with her lack of response. He kept at her earlobe, knowing she found pleasure there. His hands glided over her body, first on her breasts then down to her vulva. He then delicately massaged the clitoral region and once again passionately kissed her. This time he put his tongue in her mouth. The longer he played with her, the more excited he became. His penis throbbed and he wanted to enter her in the worst way. However, he knew she was not yet ready. She would as usual allow him to enter but would not join him in united pleasure.

The warmth of his groin had by now completely spread throughout his body. His fingers sent off heat, his touch sent out sexual energy. Paul, after all these years, had learned how to gently arouse his wife. She slowly started to respond with small unconscious waves of movement. She then began to kiss him back; at first gently, then with more and more fervor. These responses again created in Paul a strong desire to enter her, to take her in love. When he felt some moisture in her vagina, he got on top of her and slowly pushed into her.

Paul was aware that though Mary was more sexually excited than she had been in years, she was still not ready to have an orgasm. However he could not hold back any longer and with a few quick deep thrusts climaxed, yelling and moaning, "Oh, Mary, ohh my love, ohhhh."

Not letting go, he remained in her as he came down from his peak of pleasure. He began to nibble her ear while his hand continued to rub her clitoris.

"You're still hard," she said with some surprise.

"Yes, Mary, I love you." He now started a small and gentle rhythmic thrust. Back and forth, back and forth, all the while playing with her clitoris. He let go of her earlobe and dropped his mouth onto the side of her neck. He nipped and took playful but sharp bites. He was aware his sexual heat was finally reaching her. She reacted to his lust with her own: she began to tighten her hold on him. Suddenly he raised her legs, leaned on her buttocks, and sped up the tempo.

"Paul, what's happppennnnn, ahhhh, Paullll." She moaned and moaned as she was enveloped in her climax, her orgasm.

She snuggled in his arms while Paul lay back, his mind clear of thoughts though full of emotions.

"What happened Paul? How come now after all these years?"

He didn't answer with words. Instead, he gently squeezed her shoulder with one hand as he wiped away a tear running down his cheek with the other.

ABOUT THE AUTHOR

Fritz Klein, MD, is a psychiatrist who lives in San Diego, California. His former positions include Clinical Instructor at the University of California at San Diego and co-leader of the Bisexual Forum in New York City, which he founded in 1974. Dr. Klein also established the Bisexual Forum in San Diego in 1982 and is on their Board of Directors. He is the President of the not-for-profit Bisexual Foundation. His Web site, www.bisexual.org, is a leading Internet source for all things bisexual. He is editor of the *Journal of Bisexuality,* the author of *The Bisexual Option,* co-editor of *Bisexualities, Theory, and Research,* and *Bisexual and Gay Husbands: Their Stories, Their Words* (all from Haworth Press), and co-author of *Man, His Body, His Sex.*

Order a copy of this book with this form or online at:
http://www.haworthpress.com/store/product.asp?sku=5601

LIFE, SEX, AND THE PURSUIT OF HAPPINESS

_____in softbound at $19.95 (ISBN-13: 978-1-56023-577-4; ISBN-10: 1-56023-577-2)

Or order online and use special offer code HEC25 in the shopping cart.

COST OF BOOKS_____

POSTAGE & HANDLING_____
(US: $4.00 for first book & $1.50
for each additional book)
(Outside US: $5.00 for first book
& $2.00 for each additional book)

SUBTOTAL_____

IN CANADA: ADD 7% GST_____

STATE TAX_____
(NJ, NY, OH, MN, CA, IL, IN, PA, & SD
residents, add appropriate local sales tax)

FINAL TOTAL_____
(If paying in Canadian funds,
convert using the current
exchange rate, UNESCO
coupons welcome)

☐ **BILL ME LATER:** (Bill-me option is good on US/Canada/Mexico orders only; not good to jobbers, wholesalers, or subscription agencies.)

☐ Check here if billing address is different from shipping address and attach purchase order and billing address information.

Signature_____

☐ **PAYMENT ENCLOSED: $**_____

☐ **PLEASE CHARGE TO MY CREDIT CARD.**

☐ Visa ☐ MasterCard ☐ AmEx ☐ Discover
☐ Diner's Club ☐ Eurocard ☐ JCB

Account # _____

Exp. Date_____

Signature_____

Prices in US dollars and subject to change without notice.

NAME_____

INSTITUTION_____

ADDRESS_____

CITY_____

STATE/ZIP_____

COUNTRY_____ COUNTY (NY residents only)_____

TEL_____ FAX_____

E-MAIL_____

May we use your e-mail address for confirmations and other types of information? ☐ Yes ☐ No
We appreciate receiving your e-mail address and fax number. Haworth would like to e-mail or fax special discount offers to you, as a preferred customer. **We will never share, rent, or exchange your e-mail address or fax number.** We regard such actions as an invasion of your privacy.

Order From Your Local Bookstore or Directly From
The Haworth Press, Inc.
10 Alice Street, Binghamton, New York 13904-1580 • USA
TELEPHONE: 1-800-HAWORTH (1-800-429-6784) / Outside US/Canada: (607) 722-5857
FAX: 1-800-895-0582 / Outside US/Canada: (607) 771-0012
E-mail to: orders@haworthpress.com

For orders outside US and Canada, you may wish to order through your local
sales representative, distributor, or bookseller.
For information, see http://haworthpress.com/distributors

(Discounts are available for individual orders in US and Canada only, not booksellers/distributors.)

PLEASE PHOTOCOPY THIS FORM FOR YOUR PERSONAL USE.
http://www.HaworthPress.com   BOF04